Jax Sheppard

AND

the Seven Mirrors

D1091714

Sharon Warchol

Jax Sheppard

AND

the Seven Mirrors

Book One

Sharon Warchol

PANDAS PRESS

ISBN: 978-0-9904499-3-5

Illustrations by Yoko Matsuoka
Edited by Tomoko Matsuoka

This book is a work of fiction. Any references to real people, real places, or historical events are used fictitiously. All other names, characters, places, and events are the product of the author's imagination, and any likeness to actual locations, events, or persons, living or dead, is entirely coincidental.

For Luke, Zack, and Jillie, my creative team
Little Skerb and Very Little Skerb, my alphas
and Jeremy, my cheerleader

CONTENTS

CHAPTER 1
Creepy Clowns and a Dodgeball Diva

Be yourself? Just keep it real?
Well, guess what? BAD advice! Plain old, misguided, rotten advice that could only come from a Normal. I might have bought that nonsense when I was four. Maybe even when I was six—when I was still under the delusion that I, Jax Sheppard, *was* a Normal. But fast forward to my seventh birthday—the day I got my first inkling that I was anything but normal, courtesy of a dozen creepy circus clowns.

My mom had managed to snag backstage passes to the circus for me and my friend, Petey. I'm sure we'd all agree any seven-year-old would be tempted with the idea of owning his own clown car. Especially one packed full of twelve ultra-small and ultra-creepy clowns.

So when Mom stopped to use the restroom, I made my move. I grabbed Petey and the two of us sneaked out while my mom was in the stall. I looked around to make sure no one was watching, took a deep breath, and squatted low. With just a little grunt, I hoisted the nineteen hundred pound Volkswagen up over my head. We were halfway out the service entrance when those

1

lousy clowns started to climb out. Wouldn't you know one of them landed right on Petey!

Mr. Bringling tried to cut us a deal—if Mom agreed to let me work as a circus freak for the next fifteen years, he would overlook Blinky's hospital bill and Bobo's mental distress claim. Instead, Mom opted for the sixty-month payment plan.

I couldn't understand why, but for some reason Petey's parents never let him play with me anymore. Not even after his body cast came off.

Fast forward again to the third grade. We were playing dodgeball in gym class. Chelsea Pendleton kept pummeling me with the ball, and everyone knew when a girl kept nailing you in dodgeball it meant you had to be her boyfriend. It didn't seem like Ms. Rattner, the P.E. teacher, even cared.

Well, I wasn't about to be the boyfriend of a girl who outweighed me by forty-five pounds and was two feet taller than me. The next time she threw the ball, I was ready. I snagged it out of the air and whipped it back at her. I threw the ball with superhero force. When it hit her in the gut you could actually hear the air leave her lungs and pop right out of her mouth. Her gum shot halfway across the gym and she flew backwards. Her legs and arms were parallel to the floor, and the ball was lodged in her mid-section. She smashed into the bleachers with a deafening crash.

I was super pleased with myself. So I was shocked when I turned around to complete and utter silence. Twelve boys, sixteen girls, and one very masculine gym teacher stared at me with their mouths wide open. After what seemed like forever, they all spun and ran screaming from the gym, Ms. Rattner included. Michael Flack could be heard whimpering, "I want my mommy!" from the guidance office for the next two hours. Chelsea was totally fine—she only had some slight bruising on her back, two cracked ribs, and the round, dimpled imprint of the dodgeball on her stomach. But I got detention anyway.

The other kids pretty much avoided me after that, so it was probably a good thing I transferred to Beyhaven Elementary the next year. I would have to have been a complete idiot to "be myself" and "keep it real" when I met my new classmates. From that point on, Gram and Grandpap had thought it best I not show or tell anyone about the unusual things I could do. In fact, I could count on one hand and one thumb the number of people who even knew about my tricks. Mom and Grandpap had known. But of course, they were both gone now. I squashed down the lump that clawed its way up my throat every time I thought about them. That meant Gram, Sebastian, Dad, and Andie were the only people left who knew my secret. Gram and Sebastian wouldn't tell anyone, I hadn't heard a word from Dad in years, and Andie was my best friend.

But, really—thanks for the advice. NOT! Next time, just stop and think for a minute or two before offering worthless and potentially harmful advice to a kid unless you know for a fact he's a Normal.

CHAPTER 2
A Bolt, My Fear, and a Mysterious Mirror

"Shhhh! Someone's coming!" Andie threw herself on the pavement. She totally misjudged her distance from the edge of the sidewalk. The next thing I know, her feet flipped up over her head, and she was tumbling down the steep, landscaped hill just a few feet from the steps we were about to go down.

I cupped my mouth. "Watch out for the—"

Thud!

"...tree!" I finished, a second too late. "I give it an eight point nine! It would've been a perfect ten, but you didn't stick the landing!"

My little brother, Sebastian, busted out laughing. Just then, the headlights of an oncoming car sliced through the fog. I crammed the rest of the Ding Dong I was eating into my mouth and grabbed Sebastian's hand. We hustled down the steps to avoid being seen.

At the bottom, Andie scowled up at me through a face full of caramel-colored hair.

"What?" I asked. "You think you deserved a solid nine?"

"You know what, Jax? This is officially the dumbest

idea you've ever had." She pinned with me her coldest, hardest glare. If there was more light, I'm sure I would've seen smoke pouring out of her ears. "That's it! I'm going home!"

"Awww, c'mon Andie. You always do this. You always say you'll try something and then you always back out. Why do you have to be such a rule-follower?"

"Rules are made for—"

"Breaking." With one freakishly strong hand, I lifted her high in the air. Her legs just dangled there, but she kept kicking and trying to nail me in the kneecaps. Each time she kicked and missed, Sebastian giggled even harder.

Some kind of half-cat, half-sheep, half-turkey, one-third baby bear sound screeched in the back of her throat. And I knew what that meant: she was about to go all psycho-Andie on us. As soon as I put her down on the pavement next to the fence surrounding Beyhaven Community Pool, she shoved me good and hard in the chest. I didn't even wobble.

"Show off!" Andie spit a piece of mulch out of her mouth and flung a branch out of her hair.

"Glad I could help." I struck my best pose and flexed my muscles, small as they were.

Sebastian copied my moves. "Jax, feel my muscles. They're as big as yours!"

Too bad it wasn't far from the truth. I might be strong and fast, but I was definitely a runt of a thirteen-year-old. It didn't make any sense at all.

Andie's teeth were clenched. "How can you two stand

there comparing those…those…pipe cleaners you call arms when we could get caught any minute?"

I shrugged and kissed my left pipe cleaner.

I might have gone too far because Andie didn't care about whispering anymore. "I knew I shouldn't have let you talk me into this, Jax!" She spun around and tried to scramble back up the hill.

Sebastian chased her and caught her hand. "Andie, wait! Just wait! Jax will never bring me back. If you leave, I'll never get to do it! Please, please, please."

Andie stopped. "Jax never should have agreed to bring an eight-year-old in the first place," she said, but her voice softened when she looked at Sebastian. She turned to me. "Honestly, Jax. Once you found out you had to babysit, you should have changed the plan. You're going to turn him into a little delinquent. You know," she said, turning back to Sebastian, "Jax will *never* visit you in juvie."

Sebastian screwed up his face. "What's 'juvie'?"

"It's jail for kids," I said. "But don't worry. I'm pretty sure sneaking into the pool for a quick night swim won't land you in the big house."

Sebastian cracked up again. He was like my one-man fan club.

"Now hurry up and climb the fence, you wimp," I said. "If you don't, I'll tell everyone you kissed Roger Schnoppenhoffer at—"

"I was five!"

I was expecting little darts to shoot out of her blue eyes and poke holes all through my favorite shirt. Instead, she snatched the flip-flop from her foot and chucked it boomerang style at my head. I caught it, mid-air, and prepared for her next attack. Then, without warning, she turned and scaled the chain link fence. She hopped down on the other side and glared.

"I am NOT a wimp!" Her thick hair was whipping in the wind.

I gave a little whoop and smiled at Sebastian. "C'mon." I looked at the sky. "We better hurry. I think it's going to rain."

The wind was hollering and howling. The moon had taken cover behind a group of sinister-looking clouds. There was barely enough light left to see Andie or the pool. I wrapped my arm around Sebastian's chest and hooked him under his arms. After a quick scan to make sure no one was watching, I took two small steps and jumped. I cleared the top of the six-foot fence, no problem.

Sebastian squealed. "Cool!"

Andie's eyebrow popped up like a piece of perfectly toasted toast. "That's a new trick."

I shrugged, set Sebastian on the concrete deck, and tossed Andie her shoe. "I dunno." I looked down and scuffed the toe of my sneaker on the ground. I always felt awkward talking about my strange abilities. No one wants to hang out with the friendly neighborhood freak. Just then, Petey's smiling, chubby face invaded my brain. Violins and harps played. Petey ran to me in slow motion across a sunny field of waving, golden wheat. Right as we were about to act out our joyful and dramatic reunion with the slow-mo-bro chest bump, POW! Bobo popped up between us.

I shook my head like I could jiggle that dreadful picture right out of my ears. Petey was a thing of the past. Just like Mom, Dad, and Grandpap. And it was best to leave bad memories in the past.

"All right, Monkey," I said to Sebastian. "Let's do this!" I kicked off my shoes, ran, and pulled off a masterful cannonball into the deep end.

Sebastian did a cannonball of his own. He surfaced and asked, "Andie, did I make a big splash?"

"The biggest." She blinked when a fat drop of rain hit her right in the eye.

The wind had picked up even more, and it was jostling Andie around. When she glanced at the clouds, she looked worried.

I swam to Sebastian and grabbed his waist. "Ready?"

"Go, go, go!" He tucked his knees into his chest.

"See how high you can count before you hit the water." I tossed him high in the air.

"One, two, three…" He flew way above the lifeguard tower and even higher than the roof of the two-story clubhouse. "…eighteen, nineteen!" Sebastian hit the water. He popped up laughing and sputtering water. "That's a new record, Jax!" I reached for him, and he squeezed me around the neck. His teeth chattered behind his blue lips.

"You and me, Monkey. Forever," I whispered and guided him to the shallow end. I looked at Andie. "Dive in. If you don't, I'll make you regret the day I ever moved in next door to you."

"I already do!" Andie took one step closer to the pool, but then stopped. She chewed on a thick strand of hair. "It's not that I don't want to come in, Jax—you know I do." Her courage from earlier was fading. "But if I get caught, my dad will *kill* me. I'll be grounded 'til I'm like, thirty, and then I'll never get my new telescope."

Right then, up on the road, a car splashed through a puddle. Andie took two quick steps back. Above us, those sinister clouds were now happily dumping rain. The sky rumbled in the distance.

"That's thunder. Check out the sky," Andie said.

Her eyebrows were creased. She studied the clouds that literally swirled above us like water in a toilet bowl. Unfortunately, I didn't bother to wonder why the clouds had taken on an eerie, greenish glow. As they circled, they created some kind of vortex in the sky.

As for Andie, she was pacing faster than a Ping-Pong ball at the Chinese Olympic trials. I couldn't tell what she was more nervous about—getting busted or the bad weather. But I did know if I didn't act soon, she would wear the rubber right off the bottoms of her flip-flops.

"You need to get out, Jax. *Now.*" She shivered. She was wet as a mop, and she hugged her arms across her chest.

"We will." I hopped out of the pool, still not worrying about the sky. "But not until *you* go in!" I lunged toward Andie. She shrieked and bolted away from me.

"Don't you dare!"

Sebastian giggled from the shallow end. "Get her, Jax!"

At that moment, a deafening crack of thunder rocked the ground under my feet. Before I could think, a blinding, unearthly green bolt of lightning pierced the clouds. I spun toward Sebastian as the green lightning struck the pool's surface. It exploded in a huge plume of water and sparks. I didn't spare a thought for the shiny, glowing object that dropped from the vortex and fluttered to the pool floor.

Sebastian's small body shook for a second. His terror-stricken eyes were fixed on me. In an instant, he went limp in the water.

"MONKEY! NOOOOOOOO!"

It was four weeks later. I was on the front porch drinking a glass of Gram's freshly squeezed lemonade. Sebastian came running up the driveway from the bus stop. Happy tears puddled in my eyes.

"Monkey, you're here! You're okay!" I repeated over and over. I was completely thrilled and completely confused. That whole night at the pool—maybe it had all been just a terrible nightmare.

Either way, I was so happy to see my little brother alive. My heart swelled with joy—like someone had filled it to the top with pure, sweet honey.

"Jax, Jax! I got a perfect score on my spelling test!" Sebastian waved a bright yellow paper at me.

His hair was just like mine—dark and wild. It was shoved under a paper pirate hat he must have made in school. He looked exactly like I did when I was a little kid, except his eyes were a deep hazel, like Mom's. Gram had always said mine were a warm, chocolaty brown.

I jumped off the porch. My arms could actually feel

themselves hugging Sebastian before I even got to him. But suddenly, Sebastian's face twisted and morphed. I blinked in horror and watched as his big hazel eyes changed to an icy, empty blue. They were so pale they were almost white. His playful grin was replaced with small, sharp teeth. His skin shriveled up and turned gray, and his hair grew long, stringy, and white. The thin lips pulled back in an evil smile. When his eyes met mine, they drilled right into my soul.

I shot up in bed and gasped for breath. My heart pounded on my chest wall like it was trying to escape. My pajamas were sweat-soaked. I looked around at the familiar bedroom that had been mine since we moved in with Gram and Grandpap after Mom's accident. *Mom's accident*—it was still hard to think about all these years later.

The clock read three o'clock in the morning. I squeezed Sebastian's little stuffed monkey and swiped at the tears that stung my cheeks. It had been almost a month since Sebastian's funeral. And that stupid dream had haunted me every night since then.

I slid out of bed and pulled a hoodie over my head. I made my way down the stairs and past the photo collage on the wall. The eyes from the photos—Gram's, Grandpap's, Mom's, Sebastian's, and even my own—condemned me as I crept down the stairs. "It's all *your* fault," they called after me. "*You* did this. Why couldn't it have been *you*, instead?" My guilt and sorrow hung on me like a thick wet blanket. I prayed every night that I could trade places with Sebastian, but I was still here, and he was still gone.

I slipped on my shoes and sneaked out the front door. The night air was cool, and I gulped it down. Outside, it was quiet except for the chirping of crickets and the long low croak of a lonely tree frog. That croaking really annoyed me, but then, everything annoyed me these days.

Zip it, Kermit!

I shot the tree an evil look. But the dumb old frog didn't seem at all concerned about being quiet. Its accusing croaks echoed inside my skull—like the frog knew what I had done to my brother.

I started to walk. I didn't know where I was going—just that I had to get away from those croaks. I walked past Andie's house, and past the Gibsons' and the Nortons' houses. I had no set destination in mind. When I finally looked up, I was standing in front of Beyhaven Community Pool. I climbed down the hill and stood at the fence. Anger bubbled up from somewhere deep down inside. I grabbed the chain link on the fence and ripped off an entire panel. I raised it over my head and hurled it across the parking lot. It sailed high into the air and out of sight.

The cement seemed harder and colder; it didn't care one bit that my heart had broken. I walked across it to the pool's edge. The lightning strike had fried the pool's equipment, so the pool wasn't able to open on Memorial Day like every other year. It was still closed, and I didn't care if it ever reopened. I hated this place.

I stared at the water, which was still and smooth as glass. It was doing a pretty good job of acting innocent after the part it had played in my tragedy. Then, a faint glint of light at the bottom of the deep end caught my eye. I peered into the water at the glimmering object. It was actually giving off its own light. Mesmerized, I kicked off my shoes and dove in. Even under the cool water, the thing was warm in my hand. I kicked back up to the surface and swam to the side.

By the light of the moon, I studied it. It was small—only about two inches wide—and appeared to be a shiny piece of broken mirror. It was misshapen on one side with jagged edges. The other side was smooth and curved. Some kind of mysterious-looking symbol was carved multiple times around the border of the curve.

The broken edges looked super sharp, as if they could cut me, but instead were super smooth. Mounted underneath the mirror was an old, tarnished piece of brass. It created a kind of frame, and the same strange symbol was etched around it too.

The coolest part, though, was the glow. From somewhere deep inside, a green light radiated. It even gave off a little heat. The thing actually vibrated in my hand. I turned it over to look for the battery compartment, but there wasn't one! Instead, there was some type of inscription scratched into the brass. It had letters that looked like Chinese or hieroglyphics or something.

What the heck is this thing? I stared at my reflection in the mirror for what felt like forever. I was glad for the distraction. Eventually, I put it in my hoodie pocket and headed home.

When I neared my house, that same annoying tree frog was still croaking away.

"I'm pretty sure I told you to shut up." I looked up at the big maple tree where the noise lived.

I swear it—a low voice rumbled, "No problem, dude." And at that second there was silence.

"Hmmm." I almost chuckled for the first time since the accident. "Thanks."

CHAPTER 3
Ding Dongs, Demons, and Dobermans

"I can't believe you'll be gone for the rest of summer," I said.

It was the next day, and Andie had talked me into joining Drake and her for lunch at Taco Tico's. After lunch, we had stopped by the Four Circles supermarket so Andie could pick up some groceries. Drake pushed the cart while Andie loaded it with the ingredients she needed to make brownies for the women's shelter, where she delivered baked goods every Friday.

"I won't be going." Andie's lip quivered. She lowered her eyes. "My dad's not letting me. It's punishment for… for sneaking out…that night."

I couldn't believe Andie's old man wasn't letting her go. It was just one more reason for me to feel horrible about the accident. Andie had worked so hard to win the scholarship for the technology camp. The camp was for super brainiacs, and Andie was one of only two kids from Pennsylvania to get picked. I kind of suspected her dad just wanted an excuse to keep her around since Andie did most of the cooking and cleaning.

Drake tried to cheer her up. "Well, I, for one, am

glad. This way you'll be around to write my summer school history report. Now there's no way they'll make me repeat eighth grade. Just be sure to double-space. And use bad grammar sometimes. Oh, and shoot for a B minus—you know...so they'll believe I wrote it myself."

Andie grabbed a bag of marshmallows from the cart. Drake ducked a second too late. She whacked him on the head with the bag and then tossed it to me, but she made an effort to smile now.

"Hmmm. For some reason, these marshmallows are all smashed, Jax. Would you go grab another bag?"

"Sure." I backed up and headed toward the end of the aisle. I eyeballed the box of chocolate Ding Dongs on the bottom shelf.

"Me, you,"—I pointed to myself and then the box—"later." Even though I tried, I still couldn't find amusement in my own half-hearted attempt at humor.

I turned to go to the next aisle when I bumped square into someone coming the other way. The marshmallows slipped from my hand. I bent to pick them up and started to apologize.

"Sorry. My fault." I stood, and my eyes landed on the face of a super creepy figure in a hooded cloak. My veins filled with ice. I recognized those white eyes and sharp teeth from the demonic face in my dream. I was too terrified to scream.

The man grabbed my wrist and squeezed with his cold, pale, bony fingers. I tried to jerk away. I wanted to run with every last bit of my super speed, but my entire body was paralyzed with fear. Not to mention that for an old guy, he was ridiculously strong. He forced me onto my knees, and it was all I could do to just stare up into those horrible eyes. He smiled that same frightening smile from my dream.

"You have the Kaptrofractus. Return it to me now, Komitari!"

"I d-d-don't know w-what you're talking about!" My voice was a whisper.

His grip was freezing. It stung my skin at first, but then burned.

"Liar!" He held out his thin arm. The excess material from his dark robe blew in some unknown wind that I couldn't feel or hear in aisle number six of the Four Circles. His hand just hovered there above my head. The nasty paper-like skin hung loosely at his wrist. His long, black fingernails curled toward my skull. I became nauseous and dizzy. Pain plagued my body as the energy was sucked from my toes, my feet, and my legs. It was like he was sucking the life right out of me through the top of my head. I gasped for breath, but my lungs wouldn't fill. My ribs felt like they were being crushed in the massive coils of a python.

"I don't...know...what...you're—"

"Jax!" In the distance, Andie and Drake called my name.

I collapsed. When I finally looked up, the man was gone, and Andie and Drake were rushing to me.

"Oh my gosh, Jax! Are you okay? What are you doing down there? What happened to you?" Andie was firing so many questions I felt as if I was getting hit by spitballs. But I was still shaken and drained. My brain just wouldn't signal my mouth to speak.

Drake was on his cell phone. "I'm calling 911."

"No!" I managed to bark. The whole situation was so unreal, I was sure I must have imagined it. I didn't want my friends to think I was crazy. "I'm fine. I slipped on... on...a banana peel." I was never very good at cover-ups.

"A banana peel? Where?" Andie's doubting eyes scanned the floor. "Honestly, Jax! You sure have had a lot of accidents lately." She tugged me to my feet. "First, there was that malfunction at the go-cart track over spring break, and then there was the freak accident last week at the bowling alley..." She threw her hands up. "...and now this."

"And don't forget the aquarium field trip," Drake said. "That was insane the way that glass wall gave out. You actually fell in the shark tank! I never saw someone swim so fast!"

"You do really need to be more careful," Andie said.

"Um...yeah. I'll try. Now please, let's just get the heck out of here."

� 攵 ⟍

That night, I was in bed having the dream again. I ran toward Sebastian as his face began to transform. This time, when the guy with the frozen fingers looked at me, he said, "Give me the Kaptrofractus, Komitari."

I bolted upright. My pulse raced like it always did after the dream. I put Sebastian's monkey down on the bed—I had taken to sleeping with it every night. Like last night, I grabbed my hoodie and sneaked down the stairs. I needed fresh air. There was no doubt I was losing it.

Maybe I should go see that shrink Gram keeps telling me about.

Everything pointed to me being 100 percent nuts. The dreams, the incident at the Four Circles—I must have imagined that. I was totally messed up because of what happened with Sebastian. Maybe I did need therapy. I tried to ignore the huge bruise on my newly blistered wrist. I probably did that to myself, I reasoned.

The tree frog croaked.

"Shut it, Kermit."

"Sorry, bro. I'll keep it down," the deep voice answered.

That's it! I'm officially a nut-job! I see demons and chat with frogs!

I jammed my hands in my pockets, and my fingertips closed in on a small object. It was that strange little mirror fragment from last night. I turned it over in my hand and studied it. It was still warm and vibrated just like it had before.

A surge of energy radiated from the mirror and coursed through my body. It made me feel better—my thoughts were clearer—my body felt even stronger. It was weird, but I liked it. It made me feel…alive again. I hadn't felt this good since before the accident.

I started running, and without thinking I cranked it up to full super speed, something my Grandpap had called "flashing." I was a speeding bullet. I flashed past the school and sailed over the fence onto the track. I ran one, two, twenty, fifty laps around the track in just minutes. Everything about me felt amazing—like I just aced my math test, got a note from Olivia Delaney in homeroom, and found the sticker under my cafeteria tray that meant I won a free serving of tater tots, all on the same day.

I left the track and headed toward home. As I strolled, I took the mirror out of my pocket and examined it again. Somehow, this thing was responsible for the way I felt—I just knew it.

I continued walking past the Steiners' house and past the Nortons'. Just as I started past the row of hedges in front of the Gibsons' house, a female voice yelled, "Watch out! Get out of my way!"

Before I could react, someone crashed into me, knocking me back through the hedges onto the Gibsons' front lawn. The next thing I knew, I was lying flat on my back, and face down on top of me was the owner of that voice.

I pushed the girl off and jumped to my feet. "*You* watch it! What do you think you're doing?" Still, I couldn't help but notice she smelled like roses.

"Hush!" she whispered with one finger at her lips. She grabbed my hand and yanked me back to the ground. I was surprised by how strong she was. She clamped her hand over my mouth and hushed me again.

I scowled at her for a second, but I didn't scowl for long.

Man, she might be the prettiest girl I've ever seen.

The street lamp cast just enough light for me to make out her features. Her hair was jet black—like a crow—only pretty and without the feathers. It lay on her shoulder in one long, fat braid. Her eyes were bigger than a camel's and her lashes were just as long. And those lips! They were as full as two plump breakfast sausages, but red and not greasy either.

Geez! This girl was making me so nervous, I even sounded like an idiot in my own head! I was starting to understand why I got a "D" on my poetry unit last year.

Suddenly, from the sidewalk, I heard—or felt—someone or something coming. I peeked through the shrubs. Way at the end of the block I could make out the form of a giant, dopey-looking creature running in our direction. Chunks of asphalt crumbled and kicked up around its ankles each time its huge feet made contact with the road. I couldn't believe how fast that thing moved. While I thought I could probably outrun it if I flashed, my crushing fear made me doubt my own abilities. Every one of its steps was like four of mine.

"What *is* that thing?" I whispered to the girl huddled beside me. She clapped her hand across my mouth for a second time.

"A Pygmy Gorg," she whispered. "Shhhh."

I swiped at her hand. "What do you mean, 'Pygmy'? Are you saying they grow those things *bigger?*"

"You are going to get us killed!"

The Gorg stopped in the light of the street lamp, scanning the yards for the girl. It had to be at least nine feet tall and was even thicker than the old sequoia tree in front of Beyhaven Elementary. It had a huge, caveman-like forehead, a round, pudgy nose, and at the end of its long arms hung extremely meaty fists. Its skin was a sickly looking grayish-green color, and all told, it was ugly. I shuddered.

The Gorg took five short whiffs as he swung his head in a slow arc. He thudded one giant step in our direction and sniffed again. His big nostrils flared. With the size of those steps, three or four more sniffs were sure to do us in. I hoped it wasn't my new Stink Away Body Spray that was leading him to us.

Then, without warning, the Gibsons' three Dobermans came charging at full speed from around the back of the house. They barked so loudly I was sure the Gorg would come to investigate. And worse, I was worried the Dobermans were going to make a midnight snack out of me. They were headed right toward me. I squeezed my eyes shut.

Not me! Eat the girl! I was definitely not thinking straight.

The dogs stopped in their tracks. They snarled at me for an instant and then set their sights on the girl. They barked and growled at her and sized her up like a juicy New York strip steak.

The bigger Doberman looked at me and, I swear it, he said, "You're right, kid. She does look better than you. You'd be nothing but gristle and bone. Way too scrawny, that's what you are."

I blinked in disbelief. The dog returned his attention to the girl, who was backed all the way into the hedgerow. She didn't seem even a little shocked to hear a talking dog. All the while, I was tuned in to the slow, deliberate thud of the Gorg's footsteps getting closer. I squeezed my eyes shut again. I was frantic.

I didn't mean it! Don't eat the girl! Eat the Gorg! Eat the Gorg!

All at once, the three Dobermans backed off from their threatening stance in front of the girl. They drew back a few feet and then charged full steam toward us. I curled up in a ball and prepared to be puppy chow. But as I watched, the dogs leaped right over us and over the hedges. They took off in the direction of the Gorg.

The girl and I both got on our knees and peeked over the top of the hedges. The Gorg had turned and was running from the dogs. The Dobermans nipped at its heels. They made quite a racket, even though the Gorg was quickly outpacing them. We continued watching in stunned silence until the Gorg disappeared over the crest of a distant hill.

"No thanks are necessary," I said.

"Thanks for what?"

"I told the dogs not to eat you. Didn't you hear?" As soon as I said it I realized how dumb I sounded.

"Oh, I see." She flipped her braid over her shoulder. "And here I presumed you were playing possum while three vicious creatures drooled over me." She had a strange accent that I couldn't place, but I could definitely place the sarcasm in her voice. Something told me she wasn't actually grateful. "Well, thank you, brave sir, for telling the dogs not to eat me. I am forever in your debt." As she turned away, she muttered under her breath, "I cannot believe *this* kid is a Komitari, much less the Ark."

My ears burned. *Komitari?* My mind raced. That's what Freezer Fingers from the Four Circles had called me. Before I could ask her about it, the Gibsons' porch light flicked on.

"What's going on out there?" Old Man Gibson yelled from the doorway.

"Let's get out of here!" I reached for her hand, but she was gone. I didn't waste a second wondering where she had disappeared to. I didn't want to get busted by Old Man Gibson. When a black cat brushed up against my legs, I was sure it was a sign of bad things to come. I jumped over the hedges and was just about to flash to my house when I was stopped dead in my tracks by a flashlight beaming directly in my eyes.

"Stop and put your hands on your head! This is the police."

CHAPTER 4
Really Old Stuff in a Really Old Box

"Sorry, Gram." I was slouched in the passenger side of Gram's old Buick. My arms were crossed, and my head hung low. Apparently, the town had some lame eleven o'clock curfew for minors. Good thing Grandpap had been friends with the police chief. Otherwise, I'd have been stuck scooping dog poop at Beyhaven Community Park or some other dumb court-appointed community service.

Even so, I felt pretty guilty for making Gram go through this. She had dealt with so much pain in the past several years. I still couldn't even think about the fire with Mom, and Grandpap's death two months ago was tough on both of us. And then...Sebastian. Now, here she was, in the middle of the night, picking up her grandson at the police department. I nervously rubbed the bruise on my wrist.

She frowned. "Jackson, honey. I'm really worried about you. You've been through so much—too much. It'd be a lot for anyone to handle, never mind a teenager. You know, there's nothing wrong with talking to someone about your feelings." She paused and then added, "I wish you would reconsider meeting with Dr. Mann." She was talking about the psychiatrist again.

I hesitated. I didn't know how to tell her everything without worrying her even more. It would be a major shock for any old lady to learn her grandson was a full-out loony bird.

"You're right, Gram. I need help—serious help. I think I'm losing it." I swallowed hard. I knew what I was about to say would probably land me in a rubber room with a small cot and a helmet for my own protection. But I didn't know how to stop all this insanity. With my eyes focused straight ahead, I blurted, "I talk to frogs and I talk to dogs and they talk back and I hide from Gorgs behind shrubs with strange girls and I play with broken mirrors and I see bad guys in the Four Circles."

I exhaled and then looked at Gram, but she kept her eyes glued to the road. A look of horror might have flashed across her face, but she quickly disguised it. For the rest of the ride, her expression was blank. She didn't say a word, and she never even glanced at me. I worried it was only a matter of time before the padded van showed up to take me away forever. I thought about telling her to make sure Drake got my video game collection and Andie my telescope; I was pretty sure no one would want my chewed-gum collection. I stared out the window the rest of the way home.

We pulled into the garage, and I dragged myself up the steps to my bedroom. My mood was the complete opposite of the total invincibility I had felt just a few hours ago when I flashed around the track. I picked up

Sebastian's monkey and plopped down on the side of the bed. I scanned my room.

Good-bye, oversized beanbag chair with the stuffing coming out. Good-bye, Scooby Doo bedspread with the root beer stain on Shaggy's beard. Good-bye, extremely rare and vintage 1970s chewed piece of pink Chum Gum, which I found under my seat at Cinemart when we went to see the horror film, Run for Your Life. *Good-bye, choo-choo train wallpaper, which was cool when I was a kid but pretty lame and embarrassing now. Thanks for the memories—I'm going to miss you all when they lock me up.* I might have been a touch overdramatic.

"Jackson," Gram called from her room down the hall. "Come here, please." It was the first she had spoken since my bizarre confession.

Gram was sitting at her vanity. She held an old wooden box about the size of a toaster on her lap. When she looked at me, her soft wrinkled face showed signs of the stress of the past few months. Her silver hair was tied in a loose knot at the back of her neck. You could tell she had probably been pretty good-looking when she was younger. In fact, I'd bet if they had a beauty contest for old people, my Gram would definitely place in the top twelve or thirteen.

"I was hoping I could get away without ever giving this to you. It seems now though, I should have given it to you right after Grandpap passed, but"—her voice broke—"I just wanted to protect you. I wouldn't be able to bear it if anything happened to you, Jackson. I don't know how I would go on." She dabbed a tear from her cheek with a handkerchief she had taken from the vanity. "You're all I have left."

It broke my heart to see Gram in so much pain. I wrapped my arms around her small shoulders. She took a deep breath and sat up tall. "This box belonged to Grandpap. He left me with orders it was not to be opened by anyone but you—*only* you." She handed me the box and left the room. The door clicked shut behind her.

I put the box on the bed. Then I slapped myself on the cheek just in case I had fallen asleep and was dreaming again. I didn't wake up.

Gram was obviously completely off her rocker, just like me. Her reaction wasn't what I expected at all. I had just told her I had a conversation with a frog, and all she did was look at me and say, "Here, have a box." Maybe they'd let us share a room at the funny farm.

I tried another slap. "Ouch! Darn super strength."

I sat on the edge of the bed and lifted the heavy wooden box onto my lap. This thing was ancient. It was totally beat up and all nicked on the edges. I ran my hand across the lid, which was worn smooth from what looked like centuries of use. It had multiple carvings that were partially rubbed away. The carvings seemed somewhat familiar but were so worn I couldn't remember where I had seen them before. An old, tarnished brass lock on the front of the box held a small key, which someone had left in the hole.

I turned the key. My nerves were out of control; it felt as though a bunch of grasshoppers were playing leap frog in my stomach. I removed the lock and lifted the latch. Ever so slowly, I opened the lid. I was expecting a bunch of springy snakes to pop out and a recording to shout, "Gotcha!" I looked around to see if there were any hidden cameras.

A rich, golden-hued velvet bag was nestled in the center of the box. It was pinched shut with a thick, golden drawstring. I picked it up and held it in the palm of my hand, measuring its weight. It smelled like Gram's friend's, Mrs. Putts's, sweater. Every time I cut the grass for her, she paid me with one big hug and one thick slice of her homemade top-secret meatloaf. I never really wanted the hug, but it was the only way to get the meatloaf. Unfortunately, when you hugged Mrs. Putts, you ended up with your face smashed up against that old scratchy brown mothball-smelling sweater. But unlike Mrs. Putts's sweater, this bag was soft and looked like something that belonged to a king or someone else important. Underneath it was a folded piece of cloth. I don't know why, but I wasn't ready to open that bag. I set it aside and pulled out the cloth. It also stank like mothballs, but the colors were still bright—as if the cloth had just been woven yesterday. I put it on the bed and unfolded it.

I laid it out and took extra care to smooth out the wrinkles. The cloth was about two feet square and was embroidered with blues, reds, greens, and golds. A large circle with rays of various shades of gold swirling about it was woven into the middle. It reminded me of the pictures of supernovas we learned about last year in science class.

A strange symbol ran around the inside of the circle's border. *Wait a minute!* I fumbled in my pocket and pulled out the broken piece of mirror. It was glowing even greener than before.

It's the same! The symbol—it's the same!

I returned the mirror to my pocket, and removed the last object from the box: a small envelope. It was sealed with a gold wax stamp—the kind you see in war movies when the secret agent sends a coded message to the general. On the front, in Grandpap's strong handwriting was printed:

> For Jackson Everett Sheppard
> On Your Sixteenth Birthday or in the Event
> of My Death

I slid my finger under the envelope's flap and broke the wax seal. My hands were jittery. I pulled out the neatly creased letter, unfolded it, and read:

> Dearest Jax,
> This letter either finds you on the momentous occasion of your sixteenth birthday or the more unfortunate event of my death. If you are reading this because I have passed, you must never forget how much I love you. My spirit will always be with you.
> You have always known you were different from other children. Your grandmother,

mother, and I pretended your extraordinary physical abilities were nothing more than a unique trait that you were fortunate to possess. In fact, the truth is there is nothing random about your gifts of strength and speed. You have been chosen, as was your mother, as was I, and as was our family for generations before me to serve humanity. We are members of an elite group of guardians selected to preserve and protect the seven fragments of the Kaptropoten and ensure they are never reunited.

I dropped the letter as quickly as if it had grown fangs and bitten me.

Kaptropoten? That word…It was so much like that word from my dream, Kaptrofractus. I looked around for the cameras again. I was sure at any minute Gram would burst in with a bunch of producers from some TV show with a name like, "You've Been Made a Fool of, Punk!" When no one showed, I tried to make sense of what I had just read.

What was a Kaptropoten, anyway? And Mom? How was she involved in this? I swallowed hard to push down the knot that appeared in my throat every time I thought of my mother. It still hurt almost four years later—like a toothache deep inside my chest.

I continued reading:

We are called the Komitari.

I felt queasy. The girl with the accent and Freezer Fingers both had called me Komitari.

It is your great privilege, your responsibility, and your destiny to be part of this elite membership. The Ostium cloth will provide you transport to and from the Isle of Mirrors where you will learn the details of our mission. You are to place the Ostium on the ground in the light of the moon. Stand directly in the center while gazing at your reflection in the mirror.

You must never tell anyone, particularly Normals, of your secret. If you fail to keep this secret you will jeopardize the safety of the Kaptropoten, yourself, and even your loved ones.

Good luck, Jax. I have always been proud of you, and I know you will serve the Kaptropoten with honor.

I love you,
Grandpap

My mind whirled, and the room spun. I pressed my fingers against my forehead to keep the room still. None of this made any sense. What were Normals? And how could Grandpap keep this secret from me for all these years? I folded the letter, put it back in the envelope, and stuck it back in the box. I eyed that little velvet bag.

It gave me the unsettling feeling that once I opened it, there'd be no turning back.

Just do it!

I loosened the drawstring and was surprised by the soft amber glow that surged from the bag. As if in slow motion, I turned it upside down, shaking it by its bottom until its contents plopped softly on the bed. Dumbfounded, I picked up the small piece of mirror that had fallen out.

This had to be the Kaptrofractus. I took inventory of the stuff in the box—here was the letter; the cloth, which Grandpap had called an Ostium; and this—so it must be the Kaptrofractus. This little mirror was so much like the one I had found in the pool. It too was curved on one side and jagged on the other. It was mounted on that same old piece of brass and the inscriptions were also similar. Like mine, it was warm, but it had an amber, golden glow instead of green. It even hummed and vibrated like the green mirror.

Once again, I took my little mirror from my pocket. Holding one piece in each hand, I studied the two strange things. I knew it couldn't be possible, but somehow the jagged edges looked like they would fit together like two pieces of a jigsaw puzzle! I eased them together, but as soon as they were within two inches of each other, the most bizarre thing happened. Each mirror fragment rose about an inch off the palms of my hands. They levitated there for just an instant. In the next second, they started to spin and whir like angry hornets. They spun faster and faster, whirred louder and louder, and began to glow brightly. I had to squint my eyes. Suddenly, like two strong magnets, they slammed together.

The abrupt movement startled me. I threw myself onto the old floral carpet covering the wooden floor and shielded my eyes with my forearm. I lay there for a minute until the room was swallowed in silence.

Afraid of what I might see, I pulled up to my knees and scanned the bed. There, where I had just sat, were the two mirror fragments. Except, now they were fused together in one solid piece—like two pieces of a puzzle that were never cut apart in the first place! I couldn't even find a crack where they used to be separated. It was so weird the way each original piece still glowed in its own unique color, but the colors blended pleasantly where they met. I tried to pick up the newly formed single mirror piece, but had to jerk away. It was hot and burned my fingers.

I waggled my wrist and blew on my hand to cool the sting. The clock ticked from the bedside table. I listened to it for what seemed like hours. Finally, I folded the Ostium, put the now cool Kaptrofractus in the bag, and put them both back in the box.

I dragged myself to the middle of Gram's four poster bed and lowered my head onto Grandpap's pillow. It still smelled like Grandpap—a comforting blend of spiced aftershave and pipe tobacco. I breathed it in. I wanted to hold on to this connection that was so much more real than the letter I just read.

I curled up in a ball. All of this information was overloading my brain. I could picture the tiny hamster who turned the wheel in my head scolding me in his squeaky hamster voice, "You've been up way too long! I quit!"

My eyelids felt like heavy little curtains, ready to draw shut on the last act of a very wacky play. I vaguely remember Gram entering the room. She pulled her soft down comforter over my exhausted body right before I drifted into a deep, heavy sleep.

CHAPTER 5
Poofs, Pancakes, and Missing Pucks

The glare from the sunlight streamed through the window. I pulled the blanket up over my head, trying to block it. It was no use—the sun had no stinking business shining this bright so early in the morning! I pushed back the covers and sat, confused by my surroundings. It took me a minute to remember I had fallen asleep in Gram's room last night. When I figured out where I was, everything came flooding back—the girl, the Gorg, Old Man Gibson's dogs, the box, the mirrors, and Grandpap's letter. It was way too strange to even think about. So many questions needed to be answered.

I tried to push it all out of my mind, but that darned box of Grandpap's was still there, right next to me on the bed. I couldn't help myself. I had to see that mirror again—make sure I hadn't imagined what I saw. I opened the box, pulled out the bag, and loosened the drawstring. Right away, the energy flowed from the bag, and the glow filled the room. I carefully pulled out the mirror. Sure enough, there was the Kaptrofractus, now in one piece, glowing in its strange two-colored way.

I looked at the clock. It read a quarter to four in the afternoon! I had slept like a zombie—you know, before it rises from the grave and eats your brains.

As I sat staring at my reflection in the little mirror, I realized I hadn't even had the dream. It was the first time I hadn't dreamt about Sebastian and Freezer Fingers since that night at the pool.

The sunlight shone through the window. It reflected off the mirror and glared directly into my eyes.

"Go away, sun!"

Well, wouldn't you know, right then, the sun went ahead and glided behind a cloud. For a brief instant, the mirror lit up, exploding in color. It seemed like a really strange coincidence. Of course, I assumed, like anyone would, that the sun had glinted off the mirror in its rush behind the cloud. Soon enough, I would find out just how wrong I was.

A loud growl from my stomach snapped me back to reality. Man, was I hungry!

What I wouldn't give for some of Gram's blueberry pancakes smothered in whipped cream and syrup, I wished, looking at myself in the mirror.

All of a sudden, the mirror lit up again, and I was hit with a small burst of air. *POOF!* Right in front of me appeared a plate piled high with pancakes topped with a mound of whipped cream and dripping with syrup!

"Whoa!" I jumped back against the headboard. The plate fell onto the floor. I leaped from the bed and ran screaming from the room.

"Gram! Where are you? Gram, I need you!"

I raced down the steps three at a time and skidded around the corner into the kitchen. I bumped square into Gram who must have heard me hollering.

"Jackson, what's the matter?"

"P-p-p-pan-c-c-cakes!" I made an explosion-like motion with my fingers and arms. "P-p-poof!" I panted. "No pancakes…then…" I made the explosion motion again. "…pancakes!" I couldn't complete an intelligent sentence. I made the explosion motion one last time for extra effect. "POOF!"

Gram put her palm on my forehead. "Are you getting sick, honey?"

Feeling idiotic, I tried to smile. I think it came out more like the grin of a half-insane jackal.

Gram took me by my arm, steered me to the living room, and sat me on the worn, but comfy pink sofa. She took the spot beside me and rubbed my knee.

"Jackson, honey, I know whatever was in that rotten old box of Grandpap's was very important. And I know whatever it was must have been very alarming. I also know whenever Grandpap got that miserable box out, strange things would start to happen. I was never allowed to open that box or even ask about it. Even though I didn't like it, I have always respected that. But if you need to tell me anything—anything at all—I want you to know I will do whatever it takes to help you." She paused. I could tell she was trying hard to be strong. "I never wanted to give you that miserable box in the first place. But with everything you told me last night…and with all the horrible 'accidents' you've had lately…" She shuddered and made air quotes when she said the word, "accidents." She had to be thinking about the shark tank incident. "I should have given it to you months ago. I don't think I ever had a choice."

I looked into Gram's eyes. I knew she was hurting. Then I remembered the warning in Grandpap's letter: "Failure to keep this secret will jeopardize the safety of the Kaptropoten, you, and your loved ones." I wasn't sure what that meant, but I realized I needed to be strong for Gram—*I* needed to protect *her*.

"Pfffff." I waved my hand in the air. My voice was suspiciously high. "I don't even know what you're talking about. I was just kidding about the pancakes. It's just something we kids say nowadays. We're like, 'Hey, pancakes. Poof! Catch ya' later.'"

I made double-guns with my hands and pointed them at Gram. I pulled the triggers, winked, and clicked my tongue.

Jax Sheppard, I thought sarcastically, *master of the cover-up.* I forced a weak chuckle.

Gram looked at me as if I had sprouted whiskers and a cute cottony tail. She didn't say anything else. I dropped a soft kiss on her cheek. "Don't worry about me, Gram. I'll be fine."

But I had to wonder why Gram mentioned all the recent accidents. Did she think they were somehow related to Grandpap's box? I rubbed the spot on my chest where that bowling ball had nailed me last week. It still baffled me how the ball return machine malfunctioned like that. It had shot the ball out its return hole like a missile. Lucky for me, I had been celebrating my last strike with my original, patented "Eastside Bob" dance—which, by the way, is sure to become a sensation if only a few hundred thousand more kids "like" my video. If I hadn't just bobbed up, that ball would have knocked my head square off my shoulders.

But really. I'm sure I was just having a run of extremely bad luck.

I went upstairs and quickly cleaned the mess I had made when I knocked the pancakes off the bed. On the floor beside the plate was the mirror, which I had dropped in the middle of my panic. I grabbed it, snatched the box from the bed, and ran to my own room where I locked the door. I hid the box in the bottom of the dirty clothes basket in my closet. Anyone looking for the box would have to be a fool or have zero sense of smell to dig past my stinky old sweat socks. I showered and dressed, keeping the mirror close by at all times.

Feeling refreshed, I returned to my room and sat cross-legged on the floor. I tried to concentrate.

I'm sure it was this mirror. I looked at my reflection in the mirror. *Okay. Let's try this.*

"All right. What do I want…what do I want?" But actually, I already knew what I wanted more than anything in the world.

"I want my brother back." Nothing happened. "I wish for Sebastian back," I said louder, concentrating hard on the mirror. "I…want…Sebastian…back!" Still, nothing happened. I tried to shake off the disappointment. I didn't really think it would work anyway.

"All right, let's try this again...Hmmm..." I pondered for a minute. "I wish for the extremely rare and vintage 1970s chewed piece of *blue* Chum Gum to go with the pink piece I already have." My hair blew back from a little burst of wind. A glowing flash of amber lit the room. POOF! There, in my hand, was a small, hardened, chewed-up piece of blue gum. Chills snaked down my back. This was AMAZING!

I HAVE A MAGIC MIRROR!

I thought of all the things I was going to conjure up: cars, boats, cash, Ding Dongs—you name it!

I was interrupted by a knock on the door. "Jackson, honey. Andie is downstairs waiting for you."

"Okay, Gram. Tell her I'll be right down." I stuffed the mirror in the bag, tightened the drawstring, and hung it around my neck like a necklace. I tucked it inside my T-shirt.

Andie was waiting for me in the kitchen, sipping a glass of lemonade Gram had poured for her.

"Hi, Jax. I thought we could go check out the carnival tonight."

The Beyhaven Volunteer Fire Department was holding their annual fundraising carnival in the parking lot of the fire station. The BVFD Carnival was the largest of its kind in the state. They always had tons of carnival rides, a bunch of games of chance and skill, and all sorts of great festival foods.

"I don't know." I was thinking about the mirror and Grandpap's letter. And there was still the matter of the Ostium-cloth-in-the-moonlight business to investigate. I didn't want to wait to check that out. Besides, I hadn't felt like doing anything fun since Sebastian's death. I didn't deserve to have fun. "Maybe we can go tomorrow."

"Jax," Andie said softly, "you know it's okay to let yourself have fun again."

Gram's eyes were hopeful. "Go ahead, honey. You need to have a good time." Very quietly she added, "Sebastian wouldn't want you to keep punishing yourself."

I felt guilty telling her *no*, so I gave in, just as I did when Gram and Andie schemed to get me to go bowling last week.

"All right, I guess. Just let me get my shoes. I'll be right back." I ran up the steps to my room and rifled through my dirty clothes for the box—I was already immune to the smell. I removed the Ostium cloth and rolled it tightly, making it as small as I could. I stuffed it in my waistband, pulled my shirt down over it, and slipped on my sneakers. After a quick check in the mirror to make sure there wasn't a huge lump under my shirt, I ran back downstairs.

"See you later, Gram."

Andie and I hopped on our bikes and pedaled toward town.

As we passed the Gibsons' house, Andie asked, "Did you hear all that barking and commotion at the Gibsons' last night? What was that all about? I could hardly sleep. Man, those three dogs scare the heck out of me!"

"I didn't hear anything." I felt instant guilt. I never kept secrets from Andie, and lying to her just didn't feel right. *Don't tell her! Don't tell her!* I fought the urge to tell her about the mirror.

"I don't know how you could have slept through it. It was crazy loud."

We steered our bikes around the road crew that was patching the potholes left by the Gorg.

"I wonder what happened here."

Don't tell her! Don't tell—but before I could complete the thought, I blurted, "I have a magic mirror around my neck!" Oh my gosh! I couldn't believe I said that out loud! I smacked my forehead. *Dumb, dumb, dumb!*

"What? You have a magic what around your neck?" We stopped our bikes and waited at the intersection for the light to turn green. Andie raised an eyebrow.

I fumbled to cover up my slip. "No. You heard me wrong. I said, 'I have a *plastic deer* on my back *deck*.' You know, for Christmas. We didn't put it away yet."

Andie wasn't buying it, so I followed up with a weak, "Hey, pancakes." I raised my eyebrows, gave her the insane jackal smile, and did a half-hearted double-guns click. "Another great cover-up, Jax," I muttered, shaking my head at my own stupidity.

Andie looked unconvinced. I gave up and fixed my eyes straight ahead on the stop light.

"No, you did *not* say that, Jax." She wasn't one bit distracted by the pancakes comment. "You said you have a magic mirror around your neck. I heard you." She walked her bike in front of mine to block my way. Without any warning, she reached over and grabbed the rope around my neck. She gave a quick flick of her wrist and freed the small velvet bag from my shirt. "What's this?"

Just then, the light changed. I yanked the bag away from Andie. Using my super speed, I steered around her and began pedaling.

"See you at the carnival," I called over my shoulder.

As I zoomed down the street, I was a blur. But the stupid gears on my bike rebelled when they couldn't keep up with me. The chain popped off, and I had to hop off the bike. Darn super speed!

I grappled with the chain for a few minutes but in the end, the chain claimed victory. Then, I remembered the mirror around my neck. I pulled it out, looked at my reflection, and concentrated with all the intensity I could muster.

"I wish my bike was fixed." I waited for that little pop of air and the burst of color. Nothing happened. I had to wonder if this thing came with an instruction manual. And then a thought entered my mind that I couldn't deny: *If it does, I'm going to find out how to get Sebastian back.*

When Andie caught up with me, I had just slipped the mirror back in the bag. I was on my fourth failed attempt at reattaching the chain to the gears.

"Serves you right. Let me do it." She dropped her bike in a nearby yard and shoved me out of the way. She fixed the chain with the ease of a bike shop mechanic. "You're not off the hook, Jax. I want to know what you have in that bag."

"It's a long story." I sighed. "I promise I'll tell you later."

For a second, Andie looked like she was going to let

it go. I figured I had bought myself some time to come up with a good story, but she didn't stop.

"And don't think I haven't noticed you've been getting even faster and stronger lately. Were you planning on telling me about *that* anytime soon?"

It was obvious Andie wasn't going to let me brush her off completely. But honestly, I couldn't talk about it. It was like my thoughts were all jumbled up in a giant word-search puzzle inside my head. They were sprinkled in with terms like *Kaptrofractus*, *secret*, *Gorg*, and *pancakes*. There was no way I could find the exact words I needed to explain everything. I wanted more time to figure out how much to say and exactly how to say it. I rode ahead and ignored Andie's question.

When we got to the carnival, Andie seemed willing to drop the subject. We stowed our bikes on the rack and headed for the hot dog stand. The music from the carousel drifted through the air. Throngs of people zipped from one brightly colored attraction to the next. It looked like all of Beyhaven was here. The smell of french fries and funnel cakes danced in my nostrils. But still, I couldn't get into the carnival spirit. Sebastian had looked forward to coming to the BVFD Carnival every year. It was his favorite thing to do each summer. Standing here, I could almost feel him tugging on my arm, trying to drag me toward the Tea Cup ride.

At once, I didn't feel like hanging out at the fair anymore. I shouldn't be here after what I did to Sebastian.

"Andie." My eyes burned from the unshed tears. "I'm ready to go."

Andie studied my face for a second. I knew she understood.

"Okay." She nodded. "Can we just grab a bite before we go? I'm starving." Before I could protest, she stepped in line at the hot dog stand. She bought a bunch of dogs for us to share.

The sight of those hot dogs reminded me of the magical pancakes that never did make their way into my mouth. My stomach orchestrated a mutiny, clearly siding with Andie. I had just inhaled my second chili-cheese dog when we spotted Drake at the High Striker booth. He was with a group of kids from school and was drooling all over Marisa Roth, a girl from my science class.

"Let me just say a quick hi before we go." Andie went over to Drake and the crowd of kids. It didn't seem like she ever had any intention of leaving the carnival. I sighed and followed her over to the High Striker.

"Hey, Drake!" Andie said just as he swung the large hammer. The puck rose about halfway up the twenty-foot tower before falling back to the base. A buzzer sounded, and a light flicked on illuminating a sign that read, "Dud!"

The crowd booed, and Drake stepped aside. "Awww! C'mon! You guys distracted me. I was about to win that big purple gorilla."

"How about you, son?" the operator called out to me. "Step on up and test your strength on the High Striker! Let's see what a real man can do."

I shook my head. Everyone was staring at me. "No thanks, I'm not very strong."

But this guy was relentless. "Don't be a sissy, son! Step on up and win a prize for your beautiful lady."

Andie shook her head. She made a face that looked like she had just eaten freshly ground earthworms. "He's not my boyfriend."

The man kept pushing. "Show us what you're made of!"

Pretty soon the kids from school joined in chanting, "Do it, do it, do it!"

Drake pushed me to the front of the crowd. He stuck the giant hammer in my hand.

"Traitor," I muttered. "Shouldn't you be home writing your term paper?"

He grinned and put his arm around Marisa's shoulders. I stepped up to the High Striker. Past experience had taught me these types of games never went too well for me. I usually tried to avoid them. So for now, my plan was to give it just a light tap. I made a big scene of heaving the mallet up over my head. I grunted and panted for effect. Then I let it drop ever so gently on the target. Apparently, it wasn't gentle enough, though. The puck whistled to the top of the twenty-foot tower. It whacked the bell so hard it gave one loud clang, cracking the bell, which fell off the board. Believe it or not, that stinking puck wasn't slowed one bit by its collision with the bell. It kept right on going and flew off the top of the tower. It actually seemed excited to be free from its track. The stupid thing sailed high above the crowd, plotting its escape. Darn super strength!

The crowd all gasped. I had flashbacks of the traumatic dodgeball incident.

The operator was not the least bit pleased. "What do you think you're doing, kid? You broke it! You broke my game! Who's going to pay to repair this?" His head whipped from left to right. He searched for the puck like he had lost his winning lottery ticket. "Where'd my puck go?"

Before the crowd had a chance to figure out what I had done, Andie rushed to my rescue.

"That game was fixed!" She pointed theatrically at the tower. "There's no way my wimpy boyfriend could have done that. Look how pathetically small he is. Even *my* arms are bigger than his."

I didn't know if I should be thankful for her passionate defense—she actually pretended I was her boyfriend!—or offended by the "pathetically small" comment.

Andie continued, "You owe us a gorilla!"

"And your pathetically small boyfriend owes me a puck!"

Not knowing what else to do, I offered up a nervous, "Don't worry, I'll go find it."

I took off in the direction I thought I had seen the puck fly. I was searching over by the Duck Pond game when a voice with a familiar accent asked, "Looking for this?"

I stopped cold. There, straight in front of me, was the girl from last night. She stood tall and proud, and in her outstretched hand was the missing puck.

In the bright overhead lights of the carnival, I'd have to have been a complete moron not to notice she was even prettier than she had looked behind the bushes.

She seemed about nineteen. And trust me, those nineteen years had been very, *very* kind to her. Last night, I didn't notice how clear and green her eyes were—kind of like new moss growing on a rotting log—only not furry. And her skin—it was pure white and looked so soft—like quilted toilet paper.

Oh man. Here I go again!

She was dressed in some kind of unusual costume. It was a cross between medieval warrior and gladiator princess. There were all sorts of props attached to her, like daggers, swords, and bow and arrows. On her right ring finger was an obnoxiously large gold ring with a huge red ruby stone. It was definitely over the top, even for a costume. Maybe she was one of those Spaceys who was obsessed with the movie *Space Wars*. She was probably participating in one of those weird reenactments.

Whatever the costume was for, it didn't matter to me. If anyone could pull it off, it was this girl. I made a mental note to watch my *Space Wars II* DVD when I got home. My knees felt weak, and I tried to remember what it felt like before the bones in my legs vaporized like the droids in *Space Wars III*.

"You!" was all I could manage to choke out.

I barely noticed Andie, who had found me and was staring at me staring at the girl. We all just stood there saying nothing until Andie finally spoke. She snatched the puck from the girl's hand.

"Thanks for this." She gave the girl a bored glance. "You can go back to whatever it was you were doing now." She made a shooing motion and took my arm. "Let's go, Jax."

I pulled against her. "Wait." I shook free of Andie's grip. I drew myself up as tall as I could, puffed out my chest, and did my best cool-guy impression. "W-w-what you name?" It didn't come out exactly as I planned.

"Excuse me?" She tilted her head.

"You name." I tried again. "What it called?" There was definitely something different about this girl. She made me feel like my brain had been traded for mashed potatoes.

Andie rolled her eyes. "Your name." She sighed. "He wants to know your name."

"My name is Princess Katriana, and I have come to escort you to the Isle of Mirrors."

CHAPTER 6
The Princess and the Portal

The princess' words rang in my ears like a thousand cracked High Striker bells.

She wants to take me to the Isle of Mirrors! I gulped. I touched the lump created by the rolled-up Ostium cloth under my shirt. Grandpap's letter had told me to go to the Isle of Mirrors. Andie's shocked expression would have been funny—except I knew Princess Katriana was dead serious.

"Of course, Your Highness," Andie said, drawing out the words. She bowed her head and curtsied. With the back of her hand by the side of her mouth, she pretended to whisper. Instead, she was ridiculously loud. "Pack your bags, Jax. She's taking you to Mirror Island." Her next comment was to Katriana. "Are you nuts?"

Man, Andie was being rude. It wasn't like her at all. She was normally super nice to people. But I got the feeling Andie didn't like this girl. Luckily, Katriana either didn't notice or didn't care.

"The name of the island is *Isle of Mirrors*." She never took her eyes off of me. "And we must leave without delay."

I grabbed Andie's arm. "Princess Katriana, I need to talk to my friend. Alone."

"Of course. But you must hurry. Dusk is nearly upon us, and we must leave at the moon's first light if we are to make it in time for Council to convene. And please, call me Kat."

I pulled Andie between the Duck Pond booth and the Skeeball booth. Kat stared at us, but she stayed far enough away for me to have a private chat with Andie.

I hesitated. I had no idea what to tell Andie. It didn't matter though, because she blurted, "Do you know this girl, Jax? I mean, this chick is capital C-R-A-Z-Y. She's a total freak—she actually scares me! Let's get out of here."

I took a breath. "I—uh—sort of know her. I saved her from the Gibsons' dogs last night."

"You were involved in that?" She whacked me on the arm. "Why did you lie to me?"

"Andie, please, let me finish. Remember the...uh... mirror I told you about?" I lifted the bag out of my shirt. Before I could take the rope off my neck, an iron grip seized my wrist.

"That would not be wise, Komitari." Kat was beside me. Just like last night, I couldn't believe how strong she was. It took every bit of my super strength to break free, and that bothered me. I had never met anyone even half as strong as I was.

"Hey, what's your problem?" Andie shouted. "Let go of my friend!"

"This does not concern you." Kat spoke to Andie for the first time. "It is honorable that you are trying to protect your friend—I understand that—but you would do best to run along, child. Leave this matter to your friend and me."

Andie's face flashed right past red and all the way to purple. "Child? Who are you calling a child? I am almost fourteen, I'll have you know! And anyway, anything that concerns my friend, concerns me. Why don't you go back to your stupid gladiator games and leave us alone?"

Kat glanced at Andie like she was just an annoying gnat. Then to me, she said, "You are new to this, Komitari, so perhaps you do not fully understand the Komitari Code. That is why it is imperative for you to accompany me at once. Caephus has sent me to retrieve you, and we cannot afford for you to make any more mistakes."

She studied Andie, peered into her eyes, and spoke real slow—like Andie didn't understand English. "Please reconsider your position. I am certain you will see reason and choose to stay here while young Jackson and I tend to our business."

As she said the words, a ridiculous fear brewed in my gut. Nobody talked to Andie that way. Not unless they were prepared to open up a whole can of psycho-Andie. I took cover behind the Skeeball booth and waited for Andie to start swinging Kat around by her beautiful braid like a lasso. Instead, Andie's response left me speechless.

"Okay. Fine." Her face was expressionless. Then, she gave the Skeeball operator five dollars! She was totally calm. "Ten balls, please." Andie hated games with balls, so I could only stand there shaking my head in disbelief!

I was stunned. I didn't resist when Kat pulled me

toward the open field behind the carnival tents and trailers. Normally, I never would have dreamed of going off by myself with a gorgeous older girl into a secluded, dark field for a private meeting. I mean, I *was* only thirteen. I was pretty sure Gram wouldn't approve—but I figured I owed it to Andie since she blew five bucks to roll balls. So I forced myself to go. And anyway, the whole situation fascinated me. Besides, it was like I was honoring Grandpap by following through on his instructions.

"I can't believe you convinced Andie to do that." I trailed behind Kat.

Kat shrugged. "You must not worry about her. I merely suggested she find something to keep herself busy. She is a reasonable girl. She must have realized how rudely she was behaving." Kat looked up at the sky. "There." She pointed at the moon. It was casting a beautiful, luminescent glow on the grass. "It is perfect."

There was no one around, and it had grown way cooler. The sounds of the music and the crowd were a distant echo, but we ventured even farther away from the bright lights of the carnival.

Kat stopped in the center of the field and reached for another bag. This one was also leather, but it was larger and strapped to her back. She opened the flap and took out a folded cloth. Once she shook out the wrinkles, she laid it on the ground. It was an Ostium and was just like mine, except hers had red rays surrounding the circle instead of gold.

"This would be much more comfortable for the both of us if you had brought your own Ostium. But since you do not have it, I suppose we will have to make the voyage together." She shuddered, like maybe I was smelly or something. Come to think of it, I hadn't used the Stink Away Body Spray after my shower today, just in case I encountered any more Gorgs.

"I do have mine." I had no idea what was about to happen, but I could smell my own curiosity—it practically bubbled out of my ears.

I took the folded Ostium out of my waistband and copied Kat. When she stepped into the center of the circle on her Ostium, I did the same. Then she took a small mirror from the front pocket of her backpack. I wasn't even surprised when it glowed red. I wondered what would happen if we put our mirrors beside each other.

I opened my velvet bag and took out the Kaptrofractus. I couldn't miss Kat's eyes. They were pinned to my hand. As soon as the little mirror was out of the bag, the two-toned light lit up the space around me.

Kat's eyebrows went higher than the High Striker puck. "What—how—why is it like that?" For a moment, she looked rattled. Then, her eyes narrowed. "*Did you reunite two fragments?* Do you realize what you have done? How did you get the second piece? Perhaps you have been deceiving me all along—perhaps you are far more involved than you have pretended to be."

I panicked. I vaguely remembered something in Grandpap's letter about not reuniting the fragments. How the heck was I supposed to know what that meant?

"Look. I didn't do it on purpose. Nobody told me not

to put them beside each other. I was just looking at them and then, bam! This happened. What's the big deal?"

Lucky for me, Kat became distracted when the light faded. A giant cloud had floated in front of the moon.

"Oh, no! We cannot transport without the moonlight. It is simply too overcast for us to travel to the island. We should leave before someone discovers us."

I was disappointed. I looked at my mirror. Liquid courage was pumping through my veins. If there was ever a time when I would be ready to try this, it was now. Otherwise, I'd probably chicken out.

"Stupid clouds," I muttered, "why can't you just go away?"

My mirror exploded in color. What happened next was totally amazing. The clouds split in half and raced away!

Kat nodded. "Ah, I see you have the Kaptro Elementum. Well played."

I didn't have any idea what she was talking about. "Yeah. The Kaptro Elementary. I use it all the time for like, pancakes and gum and stuff."

Kat rolled her eyes. "Good for you." She looked up at the night sky. "We must go."

She stood there, staring at her reflection in her mirror—I couldn't say that I blamed her! If I looked that good, I'd check myself out all day long.

Then, the craziest thing happened. The winds all joined together to form a mini cyclone around Kat. Her clothes and braid whipped against her body. At the same time, the red rays on her Ostium began to glow. At once, they lifted up off the cloth. They started rotating with the winds. As they spun, they licked at Kat like red flames devouring fresh kindling. Soon, they ate her up from head to toe. The rush of winds became deafening and then—silence. Kat was gone! The cloth was gone too. All that was left in its place was a two-foot square patch of scorched grass.

"Oh my gosh, oh my gosh, oh my gosh!" I shifted from foot to foot. I gulped down what was supposed to be a calming breath. "Okay, Jax, you can do this. It's a portal. The cloth is obviously some type of portal. You've seen this on *Space Wars*—it's no big deal. I'm sure everyone's doing it these days. Just stay calm."

I took another breath, raised the Kaptrofractus, and stared at myself. The winds began to swirl around me. The rays rose off the cloth. I was excited and frightened at the same time. Suddenly, there was a flash of movement in the mirror. Someone was coming!

Don't move, Jax! You're almost there.

As the golden flames overcame me, the person behind me called, "Jax! Stop! I'm coming to help you! Get out of there!"

It was Andie—she must have come to her senses after rolling that Skeeball a few times. In the mirror, I could see her running toward me.

It was too late, though. I felt all tingly. Like all the molecules in my body were bouncing off each other. A loud rushing sounded in my ears. The world around me began to spin, and I was in the eye of a tornado. It sucked my body matter outward and into its rotating spirals.

Andie's image flicked past over and over again. Just when I felt like I was being drawn by the top of my head into some tight, suffocating tunnel, Andie lunged at me. In the nick of time, she managed to grab on to my leg.

"Andie! No!" But I was already being sucked through the whirling, gray tunnel. My body parts stretched to inhuman lengths. I felt nauseous and was pretty sure I should've passed on the second chili-cheese dog. All the while, Andie's weight pulled me down. It caused my body to stretch out even more, if that was physically possible.

And then the spinning stopped.

CHAPTER 1
The Very Sorry Komitari

The world stopped spinning, and I stumbled. I teetered on my Ostium and tried to catch my balance. My eyeballs bounced from side to side in their sockets, like no one had told them the earth was now still. Andie groaned at my feet and rolled to her side. She was just in time. I heaved, and even though only two chili-cheese dogs went in, I'd be willing to bet three or four came out—all over the Ostium.

When the dizziness began to fade, I became aware of my surroundings. It was daylight and the sun's rays warmed my cheeks. We had been dropped on a white sand beach with the sea at our backs. The clear blue waves were welcoming as they lapped at my ankles. Andie was still on the ground, so she got soaked. She was curled up on her side and clutching her stomach.

In the shallow water, green blades of seaweed were dotted with little pearly shells. They swayed gracefully with the current. Elegant cypress trees and majestic pines lined the top of the beach past a series of gently rolling dunes. There weren't any palm trees, though, so I was guessing this wasn't a tropical island. A wide path was cut through the trees, and a flurry of people were using it to get to and from the beach.

About six feet to my right, Kat was on her Ostium. She looked just like she did before we left—collected, confident, and beautiful—and not at all rattled by her trip through the portal. She checked out the remnants of my dinner and curled her lip.

"Neophyte."

"Neo-what?"

While I waited for an answer, a sturdy hand clapped my shoulder.

"Neophyte. It means rookie, novice, greenhorn, beginner," a cheerful male voice said. "Don't feel bad, though. All the first time transporters hurl."

The guy stepped in front of me. He had a wide grin on his face, and his blue eyes sparkled. He looked about sixteen or seventeen, and he reminded me of a cartoon character. His long face was silly-looking—his nose was slightly crooked, and his eyes were too close together. It was made all the goofier by the way his funny face perched on top of a perfectly built male body.

He was about a foot taller than I was, and he wore a light-brown suede vest with no sleeves. His arms were covered with lumps and bumps and lumps *on* bumps. They could only have been described as major muscles. In fact, his arms bulged so much, I tugged at my sleeves. I was totally planning to hit the weights when I got back to Beyhaven.

"Welcome to the Isle of Mirrors." He shook my hand, pumping it up and down like he was inflating a soccer ball. "The name's Cletus, of Flaeritay. I'll be your Komitari attendant. Great to finally meet you. Caephus is waitin' for you at headquarters, so we should probably get goin' to the K-Coaster—unless you want to stop at your room first. I could use a bite to eat. You hungry? Nope—pretty sure you're not hungry." He looked down at my dirty Ostium and then called to a small, baby-faced boy on the beach. "Take care of this." He pointed to my Ostium cloth.

The boy nodded and reached inside his shirt. He pulled out a pair of kitchen tongs, which he used to pick up the dirty Ostium. His level of preparedness was impressive. I wondered if he had a pair of dry shoes for me in there too.

"I'll get this cleaned and to your room right away, Master Jax." The boy bowed and ran off toward the path.

I was so dizzy, I couldn't be sure I was seeing straight, but I swear the sturdy, little fellow had a big brawny and hairy chest.

Cletus didn't move. I felt like he was waiting for me to say something.

"I'm Jax," I said, even though the boy with the tongs had just called me by my name. My voice was still shaky from the trip through the portal. "I'm from Pennsylvania."

"I know who you are. Kat went to get you." He crouched to help Andie off the ground. "But who's your pal, here, huh?" His eyebrow was raised. He had a silly-looking smile plastered on his silly-looking face as he nodded at Andie.

I had forgotten about Andie. I felt a bit guilty about that, but mostly, I had a minor case of the willies. The way Cletus looked at Andie—it was weird. I guess some people would describe her as pretty, but let's get serious here—we were talking about Andie, my best friend.

"Are you okay?" I asked her.

She groaned again, but let Cletus help her to her feet.

"I'm Andie." Her voice was shaky, her face was pasty, and her pupils were the size of nickels. "Where are we?" She swayed before fainting into Cletus' arms.

"Now isn't that a bugger?" Cletus mused. "Usually it's only Normals who can't handle the transport like this. No worries, though. Should be only temporary." He gave Andie a once-over. "Hold on there, kid. Don't tell me you brought a *Normal* with you?" He threw back his head and laughed. "That's classic! You know your mother was the only other Komitari ever to come to the island with a Normal. Priceless. Absolutely priceless."

"You knew my mother?" A huge bubble of excitement rose in my chest. Even though Gram and I never discussed Mom, I still remembered how she would tuck me in every night. She would always rub my back and whisper her favorite quote.

"Remember, baby," she would say, "the wings of angels are often found on the backs of the least likely people." I never understood what that meant, but after she died, I would whisper it to Sebastian every night before he fell asleep.

And, of course, I had always wanted to know more about Mom's life. Maybe Cletus could answer some of the questions that buzzed about my head like bees around a honeypot.

"Never actually met her," he said. "But I was in the audience when she was awarded the Golden Speculum. And they say Rephael himself was the one who gave it to her, you know. Don't get me wrong. We didn't get to see Rephael in person. Meredith had a private audience with him. And after she received the award, Caephus presented her to the crowd. Totally exciting it was. Only time I ever saw a Golden Speculum awarded. But that's enough natterin' for now. Gotta get the Normal to Caephus, and they can brief you while we're at HQ."

"Brief me?" I was confused. Now I had even more questions.

Cletus marched up the beach carrying Andie. "Let's roll out! What are you waitin' for?"

To the right of me, a full team of people swarmed around Kat. As she marched toward the tree line, she stripped off her weapons and layers of armor. She loaded the items onto the arms of the people around her.

I followed Cletus to the path. We walked for at least a half a mile through the dense woods. I anticipated the wooden cabins, rope bridges, and campfires that I guessed were waiting at the end of the path. If it weren't for the fact that I had just seen dozens of people bustling about, I would have thought we had trekked deep into the woods. Monkeys howled while swinging from tree to tree. Birds with black-and-white feathers soared above, calling greetings to each other as they passed. We even had to wait while a huge, wrinkled elephant lumbered across the path! Strangely enough, there wasn't any chirping of insects or croaking of frogs. When I looked around, I didn't catch sight of a single bug in the air or on the forest floor.

Soon enough, we reached a clearing carved into the center of the island. What I saw was not even close to what I had expected. A massive, polished rollercoaster track stretched and twisted from one end of the clearing to the other. Its metallic rails curled around buildings, under trees, and through tunnels. I was thinking about how odd it was to have a modern coaster plopped right here in the middle of this remote island, when a car thundered across its tracks. It carried only two passengers. One had his arms raised. He screamed like a maniac as they raced around a deep bend and through a tunnel.

Rising from the center of the coaster was a shimmering glass complex. It had walls made entirely of mirrors. Spires and towers stretched toward the sky, making it feel really gothic. It looked a lot like the castles we had learned about in Social Studies. One enormous building rose from the center of the complex. It was as tall as any skyscraper. Parapets and peaks at its roofline gave it the appearance of a castle keep. The mirrored sides reflected the trees, the clouds, and all of its surroundings. It created an awesome display that played tricks on my eyes. Sunlight glinted off of every angle and cast sparkling rainbows of light over the entire island. The mirrored castle looked really odd sitting there in the middle of all that nature. But it was so indescribably beautiful that a quiet gasp escaped my mouth.

"Where are we?"

Cletus was still holding Andie. She slept peacefully in his bulging arms. His smile beamed like a flashlight. "Pretty, isn't it?" He looked at the clearing like he was seeing it for the first time. His eyes were full of pride. "Isle of Mirrors is the most beautiful place in the world. Lucky for us, it's shielded from anyone but guardians of the mirror. Only two ways on and off the island. One is with an Ostium, and the other is—well, you'll learn all that stuff later."

"But *where* are we? Where exactly is this island?"

"It's one of the six small islands that make up the Italian city of Murano in the Adriatic Sea. Won't find it on any maps, though. On the maps, they only show five of the islands because the shield makes our little island invisible. Pretty ingenious, eh?"

"Yeah, I guess so. So why am I here?"

Cletus readjusted his hold on Andie and shifted her weight. "Gettin' hot." He completely ignored my question. "Gotta find out what to do with her. Move it out!" He made his way to the courtyard in front of the castle.

For the second time, I followed along. Various groups of people hustled around, and I had to stare. There was this group of…uh…toddler boys? They were all about three to four feet tall, and they had these cute round baby faces with big bald heads. Each boy was dressed like the kid who had taken my Ostium. They wore short pants, which were cut off at the knees, and white V-neck shirts. Brown sashes were slung across their unusually wide and muscular chests. The sashes displayed various colored badges, although some had just a few and others had more than a dozen.

Every one of the boys was barefoot. Their ridiculously large feet were way too big for their small bodies—in fact, they had even bigger feet than that elephant I saw earlier! I didn't want to gawk, but if I counted right, each one had four toes per foot, with huge, big toes. I had a thing about feet, so I shuddered when their group stomped past us with their big bare feet exposed for the world to see. And my observation from before was true. These boys had hairy chests peeking out of the Vs! They weren't actually boys at all. They were little men!

"Pedamples," Cletus called over his shoulder. "They assist the Komitari here on the island. You can have your own Ped assigned to you when you leave here if you want."

The thought of having my very own little hairy-chested bigfoot was so crazy I laughed uncontrollably. I pictured myself sitting in algebra class while my baby-faced Ped massaged my shoulders, taking breaks only when I needed him to brush the eraser bits off of my notebook paper. I laughed so hard I snorted. One of the Peds shouted, "Gesundheit!"

We neared the entry to the skyscraper, which was centrally located at the end of the courtyard. There were no doors, and the lower floor stood on mirrored glass stilts. It was open on three sides except for the back wall, which held a massive elevator door.

Cletus used the tip of Andie's foot to push the button. When the door slid open, we both stepped on.

The walls of the elevator were plated with brass. Large expensive-looking mirrors were mounted on the back and sides. Fancy carpet covered the floor and the pattern resembled the one on the Ostium. Beside the door, right where the buttons would normally be, was one lonely round mirror.

Cletus leaned forward and huffed on the mirror. A small white cloud appeared on its surface. His attempt to use Andie's toe to rub something on the fresh huff mark was funny and unsuccessful. The cloud faded and the doors to the elevator popped back open.

He huffed again. "How about writin' a seventy-seven in that cloud for me?"

My finger squeaked as it traced the numbers on the mirror.

"Bing!" The elevator responded and a pleasant female voice confirmed, "Seventy-seventh floor."

Loud elevator music filled the small space. We both stared at the numbers above the door. Little lights illuminated each floor we passed.

"Bing…Bing…Bing."

My palms were sweating like they had the time I got called to the principal's office for collecting the chewed gum off the bottoms of the gym bleachers. Who knew it was inappropriate to be hanging out under the bleachers while the girls watched a film about their blossoming buds?

Seventy-seven bings later, the voice said, "You have arrived at the seventy-seventh floor. Have a nice day and thank you for visiting IOM headquarters."

We got off the elevator and stepped into a large lobby. A super tall dark-skinned woman greeted us. She told us to have a seat on one of the leather benches and wait to be called. The name plaque on her desk read, "Zara." Zara was at least six-and-a-half feet tall and super thin. She reminded me of the willow tree growing in Andie's backyard. Her hair was green and looked more like a glittery, glossy helmet than it did actual hair. It came together in a deep peak on the center of her forehead, and there was a curved point at top. The most unusual thing about this lady was the big, green jewel stuck in her forehead right at the peak of her hair. I couldn't imagine how it got there, but I guessed it had to be painful.

Cletus leaned over to me. "She's a Quinorian. Their jewels are their life force. They receive energy from the moon and convert it to fuel. Kinda like food for you and me."

I had to ask, "Is this for real?" I didn't mean just the Quinorian.

"Every bit of it."

We waited for a few more minutes. It was just long enough for my nerves to start percolating like a pot of Gram's famous coffee.

"Caephus will see you now." Zara opened the solid wooden doors to the boardroom.

Cletus carried Andie into the room, and I walked in behind them. There was a long mirrored table in the center of the room. Seated on the far side of it was none other than Kat. She shook her head and rolled her eyes at the sight of Andie in Cletus' arms. Beside Kat was a kid who was just as handsome as Kat was pretty. He was dressed in the same type of *Space Wars* costume as Kat. He was probably about seventeen.

Two chairs to Kat's right were two women, both dressed in white robes. Their hair was twisted into funky little sculptures on their heads. A delicate, nerdy-looking man with thick glasses and a tweed suit sat alone all the way at the end of the table. Since he sat at the end, I figured this guy must be Caephus. The other eleven chairs were empty.

Zara motioned to Cletus to put Andie on the sleek gray sofa against the window wall. She then showed the two of us to the seats across from Kat.

Once we were seated, I looked at tweed guy, and he looked at his notes. I looked at Kat, and she looked at the door. I looked at the lady with the pretzel sculpture on her head, and she looked at the lady with the corkscrew on her head. I looked at Cletus, and he looked at Andie. I couldn't take it anymore. The suspense was worse than waiting for the mail lady to deliver my chewed-gum-of-the-month club package. I didn't know how long I could stand it before somebody actually told me what I was doing here on this island.

As it was, I hadn't learned anything that would explain the stuff Grandpap wrote about. I hadn't learned anything about Mom, either. Worse yet, I wasn't any closer to finding out if this mirror had the power to bring someone back from the dead. I was starting to think I never would find out. My watch read a quarter past ten, even though it was still daylight here. I was sure Gram would be worried sick if I didn't get home soon. And there was no telling how Andie's dad would react to her being out so late.

Finally, I looked back at tweed guy and blurted, "Hello, Mr. Caephus. I'm Jax, son of Meredith Sheppard. My grandfather was Harold Everett. Could you please tell me why I'm here?"

Caephus didn't even look up from the papers he was studying. Nobody else said a word.

"Okay." I tried another tactic. I took out my Kaptrofractus. Kat's eyes narrowed in on my mirror with laser precision. It made me worry all over again about the reuniting snafu. One quick scan around the table was all I needed to see everyone was freaked out by my two-toned mirror. I hoped Caephus wouldn't blame me for the whole joining-the-two-pieces-together thing.

I didn't think I could get any more nervous than I already was. "Um…okay…I was wondering if there was some kind of instruction manual for this." Still, no one answered. "Something I could…download online… perhaps?"

More silence. My face burned with anger.

"All right, Mr. Caephus. Fine. I see how it is here. You know what? You can have your dumb mirrors back." I was mad, but I felt like I had to explain. "They're kind of stuck to each other, but I bet if you whack it just right with a hammer they'll break back apart." I slid the mirror to the middle of the table. "Now, if it's okay with you, sir, maybe someone can show me where my Ostium is, and I'll get Andie, and we'll be on our way home."

He looked like an owl, the way he blinked at me through his glasses. He scribbled something in his notebook.

Cletus began chuckling, quietly at first but then louder. Eventually he was laughing so hard his whole body shook. The kid with Kat tried to stay serious, but after a while he started laughing too. Before I knew it, even Caephus had joined in. He let out what sounded more like a string of snorts than a real laugh.

"What?" I knew they were laughing at me, but I couldn't tell why. "What's so funny?"

"Caephus?" Cletus pointed a finger at tweed guy. "Him? Caephus?" He laughed so hard, he was crying now. "That's a good one!"

To make things worse, tweed guy pulled a small piece of paper from his notebook. He scrawled something on it and peeled what looked like a label from the paper. He stuck it to his lapel. It said, "Hi, my name is Galen." He snorted again.

That made Cletus break into a fresh round of laughter. Even Kat was laughing. Her throat made a sound as sweet and clear as the tinkling of choir bells.

"Galen is Caephus' attendant." Cletus wiped his stupid tears with the back of his stupid hands.

Then, an enormous arched gold door on the wall behind the other end of the table opened. The laughter stopped. Everyone sat up stiff and tall, just like all the kids in my first grade class would when Ms. Schnook entered the room. The most impressive-looking man I had ever seen came through the door. He stopped beside the huge leather chair across from Galen. To say he was large would have been a serious understatement. Gigantic was more like it. Next to him Zara looked petite. He might have been eleven or twelve feet tall, and he was wide too.

I couldn't believe someone so enormous could have such a well-fitting suit. They must have a Larry's Humongous and Giant Palace here on the island, like the Larry's Big and Tall Palace at home where Grandpap used to shop.

His face was strong. It looked like someone had just finished carving his chin and cheeks out of stone. He could have been anywhere from forty-five to seventy-five. There were wrinkles on the sides of his eyes, but they might've come from smiling a lot and not from being old. He stood there in a giant bubble of confidence.

His eyes swept the room and paused briefly on each face. He greeted everyone with just a slice of a nod. When his deep blue eyes landed on me, it was pretty clear tweed guy wasn't Caephus. This guy was obviously Caephus. And physically, he couldn't have been any more different than tweed guy. I recognized my mistake. I stretched across the table like a sly cat and snatched my mirror back. It fell to the ground when I tried to stick it under the table on my lap. When I went to pick it up, I couldn't help but notice the grungy pair of leather sandals tweed guy was wearing with his suit. They had definitely seen better days—they were worn and discolored and way too big. I snatched my mirror and sat back up.

"Son," Caephus said to me. His pure, deep voice rolled across the space between us. It wrapped around the room. "I see you have brought a Normal with you. Normals are forbidden here on the island." He pressed a buzzer on a little box atop the table. Zara glided in.

"You will see to it she is taken care of," Caephus said.

Zara nodded and left the room. She had barely walked out the door when two men in white coveralls marched in carrying a cot. They were in perfect rhythm as they put the cot on the floor. They snapped on some blue rubber gloves, loaded Andie onto the cot, and marched back out the door.

"Hey!" I pushed the chair away from the table and started after the men. "Where are you taking her?"

The men ignored me.

This was ridiculous! I was already annoyed that nobody had bothered to tell me what was going on. And now these men were kidnapping my best friend!

I was racing to stop the two men from disappearing with Andie when the double doors swung shut. They locked automatically. Suddenly, I was terrified for Andie. I lifted one knee and kicked the door with the bottom of my foot. It tore from its hinges and bounced across the hall. Zara smothered a little scream when the door crashed through the wall of windows at the opposite end of the floor.

I leaped toward the elevator. But, before I could get there, Caephus materialized right in front of me! He blocked my path and put a massive hand on my shoulder.

"You have your mother's spirit, young Jackson." His

deep voice made my eardrums tickle with the vibra-
tion. "Miss Andrea is being taken to the infirmary. She
may rest there until she recovers from the effects of the
transport. She will be well-attended, and you may see her
when she regains consciousness. Now, please, rejoin us
in the boardroom. Your role here is vital to the mission.
There is much to discuss and little time."

Something about Caephus made me believe him.
Even though just a few minutes earlier I had been
ready to go straight home and slip under my nice, warm
Scooby Doo blanket, I decided to trust him—at least
for a little longer. I believed him when he said Andie
would be taken care of. I let myself feel just a little
excitement about the possibility Caephus might tell
me something about my family's role in this mirror
business. And anyway, there was still one burning question that had been melting a hole in my brain since I
discovered my mirror was magic. I figured it might be
worth it to hang on to the mirror and see what else I
could discover.

But what did he mean when he said I had a vital role
in the mission?

On the way back in the boardroom, we passed through
the hole where the door had hung just minutes ago.

"Sorry about that. If you want me to fix it, I could
probably bend those hinges back in to place."

Caephus seemed unconcerned. "The door fell seventy-
seven stories."

I guess he didn't think I could repair it, but it didn't
matter anyway. Before I could even sit, a drill whirred.

When I turned, a brand new door already replaced the one I had kung-fued out the window.

Caephus returned to the head of the table.

"Cletus," he said, "I am not surprised to see our youngest Komitari has survived the K-Coaster. He appears to be no worse for the wear."

"Well, n-n-o...I had the Normal and I...I wanted to know what you wanted me to do with her...I...I'm... real sorry. I didn't take him yet." He hung his head. "My first day as an attendant and I already messed up. Please. Can I have one more chance to prove myself?"

Caephus gave no hint of sympathy or disappointment. "It serves no purpose to lament one's failures. Do not be sorry. Be better."

I wondered what the big deal was. Cletus sure was upset about not taking me on some dumb coaster ride. I thought he might not have taken it so hard if he knew how I reacted to rollercoasters. I'm not proud to say it, but I scream like a three-year-old girl. I've been known to squeeze the kneecaps off the person riding next to me. That's not so bad when I'm riding with Andie or Drake. But try explaining it to the two hundred seventy pound biker with the letters D-E-A-D-M-E-A-T tattooed on his knuckles who sat next to me on the Screaming Python.

Cletus sat up straight and looked Caephus in the eye. "I will."

"Be certain to take him there immediately following the briefing," Caephus said. "I suppose for now we must take it on faith that Meredith's accounting of Jackson's abilities is accurate. Certainly he will prove worthy to join us at this table." He turned to me. "In the meantime, Jackson, you must do your best to make sense of the information you will gain at this meeting. Your orientation on the K-Coaster will help to clarify any questions remaining after our discussion, but it is important your mind remain open until you have completed your ride."

I nodded. "Sure. No problem. I mean, what is it? Like a three-minute ride or something? As long as Andie and I can be home before eleven, my mind can be open to a lot of things."

Really though, I was just thinking about being open to a pizza. Those chili dogs were doing me no good spewed all over the Ostium. My stomach was growling again.

Caephus said, "Your purpose here, son, is far more important than your earthly obligations. You should not concern yourself with trivialities such as curfews. The pizza, however, is a matter that can be addressed rather simply."

He pressed the buzzer again. Before I could say, "pepperoni," Zara floated into the room. She had a plate with three huge slices of bubbling-hot pizza and a frosty glass of root beer. She placed it all in front of me.

"Did I say that out loud?" I whispered to Cletus.

He shook his head. "Nope. You didn't. Pretty sweet, right?"

I tore into the pizza while Caephus continued. "I will be direct. Melchasaar has mounted a new effort to gain control of the Kaptropoten."

There was a chorus of gasps from around the table. Only Kat and Cletus didn't look surprised.

Who was this Melchasaar guy? I got goose bumps just hearing his name.

"There have been attempts to steal two of the Kaptrofracti," Caephus said. "The attempt on the Kaptro Metamorphus was thwarted, but only because Katriana was able to ward off the assailants and defend the mirror." The sculpture heads clapped politely for Kat. The guy beside her gave her a congratulatory pat on the shoulder.

"Unfortunately," Caephus continued, "the raid was not without significant loss and casualties."

The guy beside Kat tried to squeeze her hand. She yanked it away and tucked it under the table.

"The other attempt resulted in Jackson's possession of the Kaptro Elementum." My ears perked up. "Its Komitari invoked the Tegeris incantation." To me, he said, "The Tegeris incantation is a protection spell that should only be used when the Kaptrofractus is in grave danger.

"Each fragment emits its own electromagnetic field. The field radiates at a frequency that can only be detected by Rephael, or by the Kaptropoten Intelligence Agency, and, most importantly, by other Kaptrofracti. Unfortunately, whenever the mirrors are used, the frequency intensifies to a level that Melchasaar can detect as well. When a Tegeris incantation is invoked, that mirror fragment seeks out the electromagnetic field of another fragment in order to gain the protection of its

Komitari. That is how you came to be in possession of the Kaptro Elementum. The mirror, therefore, is safe. However, there is serious risk involved anytime the Tegeris incantation is used. When two Kaptrofracti are placed in close vicinity of one another, the danger is that they may reunite.

"As a result, that Komitari has lost his position. Nevertheless, the Council recognizes the difficult decisions the Komitari faced in order to prevent the Kaptrofractus from being taken. He has been assigned a penance and when he has proven his worth, I will consider reinstating his post."

When Caephus mentioned the poor guy who was being punished for losing his mirror, everyone at the table looked down. An awkward silence filled the room. I could sense the shame they felt for the Komitari who sent his mirror to me.

"Remember," Caephus said, "as long as we have the capability to track the mirrors, Melchasaar can as well. It was necessary for me to cast a Celare charm. As you know, that shuts down the electromagnetic field, except, of course, when the mirror is used. That means the Kaptrofracti can no longer be tracked or traced either by Rephael or the KIA. This also means the Tegeris incantation will be ineffective."

The young man with Kat spoke up. "I agree the Celare charm was the only way." Everyone else nodded.

As for me, I hadn't felt so lost and confused since we learned about the mysterious X in Pre-Algebra. I was still annoyed that nobody had bothered to tell me why

I was involved in this mess. I was at the point where I didn't want anyone to say one more word.

I toyed with the mirror on my lap. I found myself thinking that if I had a roll of tape, I'd tape all their mouths shut. Until they agreed to answer my questions, there'd be no more talking.

Yeah. I wish I could slap some tape across all their mouths and show them who's boss. POOF! There was that little burst of air. The next thing I knew, everyone around the table, including Caephus, had a piece of gray duct tape stretched across their mouths! Their eyes were huge, and their words were muffled behind the duct tape.

I had forgotten about my powerful little mirror. I was going to have to be more careful! There was a bunch of shrieking and squealing as everyone ripped the duct tape off their faces.

Cletus was shaking his head. His face showed a mixture of secondary embarrassment and sympathy. Kat was rolling her eyes again. Everyone else looked horrified.

"Uh...Sorry?"

Caephus frowned at me. "A Komitari never uses the Kaptrofractus to advance his own agenda. Any use of the mirror, no matter how insignificant it may seem, has the potential to alter the course of fate. And each use places the mirror in grave danger of being tracked by Melchasaar. The mirror's powers must always be used judiciously."

His expression was gloomy. "A ride on the K-Coaster would have prevented this. Take him now. Once you have completed the ride, bring him to me. Until then, we will continue the briefing without you."

Cletus pushed back from the table. "Yes, sir," he mumbled. "C'mon, Jax."

I guzzled down the rest of the root beer and swiped the last slice of pizza from the plate. Through a mouthful of sauce and cheese, I said, "I really am sorry about the tape."

I hurried out the door behind Cletus. Caephus' voice trailed after me. "And Jackson, you must not use the Kaptro Conjuration again until you have mastered your own impulses."

I didn't stop to wonder about Caephus' warning. I was too busy trying to catch up with Cletus.

In the lobby, Cletus had stormed past Zara's desk. He smashed through the heavy steel door leading to the stairwell. When I reached the stairs, Cletus was gone. I peered down the center of the stairwell. All I could make out was a fuzzy streak zipping down, down, down around the center railing.

Surely that can't be Cletus. It didn't make sense. *He's flashing…like me!*

I threw myself down the steps at full throttle. By the time I flashed to the nineteenth floor, I had almost overtaken Cletus. He was only one story below me. "Cletus, wait up!"

He stopped at the eighteenth floor landing and grumbled up to me. "Meet me at the bottom." He disappeared again in a blur of muscles.

When I got to the bottom, I found Cletus outside.

He was slouching on an iron bench set among the trees bordering the courtyard. His face was glum, and he rubbed his temples.

"You gonna eat that?" He was trying to sound cheerful. He took the last bite of pizza from my hand and crammed it in his mouth. He was still chewing when he said, "Let's head to the K-Coaster." He stood and rushed ahead. I caught up, trotting alongside him.

"How did you do that? How did you run like that?"

He didn't look at me. He didn't slow down. His tone was flat when he said, "I was the Komitari who sent you the Kaptro Elementum."

CHAPTER 8
Cousins, Coasters, and Cowards

Cletus' confession left me silent as a mute giraffe. I just stared at him.

"A Komitari's greatest shame is to fail to protect his mirror." Cletus shoulders drooped. "I'm just lucky Caephus is givin' me a chance to prove myself. Normally, I'd be totally done. Lose my mirror forever. But instead, Caephus made me your attendant. Komitari usually get to choose their own attendants. Since you aren't sixteen and aren't trained yet, he thought it might help you to have someone with actual Komitari experience."

I was confused. And I was tired. And I was tired of being confused. I snapped. "You said you were my attendant. And by the way, nobody even told me what that means. And now you're saying *you're* a Komitari, like me. And by the way, nobody even told me what *that* means! I don't have any idea what's going on here, and I'm tired of it! Well, guess what? I'm done.

"The only reason I even came here in the first place was because I was curious, and the only reason I stayed was because I wanted to get some questions answered. But all I have now is MORE QUESTIONS!" I didn't pause for a breath. "Sure, I'd love to keep that mirror and poof myself up anything I want, but you know what? I'm tired of everyone talking about all this—this—mirror crap and not bothering to tell me what any of it means!

"And every last one of you—you're all nuts! Like you—you got all upset because you forgot to take me on a stupid rollercoaster. And then everyone at HQ was freaking out because the mirrors were connected. And so what if they had a little blood on their upper lip? It was just duct tape!

"Then, to top it off, two men in white coats took my best friend away!"

When I finally stopped, Cletus looked at me and chewed on his lip for a good minute.

"Okay. I get it. But you gotta understand. We're not allowed to tell you anything. Not 'til you pass the test. It's Komitari Code. But I'll make you a deal—you agree to go on the K-Coaster with me. When the ride's over, I'll tell you anything else you want to know. Anything at all. And if you're not satisfied, I'll get Andie and your Ostium, and I'll send you two back home. Deal?" He stuck out his hand.

I considered Cletus' deal. "Okay, I guess." I shook his hand, only this time, I squeezed hard just to show him I meant business.

He jerked his hand away. "Owww!" He laughed. "You're a lot stronger than you look."

Cletus led the way past several small buildings. These buildings were totally different from IOM headquarters.

They were smaller—kind of cute, even. Each one was different. Like a whole mix of cultures and architectures had all claimed a little piece of property right here on the island. On the left, we passed a small cottage with a thatched roof. A sign hanging by the front door read, "IOM Smithing, Fine Custom Weaponry, and Armor." A thin, yellow stucco building to our right had a sign that read, "IOM Sweets and Eats." And yet another building on the left read, "IOM Book Repository." It was white with an ancient Greek look.

The streets were littered with Quinorians, sculpture-heads, and an odd assortment of other strange-looking people. There were plenty of Peds, and once again, I was creeped-out by their big bare four-toed feet.

I wish they would get some shoes on those feet.

POOF! I felt that now familiar burst of air. There was an instant buzz around town when Peds everywhere were stunned by the giant shoes that now covered their giant feet.

Oops! I had forgotten about the mirror—again!

Cletus was shaking his head. "Geez. You're dangerous with that thing! Let's get outta here." We flashed the rest of the way through town.

Eventually, we arrived at the entrance of the K-Coaster. It looked like it came straight from a theme park. It was bright and cartoony. We had to make our way through a maze of crowd control ropes before coming to the mouth of the coaster's entrance. The opening revealed a large, dark room with brightly colored neon lights that made the walls, ceilings, and floors glow. All different sizes and shapes of fun house mirrors hung on the walls, causing the lights to distort and reflect and bounce around the room. The effect was totally cool. Combined with the loud rock music blaring through the speakers, it felt like we had just stepped into another world.

We crossed under the arched opening that had "K-Coaster" written in bold, colorful graffiti-like letters. A car thundered to a stop on the rails to our left, and two passengers stepped out.

The first guy out of the car could've been a Cletus look-alike, except he was a lot less lumpy. He was shorter too. And his hair was lighter. And he didn't have that same twinkle in his eye. But other than that, he looked just like Cletus.

He was gasping for breath, and his hair was all messed up from the ride. The wide grin on his long, thin face created a bridge from one ear to the other.

There was no smile on the face of the lanky man with him, though. This guy's face was almost green, and his cheeks were puffed. One finger plugged his mouth, as if to prevent a puking episode. It wasn't hard to see this guy cared for roller coasters even less than I did. I couldn't help but check the kneecaps of the kid with the big grin, just to make certain they were still attached.

The first passenger recognized Cletus. "Hey, Cuz!" The grin never left his face.

Cletus grabbed his extended hand and yanked him in for a back-slapping dude hug.

"Glad to see you recovered from our kayakin' trip the other day, little cousin."

"Yep," Cletus' cousin said. "Arms are still killing me, though!"

"What are you talking about? I did all the rowin'!"

"Details…" the other guy joked.

"You finishin' up your orientation?"

"Yeah. You know how Caephus is. Doesn't matter that I've been your attendant for years and rode this with you when you had your orientation. He still wants to make sure I can handle being a full-blown Komitari—not that it matters, anyhow. I'm sure you're gonna be reinstated, Cuz, and then I can get back to partying and having fun." He laughed.

"From the looks of it, Yancy, you did just fine here!" Cletus swiped his hand across the top of Yancy's head and flicked the messy hairs back into place.

The guy who rode with Yancy was weaving unsteadily on his spaghetti-like legs.

"Now, Hobart, on the other hand, isn't lookin' too swell," Cletus said.

"Ahhh, he's fine. Right, Hobs?" Yancy elbowed Hobart. "You gotta toughen up if you wanna be my attendant."

Hobart looked uncertain. He stumbled out the entrance, and the cousins laughed even harder.

Cletus lowered his voice. "Why'd you pick him, anyway? He's old and doesn't seem real strong. Definitely not fun, either."

"Galen sent him over to me. Said Rephael

recommended him—owes his family a favor or something—so I didn't argue. Like I said, it doesn't matter. As soon as you finish your penance, I'll go back to being your attendant, and good ole Hobs can go back to pushin' pencils at HQ."

Yancy seemed to notice me for the first time. "Yancy,"—he jammed a thumb into his chest—"Cletus' favorite cousin!"

"Oh, sorry," Cletus said. "This is Jax Sheppard. Guardian of the Kaptro Conjuration." He cleared his throat. "And for now the Kaptro Elementum."

"Hi," I said.

"Wow. Jax Sheppard. Your mom's a legend. Nice to meet you." Yancy grinned again.

An automated voice interrupted us. It echoed through the room. "Welcome to the K-Coaster. Please place all unsecure articles, such as glasses, hats, flip-flops, loose change, cell phones, dentures, and contact lenses in the nearby bin. Any loose items will fall. Remove and dispose of any chewing gum or candy prior to boarding. For your convenience, adult-sized diapers have been provided for you in the restroom."

"Diapers?" I asked. "Are my pants going to get wet?"

Cletus and Yancy just exchanged these dumb grins. Their skinny faces nodded in rhythm. They looked like a couple of bobblehead dolls who shared the best secret ever. I dropped my cell phone, a licorice whip, and a handful of wadded up dollar bills in the bin. Cletus swiped the licorice whip. He rolled it up and popped it in his mouth.

"Please be seated and raise your arms while you wait for the safety restraint to drop," the recording said.

Cletus grabbed me and towed me onto the car. "We'll catch up later," he called to Yancy, who waved and headed out the door.

The coaster began to make a chugging sound as it prepared to launch us out of the room. Soon, it was as deafening as the engines of a jet getting ready to taxi down the runway.

The safety bar dropped over my shoulders. It pinned me to the back of the seat, and I felt trapped. A wave of panic washed over me.

The voice continued, "Please remain seated until the ride comes to a complete stop. Arms and legs are to remain in the car at all times. Please do not remove or disturb any items on or around the attraction. Passengers should be in good health and free from high blood pressure; heart, back, or neck problems; motion sickness; or other conditions that could be aggravated by this adventure. Those having had recent surgery, expectant mothers, and Normals should not attempt to ride this attraction. Passengers who are generally squeamish, wimpy, or cowardly should avoid the K-Coaster altogether."

I whipped my head around to look at Cletus. "I am ALL of those!"

Cletus' eyes darted to my belly.

"Not pregnant! Wimpy, cowardly, AFRAID!"

The voice droned on. "If you find you are unable to complete the ride, please shout, 'I am not worthy!' in a loud and clear fashion, prior to passing out."

"WHAT?"

Cletus just smiled that big dumb smile. He shot me a thumbs-up.

The recording continued, "Five, four, three, two, one!"

The coaster launched onto the tracks like it had been shot from a giant cannon. It quickly reached such ridiculous speeds I was afraid we would shoot right off the tracks. The sheer velocity of the car resulted in my cheeks being pulled back from the sides of my mouth. My teeth were exposed to the giant moth that was unfortunate enough to fly in our path. I spat, which immediately resulted in my face being sprayed with a cocktail of spit and moth guts.

We were hurled up an enormous hill at such a high speed that I could hardly see a thing.

"Approaching ten *g*'s," the voice said.

I was light-headed by the time we hit the top. Suddenly, the car slowed to a near halt. I swear the coaster was deliberately torturing me as it crept over the peak. I sneaked a glance at Cletus out of the sides of my watering eyes. He waved his arms in the air and laughed like a maniac. It dawned on me the nitwit might actually be enjoying this! He gave me another stupid thumbs-up.

And then, the bottom dropped out from under us. The car hurtled toward the earth. I screamed like the three-year-old girl who lived deep inside me.

"Approaching fifty *g*'s."

I clutched like crazy to the safety bar. The metal gave way and pulled apart, and I was terrified of falling out.

Darn super strength!

I was even more light-headed now. I squeezed my eyes shut. Before I knew what came over me, I shouted, "I am not worthy!"

CHAPTER 9
Prince Poop and High Hopes

It was silent. The thunderous noise of the coaster and the gale force winds were gone. An obnoxiously loud alarm horn blasted on and off. Through my closed lids, I could sense the flashing of a bright red light. I opened my eyes. Our car was parked just where we had started, in the room with the fun house mirrors. I looked over at Cletus. His long face was made even longer by his jaw, which was hanging low, low, low.

"What...did...you...?" He covered his face with both hands.

"What happened?"

"You failed. I failed." Cletus just sat there frozen in the little car.

"Please exit to your left and thank you for riding the K-Coaster," the voice said as Cletus' safety restraint lifted from his chest. Mine was bent and cracked. It wouldn't lift. I snapped it all the way off and tossed it on the ground. My knees were still knocking, and I was still shaking when I stepped out of the car. Eventually, I managed to pull Cletus out of the car. Together, we left the building.

The afternoon light had begun to fade. My watch now showed it was 2:30 a.m. back home. I was exhausted.

I practically whined. "I don't understand." I felt ashamed for not finishing the ride. At the same time I didn't understand why it was such a big deal. "Why are you so upset?"

"What's not to understand? You didn't even try. You failed. You said it yourself. You're not worthy. You failed, so I failed. The K-Coaster is the first part of Komitari orientation. It weeds out the weaklings—weak in the body, weak in the mind, whatever. If you can't pass the K-Coaster, you can't officially become a Komitari. Because of that, there's a good chance I won't get to be one again either. It's over." Cletus trudged off ahead. For what seemed like the millionth time today, I dashed to catch up to him.

I snatched hold of Cletus' arm. He tried to break away, but I clamped down with full super strength. As hard as he tried, he couldn't get me to budge. It was weird, but even with all his Komitari muscles, I was stronger than Cletus.

He gave up. "What? What do you want?"

"You still have to answer my questions. I rode the coaster. Now you have to answer my questions. That was the deal."

"No way." Cletus stopped. "You didn't finish the ride. Deal's off. If you don't pass the test, if you're not worthy to be a Komitari, you're not allowed to have any information about the Kaptropoten, the Komitari Code, our island…nothing. You already know way too much. And when we get back to HQ, I know exactly what's gonna happen. Caephus is gonna take your mirror and send you and Andie packin'."

That didn't sound half bad to me. I was tired and cranky and worried about Andie. Heading home actually sounded like heaven. But before I left, I had to know one last thing.

"Wait a minute. You never said I had to finish the ride. You just said I had to go on it. You at least owe me some answers. And if I'm going home anyway, what's the difference? At least tell me about my mirror." I lifted the bag. "I mean, if I'm just going to lose it, you might as well tell me about it first."

Cletus thought for a minute. "Okay." He shrugged. "Why not?"

I planted myself cross-legged in the grass beside the path. Cletus stuck his hand out. "All right, give me your Kaptrofractus."

I handed Cletus the glowing mirror from my bag. He turned it over and over again in his hands. He studied it with the same intensity Drake always has when he studies that freckle on his right arm that's shaped like Texas.

"What you got here is a fusion of the Kaptro Elementum—my mirror, and the Kaptro Conjuration—from your grandfather. The Kaptro Elementum has the power to control and communicate with nature, its elements, animals…you know. So you can make it stop rainin', you can make a tree grow, you can talk to animals…Here." He handed it back to me. "I'm not allowed to use the mirror as long as I'm only an attendant, but you can try it. Go 'head. Think of somethin'."

I drew a blank. I felt dumb, but as hard as I tried, I couldn't think of any nature-related wishes. I got up and stood beside Cletus, hoping an idea would come to me.

Cletus pointed up at one of the large black-and-white birds that soared from tree to tree. "Ask one of them somethin'."

"Okay…" What do you say to a bird? I shielded my eyes from the sun with my hand and craned my neck. "All right, here goes nothing…Hey, bird!" I shouted to the sky. "You, up there! I'm Jax. What's your name?"

The bird turned and dropped in altitude until it was about ten feet above us. It hovered over me, flying in small circles around my head. Then, plain as day, it said, "Prince Vihtori Teppo Magpie III, Supreme Ruler of the Finnish Magpies. I am pleased to make your acquaintance, Master Jax."

I jerked. "Did you hear that?"

Cletus laughed. "Only the Komitari who possesses the mirror can actually communicate with the animals. What'd he say?"

"He said…he said he's a prince." I remembered feeling just as idiotic when I told Kat about the talking Dobermans. That whole thing all made sense now. And the talking tree frog too. It was all because of the mirror.

"Ah, yes. My good friend, Prince Vihtori." Cletus bowed to the bird who continued to circle. "Hope Petri's wing is healin' well."

There was an awkward silence. Cletus poked me in the ribs. "Aren't you gonna translate for me?"

"Uh…okay…yep. I guess so." I strained my neck. "Cletus wants to know how Petri's wing is doing."

Prince Vihtori Teppo Magpie III landed on my shoulder. He said quite regally, "How kind of you to ask, Master Cletus. It is healing well, thanks to the poultice you applied for him."

There was another awkward silence.

"Well? What did he say?"

"Um, okay. He said your poultice helped him." Translating a conversation between a royal crow and a muscle-bound teenager definitely ranked up there on the top-ten list of things I never thought I would do in my lifetime.

"Good…" Cletus came over and stroked the prince's feathers with the back of his finger.

I caught a flicker of sadness in Cletus' blue eyes before the bird flew off.

As he disappeared into the treetops, Prince Vihtori called over his wing, "Use your new gift wisely, Master Jax."

In the meantime, Cletus had started brushing my shoulder with his hand.

Are you kidding me? I grimaced when I realized what Cletus was doing. Good old Prince Vihtori had left a present on my shoulder! I shuddered, but Cletus kept on swiping. Apparently, he wasn't even a little grossed out by the bird turd Vihtori left behind.

At least now I could see why Cletus was so eager

to become a Komitari again. It was obvious he missed talking to the animals.

"Okay, so where were we?" Cletus cleared his throat again. "Yes, the Kaptro Conjuration. That mirror lets you conjure up anything you want. Basically, you can make any object appear out of nothin'. I think you already know how that one works." He cupped his hand beside his mouth. He spit out the words, "Duct tape," while forcing a fake cough.

"Very funny." But I had to ask the one question, the only question I actually cared about. "What about people? Can you conjure up people?" My voice cracked, and I almost whispered, "Like dead people?"

"No way!"

I didn't think it was possible, but even so, a hole developed deep in the pit of my soul. I still hadn't accepted that Sebastian was actually gone for good.

Cletus continued, "That would be Reanimation. And you *never* want to mess with that power. And besides, the only way you get the power of Reanimation is if you possess the Kaptropoten—the whole mirror—all seven pieces back together."

The hole filled with hope. What was Cletus talking about? Reanimation? I tried not to sound too eager. "The whole mirror? And if you have the whole mirror you can bring someone back from the dead?"

"Well, basically. But this wasn't part of the agreement."

I forced myself not do a backflip. *There might be a way to bring Sebastian back!* Little goose bumps camped out on my arms. The hairs on the back of my neck did a little dance. Was there still hope?

"I said I would tell you about your Kaptrofractus. That's it."

"You're right." I tried to squeeze out a bit more information. "But I have no idea what the difference is between a Kaptrofractus and a Kaptropoten. Can you at least tell me that?"

"Simple. The Kaptropoten is the most powerful magical object ever created. It's been broken into seven fragments and each fragment is called a Kaptrofractus. Each Kaptrofractus holds one specific power of the Kaptropoten. There you go. Now that's enough natterin'." He paused and then suddenly looked sad again. "Let's get this over with."

Cletus took off around the bend in the road. I lagged behind. I needed to wrap my brain around the brand new idea that had started to hatch in my head. Seven fragments. I felt excited and nervous and afraid all at once. I already had two. Could I even hope to fix this nightmare—bring Sebastian back—make everything normal again?

I needed to stay calm and gather more information. I just had to make sure I didn't let anyone know about the thought that was churning in my head.

At once, I knew what I had to do. Somehow, I had to get back on that coaster. I had to pass that test. I had to become an official Komitari. Then maybe I could figure out how to get the other five pieces of the mirror. Then maybe I could bring my brother back home to Gram.

CHAPTER 10
Disappointment and Defeat

I squeezed through the elevator doors. Cletus was tracing the number seventy-seven in his huffed cloud on the round mirror.

"Look." I carefully picked my words. I really did feel awful about ruining things for him. "I'm sorry—really sorry—for wimping out back there. I didn't realize it was a test. I had no idea it would mess up your chances of being a Komitari again."

Cletus's eyes were glued to his feet. He didn't answer.

"Let me try it again. Let me ride the K-Coaster again, and I promise I'll make it to the end. Now that I know what's at stake, I promise I'll take it seriously."

Cletus still didn't answer.

"I mean it, Cletus. I won't let you down."

Cletus looked up and shook his head. "It's not that easy. Don't you get it? You only get one shot. That's it. It's not up to me—I don't get to decide if you can go back."

"Cletus, please. I didn't know it until now, but it means…" My voice quivered. "…everything to me."

BING! The elevator interrupted. "You have arrived at the seventy-seventh floor. Have a nice day, and thank you for visiting IOM headquarters."

Cletus stepped off the elevator. He strode past Zara, who rushed after him. She tripped over her own feet as she tried to beat him to the newly installed wooden doors. "You can go in now."

But Cletus had already busted through the doors.

The conference room was empty now except for Galen. He stood behind his chair jamming some papers into his briefcase. He was small, his spine was curved, and his tweed suit jacket hid a large hump on his back.

Cletus was impatient. "Where's Caephus?"

Galen's high nasal voice went perfectly with his nerdy appearance. "Caephus had other business requiring his attention. However, he did not leave prior to reviewing the results from Master Jax's turn on the K-Coaster. He is, to say the least, disappointed." He drew out the word "disappointed," syllable by syllable, squeezing every last, juicy bit of meaning out of the word—just in case I didn't understand what a big, fat loser I was. For some reason though, I got the feeling Galen was forcing himself to sound disgusted. There might even have been some sadness behind those thick glasses.

"Jackson is a danger to himself and others. He is of no use to us if he cannot pass the K-Coaster."

"I'm sorry. Please. Just let me prove myself. If Caephus would give me another chance…" I knew I sounded desperate. I was worried I would give myself away. "If Caephus would give me another chance, I…I know I could do better." It was lame, but it was all I had to offer.

Cletus stepped in front of me. "Look. I accept full responsibility. I overestimated his abilities. Didn't prepare him. He didn't even understand what the ride was about—didn't realize it could mess up his Komitari status. When he got here, I was distracted by the Normal. I broke protocol, and I didn't brief him before the ride." He paused, took a deep breath, and held the air in his lungs. He exhaled. "Galen, if Caephus will let Jax have another shot at the K-Coaster, I'll take the blame for everything that went wrong. Caephus can dismiss me… permanently."

I was shocked and touched and thankful. I couldn't imagine Cletus would give up his chance to get his mirror back or to talk to the animals again, all for me. Galen blinked behind those glasses. Without saying a word, he left the room.

Cletus and I waited in silence. I wanted to tell him how grateful I was, but I couldn't pick the right words. I could never explain to him why I needed this so much. Then Galen slunk back through the door.

"Caephus has agreed to your request."

"Thank you!" I crushed Galen in a giant hug and then grabbed Cletus. I lifted him off the ground, being careful not to crack his ribs.

Cletus smiled a true and genuine smile. "Don't let me down. You have a real important job to do."

He dropped his head, and darn it if a sneaky, nasty guilt didn't creep up my leg and around my torso. It snaked over my shoulder and into my ear, poisoning my brain with its venom. I couldn't stand it a second longer.

"I can't let you do it. I can't let you give up being a Komitari just to help me." I didn't want to give up my only shot at bringing Sebastian back. But I couldn't live with myself if I destroyed Cletus' dream. "I can't let you do it." I choked back tears. "I won't let you do it."

"Then it is settled. I will inform Rephael you have chosen to relinquish your mirror as originally intended." Galen spoke with a finality I didn't dare question.

That was it. It was over. I was numb.

Galen packed the rest of his papers in his briefcase. He turned to Cletus. "Escort Jax to his room. Get him a meal and a good night's rest. When he awakens in the morning, the Normal should be fully recovered. You are to supervise their departure from the island and their return home." He looked at me. "Please surrender the Kaptrofractus."

I lifted the bag over my head and put it on the table. It felt like my world had changed from high-definition color to crappy black and white.

I couldn't think or focus, which was probably a good thing. It would have been too easy to give in to the helplessness that hovered around me like a rain cloud.

In a daze, I let Cletus lead me from HQ to a medium-sized building on the other side of the courtyard. I vaguely remember passing through a fancy lobby full of fancy furniture.

My next awareness was of Cletus pulling off my sneakers and of two muffled voices murmuring words I couldn't make out. A soft, fluffy pillow against my cheek was the last thing I remembered of the most exciting, bizarre, and emotional day of my life.

CHAPTER 11
One Pinky, Two Peds, Three Powers

I woke up with a gasp. I could tell it was morning from the light streaming through the curtains. The dream had been worse than usual. This time, before Sebastian morphed, he begged me not to leave the island, but to stay and steal my mirror back.

"Do it for me. Don't you want me back?" he asked over and over, but eventually the voice wasn't his. It had changed to the snakelike hiss of Freezer Fingers, just seconds before his face morphed. I was petrified. My dream feet, in their heavy lead shoes, wouldn't run.

"Jax, do it for me!" he mocked. His terrifying face grew to the size of my entire body. It lurched at me, stopping inches from mine.

"WHERE IS THE MIRROR?" The booming force of his words blew me back and knocked me over.

"I don't have it anymore!" I had woken right before I hit the ground.

I slid out of bed and crammed my feet into the pair of warm, fuzzy slippers someone had stuck on the floor beside the bed. My first thoughts were of Gram and Andie's dad. How would we explain to them why we didn't come home last night? I fumbled for my cell phone in my back pocket, but Cletus must have placed it on the nightstand. I snatched it from the table. It had five bars—pretty impressive!

I dialed home. I didn't expect to be so happy to hear Gram's voice.

"Hello?"

"Gram! Can you hear me?" I still wasn't convinced my phone could reach Gram all the way back home.

"Yes, Jackson, honey. I hear you just fine. How is camp? I was a little worried about letting you go when Mrs. Stein first called. But I think spending some time with Drake and his family in the mountains, away from all the drama, is just what you need."

"Mrs. Stein called you?" I was totally confused.

"Well, of course, honey." Gram chuckled. "I think that fresh mountain air has addled your brain. Don't you remember putting her on the phone when you called from Drake's house last night? You know I would never let you take a trip like this without talking to a parent first." She chuckled again. "And with Andie's father finally agreeing to let her go to camp, you wouldn't have anyone here to pal around with anyway."

"Andie…at camp?" I didn't get it.

The line crackled. Gram shouted into the phone. "We must be breaking up here. Just relax and have a good time, honey. And don't forget your good manners." The line crackled again. "And if you decide to stay longer than a week, just call me! Love you!"

There was another crackle, and the phone went dead.

"Gram! Wait! Gram!"

I didn't even have a chance to tell her I was coming home today. Who had called her anyway? Obviously, someone had pretended to be me and Mrs. Stein. Whoever it was must have called Gram before the K-Coaster disaster happened. It was just one more question I would probably never have answered since I was going home today.

That thought made me aware of the knot in my stomach. I couldn't believe I had screwed up my only chance to get Sebastian back. I closed my eyes and tried not to cry. I was ready to give in to a full-blown pity party, table for one. My stomach growled.

"What's a party without refreshments?" I asked just to distract myself from my misery.

My eyes traveled around the room. I was searching for the refrigerator I knew I would find in such a ritzy hotel. When Cletus had brought me here last night, I barely noticed how fancy it was. The sheets were the softest I had ever felt, and the room was definitely fit for a celebrity. I even had my very own suite with a separate living area that included a fringed navy blue sofa. There were big, beautiful mirrors everywhere, but that seemed to be a theme here on the island.

Suddenly, I felt out of place, like I had to speak with a fancy English accent. "What's a party without refreshments?" I repeated, only this time I did my best impersonation of a Brit.

I spotted the mini fridge under the counter in the kitchenette. On top of the counter was a basket full of

Ding Dongs. I tore open the wrapper of one and shoved the whole thing in my mouth.

"Delightful," I said quite snobbishly—or at least as snobbishly as you can when you're wearing fuzzy slippers and your mouth is stuffed with Ding Dongs. A pot of freshly brewed coffee was right beside the Ding Dongs. It smelled as strong as one of Gram's pots back home. I poured myself a cup, and sipped the hot brew, my pinky in the air in spite of myself.

Three hurried raps on the door startled me. Right away, there were three more.

"Hold your horses," I called, still in full accent. I sat my coffee cup on the table and started to turn the handle, but the door crashed open, and Kat burst through. She pushed past me and into the middle of the room.

"Well, good morning to you too." I pretended to be huffy, but I felt that same giddy feeling I always had when Kat was around.

"Get dressed. There is…a situation, and we must take care of it at once. The fate of the world depends on it."

"I *am* dressed." I smacked my hands on my chest to point out the—"Wait a minute!" My hands rubbed an unfamiliar fuzzy fleece. Someone had dressed me in a warm and cozy pair of blue footie jammies! I snatched the comforter from the bed and held it in front of myself, protecting both my modesty and my manly ego.

"You wait here!" It was my turn to give the orders. I pointed to the couch where I wanted Kat to wait. I backed into the bathroom, shielding myself with the comforter and then slammed the door. There, hanging over the bathtub on scented, satin hangers were my freshly washed and ironed blue jeans and T-shirt. My underwear and socks were on the vanity. They were twisted into fancy little rolls. Blue satin bows were tied around each of them. I quickly changed and headed out to see what had Kat so fired up.

"So what seems to be the problem?" I plopped onto the striped chair beside the sofa and slung my right leg over the arm of the chair. I was going for a casual "I couldn't care less" attitude.

Kat rolled her big green eyes at me. "It is Melchasaar. He has killed a Komitari—Loryllia—from one of the planets in the galaxy you know as Andromeda. He captured her mirror, the Kaptro Enchantment. Her attendant was on the run for two days and arrived here early this morning. He was lucky to escape with his life."

"So what does this have to do with me? Me and Andie are going home today."

"Andie and I," Kat said. "And you are coming with me. We must collect all seven pieces of the Kaptropoten and reunite them. You already have two. I have one. So we only need four more. The Kaptropoten is the only way to defeat Melchasaar. It is the only thing powerful enough to challenge his magic. And once we have killed Melchasaar, the Kaptropoten can be destroyed…forever."

"So you were the one who called my Gram and Andie's dad."

"I have no idea what you are talking about."

"And Caephus has suddenly changed his mind about me?" I didn't believe that.

"You let me worry about Caephus." Her answer made it pretty clear Caephus didn't know anything about her plan.

"Okay…Tell me this…I thought you should *never*, no matter what happened, *ever* reunite pieces of the mirror. Everyone's been on me about it since we came here. Now you're telling me that's exactly what you want to do?"

"Oh, that's right. I forgot you missed the history lesson you would have gotten in your orientation…" She added under her breath, "…if you hadn't washed out on the K-Coaster."

She leaned forward and pulled off her ruby ring, toggling it back and forth between her hands. "Listen carefully. Under normal circumstances, it is safest to keep each of the Kaptrofracti as far apart as possible. It is simply too dangerous to risk Melchasaar will gain possession of the Kaptropoten—the whole mirror—in its entirety. The Kaptropoten…in the hands of the most formidable sorcerer in history…well, there is no way to predict what could happen."

"All right," I said. "Let me see if I understand. If you reunite the seven Kaptrofracti, you would have all seven powers—"

"Plus the Big Three. All seven powers *plus* the powers of Healing, Evocation, and Reanimation."

Of course I didn't forget about *that*. It was the whole reason I wanted the Kaptropoten in the first place.

"Okay. So you get all seven powers of the Kaptrofracti plus the Big Three. And this Melchasaar guy—you said he's some kind of a sorcerer? Why does he want the mirror so bad? I'm guessing it's your typical story of world domination...all the world will bow to me...I will be the most feared and respected sorcerer on the planet...blah, blah, blah..."

"Uh...no." Kat slid the ring back on her finger. "It is far more complicated than that. Now be quiet and listen." She frowned. "It has always been safest simply to keep the fragments separated. However, Melchasaar has become much more aggressive in his pursuit of the fragments in the past week. He nearly succeeded in stealing two of them and this last attempt resulted in the death of one of our best Komitari—and now he has her Kaptrofractus."

"Loryllia," I said.

"Right. I should tell you the mirror can only be broken or destroyed when it is in its fully fused state. And in just the same way, the bond between two or more Kaptrofracti can only be destroyed when the mirror is in its complete form."

I pulled my leg from the arm of the chair, and put it squarely beside my other foot. I leaned forward. "So you're saying that when I accidentally fused the Kaptro Conjuration and the Kaptro Elementum, I got them permanently stuck together. And now they can't be separated until *all* parts are joined?" I was starting to get it. "And if all the parts are fused, and Melchasaar gets a hold of it..." I let the words hang in the air while I thought about what that could possibly mean.

Kat nodded. "For centuries, just being broken— just keeping the Kaptrofracti separated—has been effective enough to keep it out of danger, but now, with Melchasaar becoming so hostile and violent, we need the full Kaptropoten to defeat him—to kill him—once and for all. He has left us no choice but to beat him at his own game. We have to reunite the mirror before Melchasaar can. We have to use it to kill him. After that, Rephael can grind the mirror down to a dust. And once all its reflective surfaces are destroyed, it will lose its magical properties."

She blew a strand of hair from her forehead and tucked it behind her ear. "I suggest you pack a few necessities while I make last-minute arrangements for our trip."

"Why do you need *me*? And anyway, I'm not going anywhere but home. I failed the test. And Galen took my mirror—I don't have it anymore. I'm done." It was the truth. I didn't like it—I needed the mirror to save Sebastian. But I knew it was over for me.

Kat got up. She loomed over my chair. She leaned forward and stuck her hands on both sides of the chair's back, trapping me between her arms. Her long black braid hung like a pendulum. It thumped my shoulder each time it swung forward, making it really hard to focus on anything but the spot where it kept hitting me. Her eyes were inches from mine. My heartbeat thumped in my ears, and I hoped Kat couldn't hear it too. But mostly, all I could think was, *She sure smells good!*

"Look. I have no doubt I could defeat Melchasaar myself. But William says he will tell Caephus about my plan if I don't involve another Komitari. He says it is certain suicide if I try to kill Melchasaar alone." She inched even closer. I could tell she was trying to bully me. "So you *are* coming."

I pressed as far back into the chair as possible. "Who's William?"

"William is my younger brother, and he is also my attendant. He was with me at Council."

I remembered the good-looking guy who sat beside Kat at HQ.

"Galen and Caephus are wrong about you, and I am giving you a chance to prove it." She straightened. Suddenly, she seemed all concerned about checking out her manicure.

She muttered to her fingernails like I wasn't even there. "Granted, I have no idea *how* he will prove it. He *has* proven himself to be a coward, and he *has* proven he is not a quick thinker. He certainly does not *look* the part. It would take a complete miracle for him to prove he *is* worthy."

I was just glad her fingernails didn't answer her. I was pretty sure they would start bashing me too.

"It doesn't matter anyhow. Galen took my mirror. Which, by the way, means you only have one, so you need to get six instead of four. Good luck with that."

Just then, someone else knocked on the door. Kat squeezed my arm and put a finger to her lips. She whipped the backpack from her shoulders and pulled out her mirror. She stared at her own reflection for a millisecond. Then, right there before my very own eyes, there was a quick flash of red. Suddenly, Kat's body lost its form. The outline of her figure became smeared. It pulled and pushed and twisted in wavy, blurred lines. And then…it happened. She was instantly transformed into the little Pedample who had taken my Ostium from the beach when we first got here!

"Whoa!" I threw my hands up and jumped at least six feet back from her…or him…ummm…her.

She put her little Pedample finger to her cute, baby-faced lips just like she had when she was still Kat. "Shhhh. Answer the door, but don't say anything." The voice was definitely not hers.

"Uh…Coming," I called.

"Jax! Open the door! It's me, Andie!"

"Andie!" I flashed the distance to the door. I threw it open and pulled Andie inside. "Thank goodness you're okay!"

"I'm fine." She hugged me. "I'm just glad you're all right."

"And I'm fine too!" Cletus peeked his head around the corner and then entered. His grin was back where it belonged again. He was followed by a Ped who carried my freshly washed Ostium—the very same Ped Kat had just changed into.

Cletus, Andie, and I turned our heads in unison from the Ostium Ped to the Kat Ped, to the Ostium Ped, to the Kat Ped, over and over again like we were watching a tennis match at Wimbledon.

Eventually Cletus' eyes locked in on Kat Ped. "Give it up, Kat." He casually bit into an apple he had snagged from the counter.

For the second time, Kat's form wiggled and waved. She snapped right back into her stunning self again.

"She guards the Kaptro Metamorphus," Cletus said. "It lets you change yourself into the form of any other livin' creature."

"Whatever!" Kat thrust her chin forward. "Obviously I cannot let Caephus discover I am here. So I took a chance at morphing into Jax's Ped. How fortunate for me it was only you and not someone who matters."

Andie, on the other hand, was standing there with her eyes as wide as silver dollars. "Did you see that?" Her voice was two full octaves higher than usual. When nobody said anything, Andie grabbed a fistful of my sleeve and towed me into the hall. "A moment, please." She yanked the door shut behind her.

"Jax, what in the world is going on here? You have to tell me. I'm frightened and…" While Andie spoke, a high-pitched tone pierced my eardrum. It sounded like a radio trying to zero in on a broadcasting signal. Andie was still talking—her lips were moving, but I couldn't hear a word she was saying. I developed an instant headache. I pressed my fingertips against my temple, squeezing my eyes shut to ward off the sound. Soon, the noise began to change, first to static, and then to voices—whispering voices—but coming through loud and clear.

"I saw him in the scrying mirror with my own eyes. I know it is hard to imagine, but it is he." It was Kat, and I could hear her as loud as if she were whispering right in my ear. "*He* is the Ark. And that means I must keep him alive. If Caephus and Rephael do not care, then it is up to me to protect him. Besides, his presence can only help. I will not stand idly by and wait for Melchasaar's army to destroy my people."

Andie whacked my arm. "Jax, are you even listening to me?" Her voice was hollow, like a faraway echo. "What's wrong with you?"

There was more static and then Cletus' voice tuned in. "I don't like it at all. If Galen and Caephus find out—I, for one, could lose everything. I'm already on probation. And what if you're wrong? It would be certain suicide. And aren't you even worried you'll get him killed too? He hasn't had any trainin', and he doesn't even have all of his powers yet. Remember, he's only thirteen."

"He will be fine," Kat said.

Cletus sounded really concerned. "Without support from the KIA you'll never find the other Komitari. Especially now—with the Celare charm on. And if Melchasaar learns you're collectin' Kaptrofracti, you'll be his target, for sure."

There was more static and then squealing. Without warning, it was Andie whose voice was clear again. My fingers were still pressed into my forehead. I forced my facial muscles to relax.

"Jax! Are you okay?" Andie grabbed my shoulders and shook me.

"Could you hear them? In there?" I gestured to the door. "Could you hear them whispering?"

"No." She frowned.

"I could hear everything they said. And they were

whispering. That never happened to me before." My headache faded as fast as it came on, but I was freaked out. "What do you think that means?"

"I don't know." She still gripped my shoulders, and her fingernails dug into my skin. "Is it a new talent? You've been getting a lot stronger and faster. Maybe you're getting a third power too! Maybe it's super hearing!"

"I don't know." I plucked her fingernails from my arms. "I guess I'll have to wait and see if it happens again."

The door opened, and Cletus poked his head in the hall. "You two mind movin' back inside? Makes me nervous havin' you in the hall, while Kat's in here conspirin' to steal your mirror back."

My ears pricked up at that. It might not be over for me after all! In fact, the more thought I gave it, the better the whole plan sounded. Kat was scheming to do all the work for me. If I agreed to go along with her, and if she collected and fused all of the Kaptrofracti, then all I'd have to do is get it from her before it was destroyed. It sounded perfect.

Looking back, I suppose I should have known it was too perfect.

CHAPTER 12

An Elweard, a Weird TV, and Very Weird History

Cletus ushered Andie through the door, and I followed behind. He was so preoccupied with Andie he almost let the stinking door slam close right in my face. Inside, Andie took a seat on one of the chairs by the sofa. I stood for a minute and watched as Cletus offered Andie a cup of coffee and a Ding Dong. It still seemed strange to see Cletus paying so much attention to Andie.

Kat sat at the desk, scratching away on a notepad. The Pedample was putting the finishing touches on the newly made bed. He turned down the sheets and put little wrapped chocolate mints on the freshly fluffed pillows.

Everyone was completely unprepared for what I was about to say.

"I'm in. Tell me what I have to do, and I'll do it."

The room went dead quiet. They all turned to stare at me.

Eventually, Kat said, "Well then, we shall leave at once."

"Slow down there, Kat." Cletus looked aggravated. "If Jax is gonna do this, I'm goin' too." He turned to me. "I'm your attendant. I didn't keep my mirror safe, but I *am* gonna keep you safe."

"No, Cletus," I said. "You could lose your chance to be a Komitari again. If you go with us and get caught, you'll never guard the Kaptro Elementum again. I can't let you risk it."

"You're my responsibility. I'm not gonna fail again. I'm going. Now that's enough natterin'. I'm gonna go pack." Cletus started toward the door, but changed his mind. He strode toward Andie who was still sitting on the couch. "Isle of Mirrors will lose some of its sparkle when you're gone. I bid you farewell, sweet lady." He bent over her hand. Then, he clasped it and kissed it!

Geez! I shuddered. *Have some dignity, man! C'mon!*

Andie's cheeks flared red. She looked way uncomfortable. She pulled her hand away and stuffed it between her leg and the sofa. "Uh, thanks," was all she said.

Cletus dashed out the door. "I'll meet you back here in an hour."

Kat stood. "It is settled. I shall instruct William to meet us here in one hour. Be sure to pack. As you likely do not have everything you require, we will stop at the hotel gift shop for any additional items you need." With that, she ripped the paper off the pad and left.

That left Andie, the Ped, and me in the room. I turned to the Ped. "Thanks for washing my clothes. That was you, right?"

"Of course I done it," he answered. His deep, gravelly voice did not go with his sweet baby-faced features at all. "I'm Elweard, Third Degree Fellow of the Pedample Guard and your faithful servant." He snapped his heels together. His chin went up and his burly chest puffed out. He made a fist with his left hand and then thumped it on his right breastbone. It stayed there in some sort of Ped salute. I glanced over my left shoulder, and I glanced over my right shoulder, and then I looked at Andie. I shrugged. No one else was there but Andie, so he must have been saluting me. Andie giggled, but didn't offer any help.

I thumped my right chest with my left fist and waited. When he finally dropped his arm, I dropped mine too. He stepped forward to shake my hand. His hands, by the way, reminded me of his feet—there were only four fingers, and his thumbs were huge!

"If you need anything, Master Jax, just ask. I hope I done well stocking the kitchen." He opened the door of the mini fridge. It was packed with cans of root beer and individually wrapped slices of what looked like Mrs. Putt's meatloaf. My eyes widened.

"That took some work," Elweard said.

"Wow," I said. "Impressive."

Elweard grinned. He led me into the bedroom. "I hung your Ostium in the closet. I also gone and got you some new gutchers and stockings." He went to the dresser and opened the drawer. It was full of crisp new underwear and neatly folded socks.

Back in the living area, Elweard pulled out a chair and I sat. "Here, now. Have yourself a hot breakfast. Miss Andie?" He pulled out a chair for Andie, and she hopped up. We were both amazed when Elweard produced two tall stacks of delicious pancakes just like Gram's and a plate full of thick sizzling bacon. He poured two glasses of orange juice and stood back while we scarfed it down.

"Thanks, Elweard," I said. "What about you? Aren't you going to eat?"

Elweard wrinkled his brows. "Why, no..." He sounded confused. "The Guard serves the Komitari. We don't eat *with* you, we eat *after* you."

"That's ridiculous," Andie said. "Sit down."

"I can't...I couldn't...but...maybe just this one time." He grabbed a plate, loaded it up, and scrambled into the chair across from mine.

We ate in silence for a bit before Andie spoke. "Finally, we're alone. No offense, Elweard."

"None taken."

"Jax, I need to know what's going on."

She was right. I spent the next twenty minutes explaining everything that had happened since that night at the pool. The only thing I left out was the part about me trying to get the mirror to save Sebastian. I knew Andie wouldn't be okay with that.

Andie blew out a long whistle. "Whew! That's some crazy stuff."

"How are we supposed to get you home? Do you think we should just take you out to the beach with the Ostium? I'll come right back after I'm sure you got home all right."

"Remember, the Ostium only works by moonlight," Elweard said.

"But I'll be gone by then."

"It doesn't matter," Andie said.

"I can't let you go home by yourself. What if you pass out again? Who's going to help you?"

"It doesn't matter," Andie repeated, "because I'm going with you."

"No way. There's nothing you can do here but get in the way. And if Melchasaar is as dangerous as they say, you could get hurt—seriously hurt."

"Well, you need someone to keep you out of trouble. Look at the mess you got yourself into without my help."

"That's why I have Cletus."

"I don't know him very well, so I can't trust him with my best friend's life." She pushed away from the table. "I'm not leaving." She planted her hands on her hips.

I tried one last tactic. "What about your dad?" It was a low blow. It wasn't fair to make Andie worry about getting into trouble with her dad when for once she wasn't even thinking about him.

"Didn't you just tell me someone convinced my dad to let me go to camp? As long as he thinks I'm at camp, then I have the whole summer." But she couldn't help adding, "There's no way he could find out, right?"

I didn't feel like fighting her. "Whatever. I'm going to pack."

"That's my job, Master Jax." Elweard jumped up and shuffled off to the bedroom, while Andie cleared the dishes.

I parked myself on the sofa and picked up the remote. Hopefully, I could find some mindless cartoon to watch. My brain needed a break. I clicked the television on. The logo on the bottom of the screen read, "The History

Channel." I was getting ready to flick past the black-and-white historical film, when I saw him. Popping out of the screen, in full 3-D technology, was the terrifying face from my dreams and the Four Circles. He looked right through me. I was filled with instant fear. I threw myself down behind the coffee table.

Andie must have heard me hit the deck. She rushed over. "What is it, Jax?"

"Get down!" I whispered, yanking her to the floor. "It's him! The demon from the Four Circles."

"What? On TV?" She looked up over the table at the image splayed out on the huge screen. "Jax, it's just a movie." She tried to help me off the floor. "It's 3-D or something. I wonder how they do that without glasses." Andie swiped her hand through the air like she thought she could actually touch the holographic figure that was bursting out of the screen. She took my hand. "You're shaking. Come on. Sit with me on the couch. We'll watch it together."

It took a second for me to realize it was actually a clip from some old news footage. Even so, I didn't feel any better when Andie pointed to the fine print at the bottom of the screen that read, "Reenactment." I covered my face with my hands and forced myself to watch through the slits between my fingers—I was too scared to worry about looking like a baby.

The actor playing Freezer Fingers sat on the front of a large desk with one foot on the floor and the other dangling. He drank from a coffee mug. Six men in military uniforms knelt in front of him. Their heads were bowed. The man on the left risked a glance at the scary man.

Suddenly, out of the blue, brown droplets burst from the television. We tried to duck, but they splattered all over our faces, our arms, and our clothes.

On the screen, Freezer Fingers had thrown the cup of hot coffee in the face of the soldier who had looked at him. The soldier screamed, but he didn't move as the scary guy approached him. Freezer Fingers put his arm over the soldier's head. His hand hovered there. His fingers were bent like he was waiting to catch something.

The man's body started to shake. Then it began to convulse. There were some pretty realistic special effects, like a white glowing orb that appeared inside the man's chest. The orb began to float upward in his body. It rose like it was made of metal and Freezer Finger's hand was a magnet. Slowly, the white orb exited the top of the man's skull. There was a blood-curdling shriek. The convulsing stopped, and the man collapsed on the floor.

The other soldiers never even lifted their heads, but they couldn't control their pathetic whimpers and sobs.

Even though I knew they were actors, I shouted, "Get up and run, you chickens!"

But they didn't run. Instead, they just stayed there while Freezer Fingers controlled the white orb. He made it levitate in the air between his hands. Then, in one last hideous act of pure evil, he hurled it at the other men. They all screamed for a second right before the huge explosion.

A sudden blast of wind jolted the sofa back against the wall. Luckily, Andie and I weren't hurt when it bucked us both onto the ground.

The film, still in black and white, cut to a news anchor. She was a sculpture head—this one had a hair swan up top. It looked like the foil swans you get when they give you your leftovers at Steak by the Lake, my favorite restaurant.

In her most professional broadcaster voice, she read: "The Kaptro Scryor hung in the Louvre, hidden in plain sight, as a gift from Queen Catherine de Medici of France, circa 1688, after which time it disappeared. Official KIA documents in the Isle of Mirrors' archives indicate Melchasaar orchestrated the theft, but was deceived by one of his own generals, who stole the mirror and reportedly used it to advance his own interests. According to sources inside Melchasaar's camp, Melchasaar was enraged and assembled his top generals, assassinating them all as a warning to any others who might attempt to double-cross him. The general in question, who stole the mirror, was reportedly never found. However, the Kaptro Scryor made several notable appearances throughout history, until eventually it was recaptured by the KIA in the early 1950s."

My whole body shook as I made the connection. *Freezer Fingers is Melchasaar!* I wanted to run and hide in the closet until evening when I could book myself and Andie on the next Ostium out of town.

Andie hadn't yet figured it out. She was totally preoccupied with finding out how a brown liquid could splash from the screen, stain our clothes, and then just as unexpectedly, fade away to nothing a few minutes later.

"This is amazing!" she said with the wonder of a kid finding his very first piece of chewed Black Jack licorice gum. "The kids at tech camp would go crazy for this. How'd they do it?" She walked up to the TV, slid her hand across its surface, and then inspected the sides and bottom. "There has to be some kind of liquid reserve chamber—"

"Andie!" I interrupted the techie trance she had fallen into. "THAT was Melchasaar! The scary guy from the Four Circles and my nightmares—he's MELCHASAAR!"

"Are you serious?" She stopped checking out the television to look at me. She stood for a bit and then said with calm confidence, "Then we have to get him before he gets you."

CHAPTER 13
A Monkey Named Sadie and a Misunderstood Lady

"You will need a few protein bars for the times we do not find food." Kat tossed a half-dozen All-Power bars in my basket. We were in the hotel gift shop with Andie, Cletus, and William. Kat was picking out stuff for me to buy and explaining how I would use it all on our trip.

Each time Kat tossed something in my basket, Andie grabbed the exact same thing for herself and threw it in the basket on top of everything else.

"And for those times when we do find food, flavor crystals will work wonders." Kat picked up a handful of little jars that looked like salt shakers. One of them said, "Pizza," and another one said, "Chocolate Chip Cookie Dough."

"I don't get it," I said. "Cletus said the island is really small. Why do we need all these supplies?"

"There's some pretty rough terrain out there," Cletus said. "Won't be an easy hike. Probably gonna take us a good, solid day. That means we'll have to camp out for the night."

Kat pulled a clear package from the shelf. It contained seven tiny, little handheld mirrors. Each one was the size of a compact powder mirror. "Single Use Kaptrofracti for Beginning Komitari. A Komitari can only ever be issued one pack of these because they are for training purposes only. They could prove quite useful on our journey."

I took the package from her. Each mirror had a small label under it with its name, and I recognized several of them: Kaptro Elementum, Kaptro Conjuration, and Kaptro Metamorphus. I also recognized the Kaptro Scryor from the History Channel, but I didn't understand what its power was. The other three were called the Kaptro Teleportation (which sounded pretty self-explanatory), Kaptro Enchantment, and the Kaptro Kinesis.

When Andie grabbed a pack to throw in the basket too, Cletus stopped her. "You won't be allowed to buy that. They only sell those to Komitari."

"Rrrrrrr!" She put the package back on the shelf and grabbed a mini first aid kit instead.

Kat threw several packs of matches in the basket. "We probably will not need these, what with you having the Kaptro Elementum, but just in case..."

"You're forgetting," I said. "I don't have my mirror anymore."

Kat shot William a look. He nodded and reached into his satchel. I recognized the gold velvet pouch right away.

"How the heck did you get that?" I asked.

Cletus scratched his head.

"Let's just say it can be useful to have a sister with the Kaptro Metamorphus. And we will leave it at that." William smiled and tossed the bag to me.

I slipped the golden rope around my neck. I was

surprised when my muscles relaxed. I liked having it there, as if it was meant for me.

Finally, we headed toward the last aisle. It contained several pieces of small-scale weaponry and armor. Kat picked one of the largest daggers with a double-edged straight blade. It was engraved with the same symbol as the mirror and Ostium. It was just like the one in my video game, *The World's Worst Villains*. The hilt was carved in a combination of bone and hardwood grips with steel and brass fittings. It had a leather scabbard, which could be attached to the top of my waistband or strapped around my leg. Kat sized it up and then dropped it in the basket.

Cletus and I hid our smiles when Andie grabbed a dagger for herself. It was smaller than the one Kat picked for me. Hers had a curved single-edged blade with an ivory hilt. It was way more girly than mine. She threw it in the basket with all the other items.

We put our purchases on the counter and waited for the clerk to check us out. "That'll be eleven, even," she said.

"Dollars? Wow! Great prices here on the island!" Andie reached into her back pocket.

"Of course not." Kat brushed us aside. "It's denarii." She pulled out a handful of ancient-looking silver coins in two sizes and dropped them in the clerk's palm.

"That's Roman silver," William told us.

I stuffed my supplies in the new backpack Elweard had gotten me, and we left the hotel. We crossed the courtyard and headed toward a small path that led to the western side of the island. I hadn't been on this side of the island yet. It was a lot less developed than the rest of the island. Soon, the path narrowed, and we entered a thickly wooded area.

Cletus, William, and Kat had all agreed we should head out as early as possible. They wanted to put as much distance between us and HQ as possible before someone discovered my mirror was missing. Kat was confident that we had at least twenty-four hours until anyone caught on. Her plan, which, by the way, she had made up and voted on all by herself, was to tell us the plan when we set up camp for the night.

I didn't understand why we didn't just hide out until dark and then zap ourselves to wherever it was we were going with our Ostiums. William explained the Ostium could only return us to our original transport location. And that would mean we would all end up in different places. Anyway, he said he didn't know where we were headed. So for now, I had to be content to trudge along at the tail end of our small caravan. I kept reminding myself the final result was all that mattered to me now. If Kat told me to walk on my hands while whistling "Mary Had a Little Lamb," I would happily do it just to get my hands on the Kaptropoten.

Kat led the way, and she set a good pace. She hacked at vines and undergrowth with a long stick she had found on the forest floor. William followed closely behind her while Cletus stayed by Andie's side. He was quick to steer her around any rocks or branches that she might trip on. Every now and again, Andie would throw a glance at me over her shoulder as if to say, "Rescue me from this extremely nice but overly enthusiastic and attentive muscle-bound boy who is treating me like a helpless damsel when in fact I am a strong and independent young woman." It was either that or, "You got any gum?"

As we walked, monkeys chattered and magpies chirped. And there was also the rhythmic cracking of the branches we stepped on as we hiked. But without the constant humming and buzzing of insects, it felt like half the symphony was missing.

The hot air was thick and soupy. It clung to our skin, soaking our clothes and making me feel like one giant, soggy noodle in a huge bowl of chicken soup. Kat's pace was challenging, but we pushed on. We traveled for most of the day and only paused when someone needed to visit the little boys' or little girls' tree. By the time the sun began to slip from the sky, William and Kat were bickering over the name of every last tree, plant, and flower. Andie was stumbling over every last twig and pebble, and Cletus had just about finished singing every last camp song ever written.

"Someone's cryin', Lord, Kumbaya! Oh, Looord! Kumbayaaaaaa!" Cletus belted out the lyrics.

"*You* are about to be crying!" Kat said to Cletus. "Now shut up!"

You didn't have to be a genius to notice everyone was hungry and cranky. I caught up to Cletus. "What do you say we stop for something to eat?"

"Sounds good to me," he said. "Go 'head. Conjure us up a little buffet."

"Not a chance." I remembered Caephus' warning about using the mirror. I was still freaked out about the duct tape and shoe episodes. It would be awhile before I used the Kaptro Conjuration again.

I thought I spotted a patch of banana plants up ahead.

"Are those bananas?" I asked. I was surprised bananas were growing on this island. It didn't seem tropical enough to me.

"Rephael grows 'em around the island. For the animals."

"What animals?" I asked, "We've only seen a few this whole time we've been in the woods. And no bugs either. What's up with that?"

"Believe it or not, the only animals on the Isle of Mirrors are the ones intelligent enough to recognize themselves in a mirror. It's called the Mirror Test. If they could pass the Mirror Test, then Rephael brought 'em here. Strange, huh? They say he didn't want a bunch of confused animals, bugs, and birds slammin' into all the mirrored buildings trying to attack themselves." Cletus shrugged. "Guess that would get pretty annoying."

I shrugged too and then called out to the group, "Who wants bananas?"

Everyone agreed a pause for some tasty yellow nutrition was in order. I was just about to scale the super tall banana plant when two small monkeys swung onto it.

"Talk to them," Cletus said.

"Uh, okay. Excuse me, monkeys."

One of the monkeys scrambled down the stem. "I beg your pardon, sir, but we are apes, yes we are—bonobos to be exact."

"Oh, I'm sorry. I'm Jax. Do you have a name?"

"My name is Saadiya, yes it is. But my friends call me Sadie, they do. We heard you're the new guardian of the Elementum. We'll be pleased to serve you, Master Jax. But we will miss Master Cletus. We will." Sadie lowered her bonobo head. She swiped at her eye with the back of her bonobo hand.

"I know Cletus misses you all too." I patted her shoulder. "Are there enough bananas up there for us too?"

"Yes, there are. Wait right here." She scampered back up the plant and hooted to the other bonobo. The monkeys plucked bananas from the branches and dropped them to me one at a time. After they picked several unripe bananas, Sadie scurried down. "My apologies, but those were the ripest bananas up there, they were."

I thanked Sadie for the bananas, and the two apes hurried off. But not before Sadie latched onto Cletus for a quick human-bonobo hug.

Andie seemed impressed with the whole situation. "That thing is amazing!" She was talking about the mirror.

Kat, Andie, William, and Cletus plopped themselves on a large boulder and waited for me to pass out the bananas. I took one step toward the rock, and my foot sunk deep in a pile of fresh monkey doo.

"Aww! Come on! What is it with these animals?" When everyone appeared puzzled, I said, "I just stepped in monkey poop!"

"Um, technically, it's ape poop." Cletus couldn't resist correcting me.

"Whatever!" I scraped the bottom of my shoe on a nearby rock and tossed bananas to everyone.

Andie tried to peel her banana. "I don't want to sound ungrateful, but this banana is totally green. I can't even get the peel off." She pouted and tossed it on the ground.

"Someone is grumpy," Kat said.

Andie scowled at her.

Kat turned to me. "Just conjure us up some meat and potatoes, for goodness' sakes."

"Nope." I didn't budge.

Once again, Cletus prompted me. "Use the Elementum."

"Really?" I was amazed the mirror could help in a situation like this. I put my hand on the bag, "Please make our bananas ripe." There was a flash of light from the sack, and Andie and I watched in awe. The brightest of yellows washed up from the bottom of each banana, swallowing the green until they were all beautifully ripe.

"That thing is amazing," Andie said again.

Cletus' chest puffed up. I think it made him like Andie all the more. "It is, isn't it? Definitely the best of all the mirrors."

Kat must have been feeling confrontational. "Are you mad? Any one of the mirrors is better than the Kaptro Elementum."

The long hike and hunger were definitely taking a toll. Everyone was testy.

Cletus hopped up. His arms were straightened and tensed, and his hands were balled into fists. He glared at Kat. "You wanna say that again?"

"The Kaptro Elementum has never held any historical significance like the other mirrors have."

"WHAT? What about Archimedes, the Greek mathematician?" Cletus seemed to be in complete disbelief that Kat would question the greatness of the Elementum. "He was the first Komitari of the Kaptro Elementum. He used it to save Syracuse from the Roman navy! Set the entire naval fleet on fire with it! What about—"

"A weak example." Kat examined her nails like she was already bored with the argument.

Cletus took two threatening steps toward Kat. She jumped to her feet and put her fists up.

This had all the makings of a brawl. Fortunately, before things got out of hand, William stepped in.

"Now, now, kids," he said in his most soothing preschool teacher voice. "Everyone's mirror is special in its own unique way. Let's play nicely."

Cletus and Kat both returned to their spots on the rock, but Kat was giving Cletus some serious evil eyeball.

Andie had already devoured her second banana. "Now I'm thirsty."

I was thirsty too. I felt like I had mastered the whole Kaptro Elementum thing. "Let me try this." I reached up and pulled several large leaves from the branch hanging over my head. I rolled them into small cone-shaped cups and passed them out. Again, I put my hand on the gold velvet bag. "Fill these cups with water."

The bag exploded in color. We watched as miniature clouds formed over the makeshift cups. They released a sparkling, little shower of rain into each.

The water was super refreshing, and we all enjoyed our supper of bananas, protein bars, and water. Soon, the sun left the sky. It took the heat and humidity with it, and it wasn't long before Andie was shivering and Kat was hugging herself against the cool night breeze.

William was the first to speak. "I would suggest we set up camp here for the night. Then we can get off to an early start in the morning."

Cletus agreed. "I second that. We'll take turns at guard—make sure the KIA doesn't catch up to us."

I used the Elementum to make a crackling, cozy fire. We all settled around the toasty flames and warmed our hands.

"Who's gonna sit guard first?" Cletus grinned. "I think we should do shifts of two, and…" He flexed his oversized bicep. "I think we should arm wrestle for it. Winners sleep first."

"No way!" Andie was no dummy. "I don't stand a chance against you genetic mutants. I'll just take the first watch."

"No offense," Kat said, "but I do not plan on leaving my fate in the hands of a Normal."

"Excuse me? I am perfectly capable of being on lookout!"

"Can't believe I'm sayin' this, but I agree with Kat, just for different reasons," Cletus said. "If the KIA comes, I don't want Andie to face them. Rather have them come up against one of us."

Andie scowled and crossed her arms.

"Andie," I said. "Cletus is right. Let us handle this."

Andie was outnumbered. For once she backed down without an argument, but she manhandled my backpack and yanked out the blanket Elweard had packed for me. She spread it on the ground by the fire, dropped down on one half, pulled the other side across herself, and snapped her eyes shut.

"Who wants a shot at me first?" Cletus knelt on the ground and rested his elbow on a big rock. His hand was poised for a bout of arm wrestling.

"I'll go." I stepped up to the rock. I knelt opposite Cletus and anchored my elbow on the rock. He interlocked his hand with mine. Andie had rolled in our direction to watch us though one narrowed eye.

William clasped his hands around ours to referee. "Ready, go!" He released our gripped hands and stepped away.

The second William let go, Cletus thrust my arm down toward the rock. He took me off guard with his quickness and strength. I had to belly up to the rock and pull his arm closer to me. My hand was suspended just two inches over the top of the rock. I needed to get enough leverage to stop it from being smashed against the rough surface. With every ounce of super strength in my body, I fought back.

Cletus' laughing eyes were locked on mine. "Not bad for a disgraced Komitari, eh? Is the boy wonder, the Ark, havin' a little trouble against his lowly and humble attendant?"

"No...trouble..."—my teeth were clenched—"...at...ALL!" I rallied with a sudden burst of strength.

Now Cletus was taken off guard. I forced his arm back slowly and steadily. Now *his* hand hovered over the rock. I intentionally didn't finish him off. "Why did you call me the 'Ark'? Kat called me the Ark at the hotel. What does it mean?"

Cletus was fighting so hard to stop me from slamming his arm on the rock he shook with the effort. I pushed just hard enough to keep his hand suspended there. To be totally honest, my arm was cramping a little, but I tried to make it look easy. I pressed his arm down another inch—like a threat to make him tell me what I wanted to know.

"Okay, okay!" He winced, still fighting to keep his hand off the rock. "The Ark." He panted. "Word is Melchasaar has a bounty out on one of the Komitari... his army is huntin' one of us. They say Melchasaar is seeking revenge on him. Also, needs him for some evil scheme. They're callin' that Komitari the Ark. After Octavius Arkin, the KIA agent who intercepted the intelligence. Also like the Ark that delivered Noah's people from harm." His palm was getting all sweaty. "They say he's supposed to have powers beyond any Komitari." He stopped to readjust his body position to try and get some leverage of his own. When he didn't continue, I forced his arm back another half inch.

"Ow! All right, all right! The Kaptro Scryor...it lets you see things...like other times and locations...and also the future. Kat asked the Scryor to show her the Ark. She says it was you."

I put him out of his misery when I tapped the back

of his hand on the rock's surface.

William rushed over and raised my right arm. "Ladies and gentleman, your winner!" He made the announcement even though Andie was pretending to sleep again, and Kat was busy plucking a piece of lint from her shirt.

Cletus stood. He cradled his right arm with his left, but he smiled. "I'd shake your hand, but I'm afraid of you."

I slapped him on the back. "Good match. And by the way, there's no way I'm the Ark. Why in the world would Melchasaar put a bounty on my head? He doesn't even know me, so he couldn't want revenge on me."

Cletus didn't answer.

"Kat's wrong. If I was the Ark, why didn't Melchasaar kill me in the Four Circles?"

Cletus shrugged. "Don't know. Maybe he didn't know it was you. But I suspect he needed to find your mirror first."

Andie's eyes were still closed. "Or maybe he would have if he didn't get interrupted by Drake and me."

"It's not me. I mean, I never even met a sorcerer before, so there's no way I could help with his plan."

Cletus changed the subject. "Let's see who's gonna take the first shift with me. Go 'head, Kat, William." He nodded toward the rock.

Kat sighed. "If I must." She looked at William. "But you cannot hold me responsible for any injuries, Brother."

William seemed uncertain as he stepped up to the rock. He was a good sport, though. "Bring it on, Sis!"

This time, Cletus was referee. As soon as their hands were locked in the correct position, Cletus stepped back.

"Go!"

Kat yawned, rolled her eyes, and slammed William's hand down. William's body crumpled over the rock. In the highest, girliest voice imaginable, he sang, "Owwww! Mommm-eee!"

Kat looked bored. She dusted the dirt from her elbow and walked back to her blanket. She lay down and proceeded to go to sleep.

Cletus and I were stunned.

Andie's eyes were wide. "Genetic mutants," she mumbled before snapping her eyes shut again.

William still hadn't lifted his arm from the rock. "Looks like it's the two of us," he said to Cletus. His voice was still high.

Cletus and I turned away. "Wasn't really a fair fight," he whispered. "Attendants never get full powers unless they actually become a Komitari."

"But Komitari—we're born with our powers, right?"

Cletus nodded. "We're born with some powers, but we get more as we get closer to our sixteenth birthday." He raised an eyebrow and looked me up and down. "Hard to believe you're gonna get even stronger." He rubbed his sore right hand. "You know, you *are* freakishly strong. Even for a Komitari. Does that make you the Ark?" Cletus scratched his chin. "Don't know the answer to that one. Anyhow, by the time you're sixteen, you should have all your powers.

"And then, not everyone is a pure-born. Rephael or Caephus can grant Komitari status to someone who isn't born a Komitari. Like my cousin Yancy. When I picked him to be my attendant, he got his attendant powers at the Bestowing ceremony. Really just makes him faster and stronger than your average Normal. If he ends up becoming Komitari of the Kaptro Elementum, then Caephus will grant him full Komitari powers. That would be a whole other ceremony." He picked up his pack and slung it over his shoulder. Then, he headed to a huge log about fifteen yards from our clearing. "Let's go, Will."

William's arm was still there, all limp on the rock. He got up and together, they walked over and settled on the log.

I curled up on the ground next to Andie, hoping to snatch as many hours of sleep as I could.

"Kind of creepy," she whispered from under the blanket.

"What's creepy?"

"These woods. They're so quiet. Why aren't there any crickets, bugs, animal noises? It's freaky."

"I think so too. Don't worry. I'm right beside you." I reached over and squeezed her hand. "I won't let anything happen."

"Thanks, Jax," she murmured and fell asleep.

♀ ⚔ ⚞

"Hey, Sleeping Beauty." It was Cletus, and he was nudging my shoulder with his toe. "It's your turn on the log. Now make room for me." He squeezed in between me and the fire. Before I could finish rubbing the sleep from my eyes, he was snoring like a hibernating bear. Even asleep, he had that silly grin on his long face.

Gotta love the guy. I yawned, cracked my neck, and trudged over to the log where Kat already sat.

"Got room for one more on this log?" My heart was beating a little faster just from being close to her.

She scooted to one side of the log, but said nothing. I sat beside her for a while just staring into the dark forest. After some time, I asked, "Why are you so desperate to get Melchasaar? I mean, why couldn't you just wait for Rephael to do something?"

Kat sighed. She glanced at me and then looked ahead again. "Look. For some reason, Melchasaar wants the Ark. Rephael and Caephus were planning to use that to their advantage. They *were* going after Melchasaar—with you. You were bait. And I suppose they hoped you could take him out. But then you had to go and prove yourself unworthy. Now, they will not take any action because they do not want to risk Melchasaar killing you or getting anyone else killed. Obviously, they no longer think you are the Ark. So instead they just sit, like cowards, waiting for the Ark to turn up."

Bait? Me? I gulped. "So why you? Why do you feel like it's *your* responsibility to get Melchasaar?"

Kat paused for a long time. She sounded like a child when she spoke. "Melchasaar killed my mother. He abducted my father along with countless others." She swallowed and thrust her chin out. "I will not wait for him to attack my home or my family again. And I *will* get my father back."

"I'm sorry," I whispered. I could feel her pain—the same pain I lived with every day. It helped explain why Kat always had such a chip on her shoulder. I touched her arm.

She pulled away. "I can handle it."

I looked down and picked at a hangnail. "I lost my mother…and my brother too."

"I know. What happened to your dad?"

"He split right after Sebastian was born. We haven't heard from him since, so Mom raised us on her own. Funny, but I really don't remember anything about him. We don't even have any pictures, and Mom never let us talk about him. She must've really hated him for ditching us like that."

We sat a little while without talking, until Kat took the ruby ring off her finger. She handed it to me. "My father gave me this. He has one just like it." She leaned close and pointed at the stone. "Do you see how the ruby is set against the crest with the two dragon heads?"

"Yeah." To be honest, I couldn't see anything in the dark, but I didn't want to ruin the moment.

"That is the royal family crest. My father's ring has been handed down from one ruler to the next, generation after generation. Only the ruling monarch of Flaeritay—that is my homeland—wears the ring. But I loved my father's ring so much when I was a little girl that he broke with royal tradition and had one made for me. It is very special."

"Was he after the mirror? Melchasaar, I mean."

Kat stood. She took back her ring and paced in front of the log. "He was after the mirror. But he was also trying to free Draemoch, one of his most ruthless captains. Melchasaar considers him to be an invaluable tool. Draemoch was captured by my father's army on one of the raids. Melchasaar has sworn to kill one prisoner a day until we hand over the Kaptro Metamorphus and release Draemoch."

She stopped pacing and peered into my eyes. The glow of the distant fire lit up parts of her face. Her features were as serious as I had ever seen them. "I cannot afford to wait until Rephael thinks he has found the Ark. I know it is you. Melchasaar must be defeated before he kills my father. If I keep you away from Melchasaar, then he will be distracted by his search for you. And that will give me more time to find the Kaptrofracti. I will do whatever it takes to save my family."

I completely understood where Kat was coming from. She wanted to kill Melchasaar as much as I wanted to get the Kaptropoten and bring Sebastian back.

"What makes you so sure I'm the Ark?"

She looked down, twisting her ruby ring around her finger. "I am not proud of my behavior, but I...borrowed Stirling's mirror—he is Komitari of the Kaptro Scryor." Her clear green eyes darted to mine and then away again. "I transformed into a spider and sneaked into Stirling's house. I asked the mirror to show me the Ark...and it showed you."

"That's ridiculous. Why would Melchasaar put a bounty out on my head? I never did anything to him."

Kat shrugged. "I do not know. I am not even certain if he knows it is you. All I know is the KIA has reported Melchasaar wants one of us. And supposedly, the reward is greater if the Ark is handed over to him alive."

That didn't even scare me. There was no way. I didn't believe for a minute I was the Ark. Even though Kat looked 100 percent confident when she said the mirror had shown me, I was certain she was wrong. I wasn't sixteen yet, I didn't have all of my powers, and I was not even trained. And let's face it…I did wimp out on the K-Coaster. I was no threat to anyone. I almost told her exactly that, but then I thought better of it. Instead, I decided it was best to let her think I was the Ark. Otherwise, she might decide she didn't need me. And no matter what, I was going to get the Kaptropoten.

CHAPTER 14
Portals and Chambers and Doors! Oh My!

We were just getting ready to start the last leg of our hike. The sun was peeking through the forest ceiling. Beautiful slivers of cheery light pierced the trees, lighting up select bits of the wooded floor all around us. Kat was finally filling us in on the details of her plan.

She leaned against a tree and chewed on a dark green leaf she had plucked from a nearby plant. Before each bite, she would sprinkle a few shakes of scrambled egg-flavored crystals on it.

"We have about a two-hour hike until we reach the westernmost point of the island. We are heading toward the Propius Portal—"

"Or as we like to call it," William said, "the Perma-Port."

"What's a Perma-Port?" Andie asked.

"It's the only way off the island besides an Ostium," Cletus said. "It's a permanent portal between here and Earth. Really just takes you to the other side of the island's shield."

"Where do you end up?" I asked.

"Not sure exactly," Cletus said. "It's gotta be

somewhere in the Venetian lagoon. None of us have ever gone through there. It's not allowed. Any time the portal's open, there's a chance someone could sneak onto the island."

"You mean Melchasaar?" I asked.

"Well, yeah…" William said, "but Melchasaar isn't the only one trying to get the Kaptropoten. Do you realize how many people have killed just to possess a piece of the mirror?"

"Really?" Andie seemed intrigued. "I guess it does make sense, though. Just think what kind of harm you could do with any one of the mirrors."

Cletus nodded. "And they have done harm. Take the Kaptro Scryor. It alone is responsible for countless acts of evil. Seems like it's a favorite for bad guys. Queen Catherine de Medici of France had it—she executed some of her own family members based on visions from the Scryor. And there was Hitler, Mary Queen of Scots, and Queen Clarice from my homeland—Flaeritay. The whole 'Mirror, Mirror, on the Wall' legend is based on her." He shuddered. "Thank goodness the KIA recovered the mirror in the fifties."

"Ahem." Kat sounded agitated. "As I was saying…" She took another nibble of her leaf. "Once we pass through the Propius Portal, we will head to the Palace of Versailles in France. We need to get inside the Hall of Mirrors. The Kaptro Teleportation is the mirror we are going after first. Number one,"—she ticked off on her finger—"it is here—close by—on Earth. Number two,"—she raised a second finger—"it will enable us to teleport to the other realms and locations where we will find the other mirrors."

"Okay, tell them about Jules," William said.

"I was getting to that." Kat sounded even more annoyed. She tossed the leaf leftovers on the ground. "Jules Batiste—he is Komitari of the Kaptro Teleportation. Well, he has gone underground." She turned to me. "While you two were off flunking orientation, Caephus told us Jules and Stirling could not be located. That is why neither of them was present at Council. And, unfortunately, we cannot track their Kaptrofracti because of the Celare charm. The KIA believes Jules and Stirling may have gone underground as a result of Melchasaar's attacks. But then, of course, it seems like Stirling can never be reached."

Cletus and William nodded.

"Then why do you think we need to go to the Hall of Mirrors?" Andie asked.

"This is the cool part," William said. "The Teleportation mirror has been in Jules' family since the Kaptropoten was broken in 218 BC. It has always been passed from generation to generation. It has never needed to pass to an alternate family. You know...no untimely deaths in the family, no scandals resulting in the Komitari losing his mirror, no mysteries...nothing.

"Well, one of his Komitari ancestors, Jules Hardouin-Mansart, was also the architect of the Hall of Mirrors back in the late 1600s. It was rumored that when Mansart designed the Hall, he built it with a secret chamber that he used to secure the Kaptro Teleportation. The chamber is said to be almost impenetrable. And it's also rumored to be the only place ever created with the capability of obscuring the electromagnetic field of a Kaptrofractus." He paused. "I guess that's one of the reasons why his family has had such success over the generations."

"So you think Jules is hiding out in that chamber?" I asked.

Kat was stuffing her backpack with her blanket and several small weapons she had held onto during her security watch. "I think he is either hiding in the chamber, or he has hidden the mirror in the chamber. Either way, we are going to find out."

"Is everyone overlooking the obvious here?" Andie asked. "If the chamber is impenetrable, how exactly are we supposed to penetrate it?"

"She's got a point." Cletus was on the ground, hammering out one-armed push-ups like he was getting paid for it.

"I am still working on that part," Kat said with a little less confidence than usual. "Anyhow, it is time for us to go."

Once again, Kat led us through the forest. She and William were way out ahead, followed by Cletus. Andie and I were at the end of the group. I was listening as Andie babbled on and on about the new microscope she was saving up for.

Suddenly, my ears were assaulted by the same loud-pitched squeal I had heard in the hotel hallway. The pain was so bad I had to stop. I pressed my hands over my ears. Then, that uncomfortable static, tuning noise began.

"Are you sure you can pull this off, Kat?" It was William's voice. He was clear as can be even though he was about a hundred yards in front of us.

"There is no other way."

"It just seems like a really bad idea to me," William said. "Melchasaar will kill him. And probably you too."

"It will be fine. The Scryor says so. Now leave the worrying to me."

There was more static and another high-pitched squeal. Andie's voice was in tune again as she listed the merits of the Telecore Deluxe Digital Microscope 3000.

I didn't like what I had just overheard at all. William sounded pretty concerned. I assumed he was talking about their father. And the thought of Kat going to all this trouble and that it could end with her father getting killed was upsetting. At the same time, Kat's courage was impressive. She was willing to risk her own life to save the king. I just hoped when the time came I would be brave enough to save Sebastian.

"So which one do you think?" Andie was waiting for my opinion.

"Yeah, that sounds good."

"Jax! Did you even hear a word I said?" She spun around and saw me covering my ears. "Super hearing again?"

I nodded. Andie must've understood I was freaked out. She turned back around and kept walking.

After another half mile or so, Kat, William, and Cletus finally reached the top of a steep ridge. They waited for Andie and me to catch up.

"This is it," Cletus called. "We're at the edge of the island. The portal has to be close."

A salty breeze wafted down the hill. I was eager to check it out. I grabbed Andie's hand and we struggled up the slope. We wound our way around trees and over rocks until we reached the peak of the ridge.

The wind up there was strong. Andie gasped when she looked over the other side of the crest. It was like we had reached the end of the earth. The ridge was treeless and only about ten feet wide. On the other side, the ground faded away into a bright but grayish wall of rowdy, rolling clouds.

Andie stabbed a curious finger into the mist. We all laughed at the loud, echoing BWONGGGG. It sounded like she had poked a giant sheet of tin. The mist rippled away from her probing finger. It sent circular waves outward as far as we could see. She pulled out her finger and giggled. "Don't worry. It didn't hurt."

In the meantime, William was searching the edge of the ridge. He had to be over a quarter of a mile north of us when he shouted, "Over here! I see it!"

Cletus, Kat, and I flashed to William. We forgot about poor Andie who took several minutes to jog to the Perma-Port.

The Propius Portal was totally mystical. It looked like the door to a bank vault, but it was just floating there in the mist! The handle wasn't really a handle. It was more like a metal wheel with spokes on it—like a ship's steering wheel. The door itself was outlined with a glowing, white halo of light. It practically begged me to open it.

"So how does it work?" I took the wheel in both hands.

Right as I was about to turn the wheel, the loud snap of a branch at the bottom of the hill startled us all. Kat put her finger to her lips. Without warning, she shape-shifted into a magpie and flew away, but within seconds, she was standing in front of us again as herself.

"KIA!" she whispered. "We must get off the island! Now!"

I tried to turn the wheel counterclockwise, but it wouldn't budge. I grunted and gave it everything I had, but I just couldn't do it. I tried turning it clockwise, and when it still didn't move, I tried counterclockwise again.

"It's rusted!" I was still attempting to force the wheel. "Aaaaaargh!" The two spokes snapped off in my hands. "Darn super strength!"

At this point, the cracking twigs and snapping branches were rapidly getting closer.

"Over there!" Andie pointed to the place where we had climbed over the ridge. "They're coming!"

About a half-dozen men and one woman pulled themselves up over the crest. They all wore dark suits and mirrored sunglasses. "Stop! We're KIA! Step away from the portal and put your hands where we can see them!"

I tossed the spokes on the ground and moved out of the way. Kat and Cletus grabbed the handle and tried to force the wheel. They couldn't budge it either. My heart pounded as the men ran toward us. I panicked. Just like when I was at HQ, I gave the door one solid kick with the bottom of my foot. It gave way, leaving a large dent. It made the door pull away from the frame in the lower right corner. The slight crack that resulted acted like a vacuum. It began sucking air through its small opening with a deafening rush of wind. Leaves, stones, twigs, and all sorts of forest debris swept violently through the hole. Andie lost her footing and found herself slammed up against the door. She couldn't fight the tremendous pull.

"Jax! Help!"

But it was Cletus who pulled her away from the door. He shielded her body from the wind with his own.

The men made quick progress. As they closed in on us, we noticed they were holding these little metal boxes in front of them. I kicked furiously at the dent. I was hoping to widen the crack just enough for us all to squeeze through.

"Hurry!" William and Cletus yelled.

The KIA agents were about a football field away. The guy in the lead flipped open the front of his box. It reminded me of the mouse motel traps Gram was always setting around the garage. Instantly, the little velvet sack around my neck flew out of my shirt. It lurched toward the box like it was late for a hot date right inside that box. It pulled against the thick gold rope with some serious force. The rope cut into the skin on the back of my neck, but I just kept kicking the metal door.

"William!" Kat said after another KIA agent flipped open his own little box. Her satchel flew in the direction of the second trap. It slid down her arm. If she moved one inch to grab it with her left hand, it would have slipped right off the end of her right hand.

William lunged at the bag. He held onto it just long enough for Kat to grip it. The closer those boxes got to us, the stronger they pulled on our mirrors. In one last desperate attempt, I kicked the door with every bit of strength I could find.

WHOOSH! The door was sucked outward into the cloudy mist. Right behind it flew William, then Kat, and then Cletus and Andie. Just as I was about to be pulled through, I caught a glimpse of the KIA retreating against the forceful suction of the portal. It was with the slightest bit of satisfaction that I surrendered to the vacuum that had swept everyone else away.

CHAPTER 15
A Close Call and a Flo Call

I let go of the door frame. I found myself hurtling through the blinding mist. There was no way to tell which way was up and which way was down. Then, all of a sudden, I was dunked into warm water. I kicked back up to the surface, sputtering water and coughing.

When Cletus said the Perma-Port led to somewhere in the Venetian lagoon, I never dreamed it would literally drop us in the lagoon. It was storming like crazy. Huge hail pellets assaulted my head like a gang of vengeful golf balls.

"Is everyone okay?" I searched the waters around me. In the distance, Andie had somehow pulled herself onto the dented portal door. She used her hands to paddle it like it was her own personal flotation device.

"I've got you!" Cletus swam to her. He held on to the back end of the door, his feet propelling him like a rocket. He steered Andie through the water and toward the rocky shore of a neighboring island.

Kat and William swam behind them. Once I saw everyone was safe, I paddled in the same direction.

Suddenly, a booming crash of thunder accompanied

a blinding flash of lightning. My mind began to relive the events of that awful night at the pool over and over. It was like a scene from a poorly directed horror movie. I watched as the eerie green lightning struck the pool again and again.

My heart raced. Panic surged through my veins like a speed boat. I tried to paddle toward the shore. My anxiety was so crushing, my arms and legs wouldn't cooperate with my brain. I thought my heart was about to stop. Even in the middle of the lagoon, with buckets of hail dropping on my head, small beads of sweat still managed to pop out. They sizzled against my burning forehead. I was light-headed and dizzy. I was about to die right here in this lagoon from a panic attack.

Another electric white bolt of lightning was the last thing I saw before I sucked in a mouthful of salty water. My nose and lungs burned. My head felt like it was about to explode. My clothes weighed me down like an anchor. They began to drag my body toward the bottom of the lagoon. The panic gave way to desperation. Finally I gave in to it, giving up my fight and sinking down, down, down.

❦ ✕ ❧

"Jax? Jax? Can you hear me?" Andie's face hovered upside down over mine. It was out of focus and only inches away. She sat cross-legged, and my head was in her lap.

I coughed and spit up salt water. Andie rolled my head to the side. When my lungs were finally clear, I gasped for breath.

Andie's tears were warm as they dripped onto my nose and off the side of my cheek. "Thank goodness you're all right. You *are* all right, right?"

Cletus', Kat's, and William's faces hung directly above Andie's. The circle of faces came into focus, each wearing expressions of fear or concern.

"W-w-what h-happened?" I asked.

"You almost drowned, but Cletus saved you. You should have seen him. He was so brave. He swam back out there in the middle of all that hail and lightning—"

I tensed. The word lightning was enough to make me remember exactly what had happened. It brought back all the anxiety I had felt in the lagoon. It terrified me. Suddenly, I noticed the sharp edges of rock digging into my back and the cool air making me shiver through my wet clothes. I struggled to get up. Cletus reached out and pulled me to my feet.

"Thank you." I looked him straight in the eye to make sure he knew I wasn't just thanking him for helping me up.

"It was nothin'."

The thought of Gram having to hear about me dying made me sick. I couldn't do that to her. I coughed a few times. "I mean it." I reached out for a handshake. "Thank you."

Cletus wrapped me up in an unexpected hug. "We're brothers."

I hugged him back—I could use a brother right now.

"What happened to you out there?" Andie asked.

"I must have swallowed too much water," I lied. I

didn't want anyone to know how much the lightning had scared me. "Will the KIA follow us?"

Kat said, "They will do whatever is necessary to stop Melchasaar from getting his hands on the Kaptropoten. It is their only objective. If they believe our actions will jeopardize the Kaptropoten's safety then...well...they will not hesitate to take us out."

"Out? As in OUT, out?" Andie dragged her thumb across her neck. She stuck her tongue out of the side of her mouth to imitate an execution.

"Out," repeated Kat. She said it as matter-of-factly as you would say, "Cheeseburgers are good."

"So you're saying we're a target for the bad guys *and* the good guys?" I asked. "That's just great."

"Then the best thing to do is not get caught," said William. "So I suggest we get moving before the KIA shows up here."

"All right," Kat said, taking control of the situation. "We are on the visible part of Murano—"

"Which, by the way," William said, "is known as the Glass Island."

"Oh! I've read about Murano," Andie said. "Did you know the glassmakers were kept as virtual prisoners on the island? They didn't want them to give away their top-secret glassmaking technique to other countries." Andie's voice was high, and her speech was fast; she was always excited to talk about science and history. "And they actually expanded the industry to include mirrors. By the sixteenth century, they dominated at mirror making."

"That's right," Cletus said. "In fact, it's no coincidence Murano became a leader for glass and mirror makin', what with the Isle of Mirrors bein' hidden right here. It's only natural that former citizens of IOM moved to the other little islands and started glass factories."

"Enough with the history lessons." Kat was impatient. "We need to get to France. There is a ferry that will take us to Venice. Once we get to Venice we can cross the Ponte della Libertà to the mainland. From there we will take a train the rest of the way."

"Wait." I had to acknowledge the hard work of my little brain hamster who had just squeaked an idea in my head. "We are going after the Kaptro Teleportation, right?" Everyone nodded. "So once we have that, we can teleport to anywhere, right?" I dug through my backpack searching for one of my gift shop purchases. "Then I don't see any reason why we shouldn't use *this* now." Triumphantly, I held up the pack of single-use Kaptrofracti and pointed to the mini Kaptro Teleportation. I mentally congratulated the hamster who was clearly running at top speed right now.

William nodded. "Heyyyyy! That's not a bad thought at all, right, Sis?" He smacked Kat on her arm with the back of his hand.

Kat shrugged. "Not bad, I suppose." But she smiled, and it was a beautiful smile. Her teeth were white and straight like a beaver's—only not as big and not at all bucky. And those dimples! They were as deep as potholes—except they weren't all full of gravel and motor oil. It made my stomach do confused little backflips, just like it did the day I scored the chewed piece of rare 1896 Pepsin Little Pinkies Gum.

"I thought good it was idea," I said, flustered by Kat's brilliant smile. I guess my mouth was as confused as my stomach. "I mean…Me idea. It good. Right?"

Andie rolled her eyes. "Yes, Jax." She sighed. "It is a good idea."

"Then what are we waiting for?" Cletus asked. "Let's do it."

I pulled the handheld mini Teleportation mirror out of the plastic.

"Everyone hold on to Jax," William said.

Kat turned to Andie. "This time," she whispered so only Andie and I could hear, "stand on one foot, close one eye, and hold your tongue."

"Like dis?" Andie held her tongue and did exactly what Kat said. It was totally cool of Kat to help Andie have a smoother trip than she did with the Ostium transport.

Cletus took my hand. I stared at my reflection in the mini mirror. "We wish to go to the Hall of Mirrors."

The little mirror glowed blue. Five ribbons of blue light emerged. They danced and swirled from its center. Winds began to rotate about us, as loud as a train thundering down the tracks. The five glowing ribbons each engulfed one of us. They rotated slowly at first and soon were spinning like a tornado. I began to feel that awful, tingly sensation. Then, the stretching and tugging began. Soon I was being squeezed through the tube. In a flash, I found myself standing in front of a tall ornate golden gate that guarded a magnificent palace. I was only slightly nauseous and hardly dizzy at all.

One glance was enough to know this place was amazing. The palace was made of stone and brick in varied tones of beige. It was so huge I could barely see from one end to the other. Endless walkways were lined with finely manicured shrubs. And there were so many statues; it had to have taken years to carve them all.

There were three rapid pops as Cletus, then Kat, and then William appeared. Andie finally popped in still holding her tongue and standing on one foot. Her face was green. She looked at me for one quick second before she collapsed at my feet.

"I thought you said that would help her!" I said.

"I never said it would help." Kat turned to study the palace.

I stooped to lift Andie, and her eyes fluttered open. "Did I do it right?" And then she passed out again.

"Don't worry," Cletus said. "Second time is never as bad. Should be fine in a few minutes. What's the plan?" he asked Kat.

"I told you, I am still working on that. But the good news is the palace is closed to the public on Mondays. That will give me some time to look around before nightfall. Everyone wait here." Kat took her mirror from her satchel.

Once again, I was mesmerized as her form waved and wiggled and then snapped into the much smaller shape of a mouse. She scampered along the path through the garden, past two sets of grand gates, and then across a black-and-white marble courtyard to the palace entrance.

I put Andie on a nearby bench. I plopped down beside her while Cletus did some squats and lunges.

William reached in his pack. He pulled out a small stack of books. Each was about the size of a deck of cards.

"Anyone up for some light reading? I stopped at the book repository before we left and borrowed a few books that might help." He tossed a small book to me. It was called *The Seven Mirrors of the Kaptropoten for Dummies*. He kept for himself a book about the Palace of Versailles.

I opened the small book, which was really more like a makeup compact than a book. A mirror was fixed on the inside of the back cover, and there were no pages. On the inside of the front cover was a compartment that held a small set of headphones.

I stuck the headphones in my ears and pressed the tiny red button under the mirror.

"Doo! Doo! Doo!" said a digitally generated robotic voice. "Please select a chapter."

Then, deep inside the mirror, a table of contents appeared. The words looked like they were floating somewhere between the back of the mirror and the glass surface. I reached out to touch them. The odd little book messed with my depth perception. My finger bumped the front of the mirror before I expected it to.

"Doo! Doo! Doo!" the book chimed, and the mechanical voice said, "You have selected Chapter Six: The Kaptro Kinesis. If this is correct, please say, 'One.' If this is incorrect, please say, 'Two.' To speak with an IOM Repository Representative, please say, 'Six.'"

Hmmm. I didn't know much about the Kaptro Kinesis. "One."

"Doo! Doo! Doo! You have selected, 'Nine.' That is not a valid option. Please select a chapter."

"No," I told the mirrored book, "I said, 'One!'"

"Doo! Doo! Doo! You have selected Chapter One: The Kaptro Elementum. If this is correct, please say, 'One.' If this is incorrect, please say, 'Two.' To speak with an IOM Repository Representative, please say, 'Six.'"

"Two!"

"Doo! Doo! Doo! Please select a chapter." The table of contents popped up again.

*Hmmm…*I wasn't sure if I was supposed to touch it or say it. "I…WANT…CHAPTER…SIX."

"Doo! Doo! Doo! You have selected 'six.' Connecting you to a customer service representative. Your current estimated wait time is two minutes."

"No! It's not that big a deal! I don't really care that much!" But the easy listening music that meant I was on hold was already playing. "Aww, c'mon!" If this book was meant for dummies, I'd hate to try and use the book for average kids!

I looked around while I waited. Cletus was on one of the walkways doing some kind of tai chi routine. William leaned against the gate reading his book, and Andie was still sleeping on the bench.

"Hello. IOM Repository. This is Flo speaking," a nasal voice said. At the same time, the face of a woman with black hair and red cat-eye-framed glasses appeared inside the mirror. "How may I help you?"

"I'm just trying to read Chapter Six," I whined.

"Yes, sir. I'll be happy to help you with that."

Buttons clicked. "Ding!" The words, "Chapter Six," appeared in front of Flo's face.

"Okay, sir. I have your chapter ready for you. Is there anything else I can help you with today?"

"No, thanks. That's it."

"Thank you for contacting the IOM Book Repository. Enjoy your book and have a great day."

I shook my head. That was definitely strange.

The book said, "Say 'start' to begin."

"Start." The words floated off the mirror and into the air in front of me. Illustrations and photographs moved across the back of the mirror. As the words floated off the page, the robotic voice read them.

"The Kaptro Kinesis is known to many as the Movement Mirror. The Kinesis provides its owner with the ability to move and control objects through thought alone."

Whoa. Pretty cool.

"When the Kaptropoten was shattered, the Kaptro Kinesis was sent to the realm known as Terreptelan." The pictures playing across the back of the mirror flicked through a multitude of sculpture-head portraits. "The Kinesis was entrusted to the Tortuos clan whose first Komitari was Ptolymus."

A moan to my right interrupted the book. Andie was stirring.

"Jax? Is that you?" She rubbed her temples. "My head…it's pounding…remind me never to do that again." She pulled herself upright.

It was then we spotted Kat scurrying back to us. Once she reached the bench she snapped back into herself.

"So, what did you find out?" William looked up from his book.

"I did not locate the secret chamber, but I did determine the best route for avoiding the security cameras. And I found the maintenance and cleaning schedules. We should be able to go in tonight immediately after sunset. The custodians will be cleaning the Queen's Bedchamber at that time, which is right next to the Hall of Mirrors. The security system in that part of the palace will be silenced while they clean. Best of all, I unlocked a door by the service entrance, so we should have no trouble getting in."

Cletus finished his calisthenics. "Good. Then it looks like we have a plan." He glanced around at our group. There was a serious expression on his face. "For now though, we have more important matters to discuss." That got our attention.

He pulled out a map of Versailles. "Should we have ratatouille for lunch or escargot?"

CHAPTER 16

Indigestion, a Naked Statue, and a Half-Naked Old Guy with Indigestion

The sun had dipped over the horizon. It had painted the evening sky with strokes of orange and pink. Our taxi had just dropped us off at the main gate of the palace. I, for one, was regretting that I had won the "Eat the Whole Duck and Your Meal Is Free" challenge. I rubbed my belly and groaned.

Cletus was wearing my duckbill hat prize. He clapped me on the back. "For a little guy, you can sure put away some waterfowl!"

"Boys!" Kat said. "Focus and follow me."

She led our group all the way around the side of the palace. We went past the wing that William said contained the opera house, and behind the north-facing side. Finally, we stopped by a door in the back. Kat surveyed the area and then cracked open the door. My heart thumped in my ears—I was both excited and anxious. I braced myself for the squeal of an alarm. Luckily, the only sound was our own nervous, shallow breaths. We all filed through the door.

Kat motioned for us to stay behind her. We tiptoed along as she led us through a maze of darkened hallways

163

with massive marble arches and impressive stone statues, and then up a set of steps to the second floor. Eventually, Kat paused in a magnificent room decked out with large panels containing bronze, stucco, and marble carvings. The centerpiece of the room was a wall panel with a massive carving showing one of the former kings riding a horse.

"This is the Salon of War," William whispered. "And that," he said, pointing to the carving, "was King Louis XIV. I saw it in my book. That means the Hall of Mirrors will be right through there." He pointed to an enormous arched opening.

Kat approached the opening. Her back was pressed against the wall. She peeked into the other room to see if it was clear. Just then, we all heard the rhythmic clicking of heels making their way across the wood floor. Someone was coming!

Kat waved us away from the door. We all crept to the other end of the room. I held my breath as a second set of footsteps joined the first. Muffled voices floated from the Hall of Mirrors.

I pressed my fingertips to my temples and tried to block out everything but the voices. There was squealing and static, and then the voices tuned in. It actually worked!

"Clearly, they are no longer here," a thickly accented woman's voice said. She sounded like a Russian spy.

"Are you sure we got the coordinates right?" It was a man's voice now.

"The repository tracked the call to here. It wasn't

flagged as suspicious until the suspects' profiles were distributed across the IOM database," the woman said. "As soon as the customer service rep recognized the photograph of Jackson Sheppard, she notified KIA command center. According to the repository's records, the call came in approximately six hours ago."

"Then they're obviously long gone by now. Let's hope they didn't find the Kaptro Teleportation."

There was more clicking and then silence.

Man! That dumb Dummies book almost gave us away! I felt pretty guilty—and stupid too. I had nearly messed everything up.

Kat motioned us back across the war salon. "That was the KIA! I have no idea how they found us this fast. Did any of you make contact with the IOM?" Her eyes narrowed. "For any reason at all?"

Everybody shook their heads. "Not me," they all said.

Kat looked at me. "Me neither," I lied, because I mean, technically, it was William's fault for giving me the stupid book in the first place—and he was such a nice guy. I wouldn't want to make everyone mad at him. It was better this way. "Let's just be glad they didn't catch us."

Kat waited a few more minutes to make sure the agents were gone. Then, she led us through the doorway. Now, let me say, the Hall of Mirrors was mind-blowing. It had to be the most spectacular room I had ever seen in my entire life.

The gallery was super long. A curved ceiling was covered with the most detailed historical paintings and murals I could imagine. To our right, seventeen huge arched glass doors gave breathtaking views of the lighted gardens. Across the hall and directly opposite the windows were seventeen mirrored arches of the exact same size and shape as the doors. They were perfectly placed to reflect the lights from the garden, and the way the lights bounced around inside the room made it magical. Each of the mirrored arches was made up of twenty-one smaller mirrors. According to William, those mirrors were the top-secret handiwork of Murano glassmakers. They had been bribed into coming to Versailles to help King Louis XIV build his masterpiece, the Hall of Mirrors.

"Historians claim the mirrors were made in Paris, but we all know they are really the product of Murano's finest," William had said.

Flat, marble columns were mounted against the walls. They were placed in between each mirrored arch. After every third mirror (and after every third glass door across the hall) were arched alcoves holding antique carved statues.

Rows of sparkling crystal chandeliers hung from the painted ceilings. Everywhere I looked was gold and crystal and glass and mirrors. It was like we had stepped inside a giant glittering diamond.

"Everyone take an area and search it," Kat said. "Check every wall panel, every statue, every pane of glass until we find something. And be thorough."

I started in the corner on the side of the hall with the doors. Andie took the space behind me on the side with the mirrors. Cletus and William both worked on the same wall as Andie, while Kat started on the other end of my wall.

I slid my hand up and down the marble wall. Reaching as high as I could, I inspected the inside of each arch, doing super-leaps to reach the tops. I took care to apply even pressure to each of the bronze carvings set in the crest of the arches—just in case they might trigger some really cool secret trap door to open up in the floor.

As I worked my way across the wall, my stomach lurched. That roasted duck must have been quacking in there because a loud rumble came from my belly. I blew out a loud burp. Kat shot me a disgusted look but then went back to searching the wall.

"Any idea what we should be looking for?" I asked.

"There was nothing about the secret chamber in the book about the Hall of Mirrors," William said. "The whole story is folklore, I know, but I think it's the only way to explain why the guardians of the Teleportation mirror have been so successful. So just look for anything out of the ordinary—a statue's arm that works like a lever...a hollow wall...a button..."

We all worked in silence as we covered every square inch of the walls. We had been there so long the moon had traveled over the hall and begun its descent in the west. Its beams were just starting to peek through the arched windows. I was making pretty good progress, when I reached a statue of a woman wearing nothing other than a blank expression on her face.

"Pardon me, ma'am," I said to the statue, "but this is going to be as awkward for me as it is for you." I closed my eyes out of respect and turned my head to the side as I patted and twisted all of her parts. My stomach roiled, and I burped again. "Excuse me, ma'am," I told the statue. Maybe sucking on a mint would help to settle my stomach. I reached in my back pocket for the complimentary one they gave me at the restaurant.

When I pulled out the mint, the used Teleportation mirror from the gift shop fell out of my pocket. It hit the floor and shattered.

"Aw, man! Seven years of bad luck." I scrambled to pick up the jagged shards, but when I lifted the first piece, something extremely strange happened.

The moon's rays were pouring through the seventeen windows in such a way that they all bounced off the mirrors on the other side of the room. The weird part was the way they formed seventeen precise lasers of white light that all converged on the one shattered piece I held in my hand. The laser beams refracted from the broken shard and formed one fat beam of light. It shone with a burning intensity on the belly button of a chubby cherub painted on the ceiling. The cherub's navel started to smoke. It was Cletus who reacted by running to snatch the broken mirror from me. Immediately, the seventeen mirrors stopped directing their beams onto that single point on my pants. Now, they just reflected random rays of moonlight onto the floor below.

"Oh my gosh!" Andie said. "How did that happen? Those beams shouldn't have all reflected to that one, single location. It's simple geometry." She walked over to one of the mirrors to inspect the spot where the moonbeam had been.

An idea flashed in my brain. "Cletus, bring me that mirror."

Cletus handed me the sharp broken shard. Instantly, the seventeen beams blazed a path to the mirror. This time, I directed the bright, fat laser of light at the wall of mirrors directly across from me. Ever so slowly, I changed the angle of the mirror. I aimed the beam on various spots of interest on the wall. When it came to rest on the center mirror panel in the middle of the seventh mirrored arch, the whole room lit up. Thousands of little lasers pin-balled around the room. They formed an elaborate web of moonbeams.

At the exact same time, we heard a grating sound as marble scraped on cement. The entire mirrored arch swung inward about a foot-and-a-half. It left a narrow opening on the left side just wide enough to squeeze through.

"You found it!" Kat seemed surprised by her own enthusiasm. "Ahem. We should go in before it closes. Cletus—you guard the north end of the hall, and William—you take the south end. Andie—you stand right here at the opening and warn us if anyone comes." She spun toward the secret chamber.

As she turned, her thick, black braid swung in an arc. It broke the stream of one of the light beams. Suddenly, a torrent of small, narrow blades with tiny feathers attached to the back came whistling right down the same path as that beam.

"Watch out!" shouted Cletus. "It's booby trapped!" Instinctively, Andie, Cletus, and William retreated from the storm of ammunition. When they did, they interrupted the path of countless other lasers. The whole room erupted with those steely little darts screaming along the moon beams from every direction.

I threw myself on Andie. We flattened ourselves on the wooden floor beneath the onslaught of barbs. But even though I had dropped the broken shard, the beams remained.

Cletus jumped high above the ruckus. He grabbed onto one of the golden cords used to hang the chandeliers from the ceiling. Kat had reacted with tiger-like reflexes. She shoved William against the wall, out of range of the ammunition. Her back was flattened against the wall beside him, but her face gave away that she had been hit. Her jaw tensed, and she held her thigh where a dark, wet stain grew.

We all waited and held our breaths until the last dart whizzed by. It lodged itself right in the stomach of the naked statue I spoke with earlier. We were all too afraid to move.

"Just wait!" Cletus stretched his leg down. Cautiously, he swiped the toe of his brown boot through the closest light ray and then jerked it back up. Again, hundreds of little blades went screaming across the hall.

I was thinking now was as good a time as any to break out the Kaptro Conjuration. I squeezed my hand under my chest until my finger grazed the velvet bag.

"I wish we all had a full coat of armor to protect us from those darts!"

POOF! A small burst of wind and a faint glow of light escaped from under me. At once, we were all covered from head to toe in full suits of heavy armor and chainmail.

It still took a few minutes before anyone was brave enough to stand. We all just lay motionless inside our armor. Unfortunately for Cletus, the added bulk of the heavy steel made it awkward to hold himself up. The weight was too much for the chandelier to support. The cord began unraveling. Each individual thread snapped one after another. Before we heard the ultimate snap, we heard Cletus' half-formed yelp. His grip slipped and he plummeted to the floor, once again breaking the paths of the lasers. The blades started flying before Cletus hit the ground, but they bounced off his armor in a chorus of noisy plinks.

"Ha! It works!" He turned so his chest took the assault head on. "Ha!" He challenged the blades again. "Is that all you got?" It was right then the frayed cord chose to snap. The chandelier dropped squarely on Cletus' head. He wobbled and then fell to the floor.

It seemed like things just kept getting worse.

"C'mon, guys!" I said. "Everyone get up. We're so close to getting the Kaptro Teleportation. We can do it."

"Put a cork in it, duck-boy." Kat's voice was weak—probably from the pain in her leg—but she made her way across the hall. Her right leg dragged a path through the littered blades as she pulled it behind her.

It was next to impossible to haul my body off the floor. The armor wasn't too heavy for me, but it made it hard to move, and it made every action awkward. After I finally got myself up, I hoisted Andie to her feet. Together, we helped Cletus up.

The five of us clomped and banged toward the secret door. Feathered darts assaulted us all the way. By the time we reached the opening to the chamber, the barrage of ammunition had slowed. Finally, the last one hit the floor.

"It stopped." William looked at Kat's leg. "We need to take care of Kat."

"I am fine. What we need is to get in there and find that mirror." Kat grimaced when she stepped and her leg gave out.

"Let's get her out of this armor," Andie said.

We all removed just enough armor to help pull Kat out of hers, although only Andie took the time to remove her helmet. We lowered Kat to the floor and watched as Andie examined the gash.

"It's not as bad as it looks. Jax, get the first aid kit from the gift shop. I put it in your pack."

Andie cleaned and bandaged the wound. "Just keep the weight off of it, and the bleeding should stop. You stay here. I'll guard the north end of the hall. Cletus can go in with Jax."

Kat protested but winced when she tried to stand. William was in complete agreement with Andie, so Kat had no choice but to give in.

Cletus and I edged through the opening created by the mirrored arch. It was really dark inside, with a tiny cement landing about two feet square. Cold, hard walls blocked our way on two sides. A steep spiral staircase on the left of the landing was the only way to go, so we did. The lower we got, the darker and colder it became. We must have descended at least four stories before we hit the bottom. A faint stripe of light on the floor meant there was a door. Cletus pushed on it, and, surprisingly, it creaked open.

I'm not sure what I expected from a secret lair— maybe a dark cave with a huge control panel built into a giant boulder, or maybe even a room as fancy as the hall we were just in with all sorts of hi-tech gadgets—but what I saw when I slid through the door behind Cletus was neither of those. Instead, we saw a schlumpy, out-dated den with shaggy orange carpeting and two worn beige recliners. The recliners faced a small old-school TV built into a piece of fake wood cabinetry. A rerun of *The Three Stooges* played on the TV, but it was dubbed in French. A folding dinner tray sat in front of each recliner. One held a plate with a half-eaten ham-and-cheese sandwich and a glass of soda. On the other, were an ashtray full of half-smoked cigarettes and a glass of water holding a set of false teeth.

I removed my helmet, setting it on one of the recliners. I picked up the soda can. Instantly, the hairs rose on the back of my neck. "It's still cold!"

We both snapped to attention, but it was a second too late. A loud THWANG sounded, and Cletus dropped to the ground like a sack of armor-clad potatoes. A craggy old man in droopy gray sweat pants and no shirt loomed over Cletus. His bushy gray eyebrows almost completely hid his eyes, and the gray hairs on his saggy chest were almost as overgrown. He held a huge frying pan, which he waved around. Who knew cookware could be so menacing?

"Whoa, whoa!" I held up my hands. "We're here looking for—"

I didn't have a chance to finish my sentence. That crazy old man let out a burp so long and loud it made my last two seem like hiccups. Then, all of a sudden, he jumped about seven feet right over Cletus's body. The second-to-the-last thing I saw was the leftover Hamburger Helper stuck to the bottom of the frying pan. The very last thing I saw was a trio of roasted ducks quacking in small circles around my head—and then everything went dark.

CHAPTER 17
Two French Dudes with Attitudes

My head screamed. I traced the source of the pain to a spot above my left eyebrow. I tried to touch the sore spot, but my arms wouldn't move. My legs wouldn't move either. And my mouth felt as dry as it did the time I tried to prove I could fit the entire box of Ding Dongs in it all at once. I was totally confused. I cracked open my eyes to see Cletus, Andie, Kat, and William, who all sat in a circle around me. Their wrists and ankles were chained to the plain wooden chairs they were propped on. Their heads dangled like they were unconscious. Andie had a handkerchief stuffed in her mouth, while everyone else had handkerchiefs stuffed through the mouth openings on their helmets. Worse yet, I realized I was in the same predicament, although the gag was tied around my mouth. I struggled, trying to spit it out.

Suddenly, that wild old man leaped in front of me. "*Qui êtes-vous?*" He waved the frying pan at my head and yelled a stream of crazy French stuff.

"No par-lay the fran-say!" I tried to enunciate through the gag. It sounded more like, "Nuh wah way la fwah say."

A pair of nimble hands behind me untied the gag and

dropped it on my lap. A young guy, maybe twenty-four or twenty-five years old, stepped in front of me. His eyebrows bore a surprising resemblance to the crazy old man's eyebrows, except they were slightly better groomed and were dark brown instead of gray.

Across from me, Kat and William moaned in their chairs. An unconscious Cletus whimpered like a puppy.

"Who are you, and who sent you?" the younger guy asked in thickly accented English. "You are one of Melchasaar's generals! Are you not?"

"What? Melchasaar? No! No way!" I said. All the while, I was trying to snap the chains behind my back without getting caught.

"Liar!" He slapped my face so hard, I had to double check to see if he had used the old guy's frying pan.

By now, Kat was alert. All sorts of muffled curses escaped through her gag. She got louder and more agitated when no one paid attention to her. She rocked, shook, and swayed her chair until her helmet fell off her head, pulling the gag with it. It clattered on the cheap linoleum floor. The noise was enough to distract the two angry French men. When they turned to confront Kat, it gave me the chance I needed.

The chains binding my wrists and ankles finally snapped. I had just sprung to action—I was already airborne and about to tackle both guys—when the younger man spoke.

"Kat?"

I could hear the recognition in his voice. When he said Kat's name, he stepped closer to her and out of my path. As a result, I landed facedown on the half-naked, old guy. He wailed on my back with the frying pan, shrieking some kind of toothless, naked, French battle cry. The good news, if you could call it that, was that his arm was bent at such an awkward angle his pan couldn't do much damage.

In the meantime, the younger man unlocked Kat's chains. "Whatever on the great green earth are you doing here?" His tone was way less angry now.

"Hello, Jules," Kat said dryly. "What a pleasure to see you again."

"What's going on?" Jules asked. "Why are you here?"

"Caephus sent us," Kat lied without even flinching. "Now, I insist you unchain my friends before I give you any more details."

"Your friends? But, of course."

He spoke rapid French to the older man. Whatever he said made the old guy stop thwacking me with the frying pan. He dropped it on the floor. Thinking it was safe to get up, I stood. And then—I'm not kidding—he did some type of double-leg, donkey-kick, ninja move and landed on his feet. He booted me hard on the shin, and it hurt like heck. Then he turned away to help Jules unbind the others.

Jules had just removed the last chain. When he turned to me, he was surprised when I handed him my two sets of broken chains. The older guy stood close by Jules, all the while scowling at us from under those wild brows. He glared at me and then spat out a few angry French words, before crossing his arms across his hairy chest.

"You have much explaining to do," Jules said to Kat. "You can start by telling me who these people are."

Kat pointed at William. His head was still bobbing around under the weight of his helmet. "You remember William, my brother and attendant?" She pulled off his helmet.

William opened his eyes, blinking with confusion.

Cletus, who just recovered, took off his own helmet. "Hey, Jules. How you doin'?" He offered an unsteady hand.

"Better than you, it would seem," Jules replied. "I heard about what happened with the Elementum. Tough break, *oui*?"

Cletus dropped his gaze to the floor. He rubbed the back of his head where he had been clobbered with the frying pan. "No big deal," he mumbled. "I'm workin' on gettin' it back."

"Just be glad you were able to save Yancy," Jules said.

That was news to me. "Yancy? He was the family member you saved when you sent me the Elementum?"

Cletus nodded.

Jules looked at me. "And you are…?"

"I'm Jax Sheppard."

Cletus added, "He's Komitari of the Kaptro Conjuration—and for now, at least, the Kaptro Elementum too."

Jules' face lit up. "Meredith's son? Splendid!" He cupped the back of my head with both hands and jerked me close for an enthusiastic kiss on each cheek. "I am delighted to meet you!" He wrapped an arm around my shoulder and steered me toward the old guy.

"Grand-père!" he called to the old man. He again fired off a bunch of stuff in French I didn't understand.

As Jules spoke, the expression in the crazy old man's eyes changed from fury to approval. He grinned at me, erasing any doubt about whose teeth were in the glass on that snack table. I was startled when he, like Jules, gripped my ears and yanked until my cheeks were smashed against his toothless mushy mouth. He planted two wet kisses, one on each side. Even though I tried not to, I had to wipe them off. And then darn it if that crazy old coot didn't go ahead and do it again!

He looked at me and rattled off more French stuff I didn't understand. All I could hear was, "Blah, blah, blah, Meredith, blah, blah, Meredith, blah, blah, blah, Meredith!" I really wished I'd paid more attention to Mademoiselle Snell in third period French class last year.

"He said your mother was a great Komitari. He was honored when she came to his retirement ceremony," Jules said. "Grand-père was Senior Training Executive at HQ for forty-two years—ever since my *pére* turned sixteen and took over as guardian of the Kaptro Teleportation."

Ahhh. The old guy was a Komitari. That explained the seven-foot jump and the wicked frying pan shot.

"He's been retired for three years now." Jules leaned close and whispered, "He's got a touch of dementia now, so he stays with me. I feel better if I can keep my eye on him."

"You meant to say he retired four years ago," I said. Surely he was wrong, because Mom had been dead for almost four years.

"No." Jules seemed baffled by my correction. "He retired three years ago. I remember it quite well because the ceremony was held on my twenty-third birthday."

"But…my mother was…dead three years ago." My words were almost too quiet to be heard.

"Hmm…Perhaps Grand-père has confused where he saw her. He does that sometimes."

"Yeah. That must be it." I accepted his answer, but the whole conversation left me feeling like something was off.

My thoughts were interrupted when Andie, who had finally come to, came to stand beside me. She had a huge shiner on her right eye where she must have been hit. I was proud of her for the way she was hanging in there with us.

When she cleared her throat, I said, "Oh. This is my friend, Andie, from Pennsylvania."

"A Normal?" Jules raised a bushy eyebrow. "It's no wonder she collapsed faster than a pop-up tent in a hurricane. My apologies." He nodded, referring to Andie's eye, and then asked Cletus, "Why would a Normal accompany you here?"

"It's a long story," Cletus said.

"I forget my manners," Jules said. "Can I offer you something to drink?"

Once we all had cracked opened the sodas Jules gave us, we put the wooden chairs in a semicircle to face the recliners where Jules and his grandfather sat. By now, Grand-père seemed to have lost interest in us. He grabbed the oversized remote control and cranked up the volume on *The Three Stooges*.

As usual, Kat spoke first. "You and Rémi were not present at the last session of Council. The KIA reported you had gone underground." She looked around. "Where is Rémi, anyway?"

"I gave Rémi some time off—he works so hard—and there is a cute little…how do you say?…yes…hottie who has caught his attention. He is no doubt enjoying himself on his father's estate in the Côte d'Azur with his little cream puff."

"Your attendant left you? With no one to look out for you? And with Melchasaar's attacks escalating?" William asked.

Jules looked bewildered. "What are you talking about? Melchasaar has attacked? Rémi only agreed to take the vacation because I promised to stay hidden in the chamber with the mirror—I thought it would give me quality time with Grand-père. We haven't left the chamber for over two weeks. We knew nothing of these attacks. I would never have sent him away, except that everything was so quiet."

"Then that means Melchasaar does not know where you are," Kat said. "And I would presume you have not heard about Loryllia yet."

"No…" Jules' brows drew together to form one large and very concerned caterpillar above his eyes. "What has happened to Loryllia?" He leaned forward.

"She's dead," Kat said. "It was Melchasaar's army. And they have taken the Kaptro Enchantment."

Jules rose abruptly and turned his face so we couldn't see it. He entered the kitchen area, and we could hear the faucet running. I suspected he was trying to cover the sounds of his own crying.

"Loryllia and Jules had a special relationship," William whispered. "He took her under his wing—helped her through training. He even saved her life once after a confrontation with Draemoch. She was like a little sister to him."

When Jules returned, his eyes were glossy. "What about Sedgwick? Loryllia's attendant. Did he survive?"

"Wicky was on the run for two days," Kat said. "He eventually made it back to IOM safely, though."

William piped in. "I heard he refused to speak to *anyone* about what happened except Rephael—not even Galen or Caephus. And then the KIA was called in to Rephael's quarters. It was all very hush, hush." William's face lit up, like he was excited to share the gossip. He lowered his voice. "Rumor has it someone on the island is under suspicion for being involved with Melchasaar in Loryllia's death. But like I said, it's all just rumor—nobody really knows what truly happened."

That was the first I had heard anything like that.

Cletus puffed out his cheeks and slowly blew out his breath. "Whoa. Pretty serious allegations there. Where'd you hear that?"

"Kat's Ped, Eugene, told me. You know those Peds—they always have all the latest info."

"You sound like a bunch of old ladies," Kat said. "No more gossip. We need to focus on the mission."

"Of course," Jules said. "What can I do? I want to help."

"We need your mirror," Kat said. "Rephael has ordered all seven Kaptrofracti be collected. We need the Kaptropoten to defeat Melchasaar, once and for all. And then it can be destroyed."

"Whew!" Jules let out a long whistle. "I can't believe it. I can't believe the time has finally come. After all these centuries, I cannot believe Rephael plans to reunite the fragments. I understand—I do…but what happens if Melchasaar gets the mirror before he's killed." He shuddered. "I don't even want to think about what he's capable of." Jules paused for a second. "I'm going with you. For Loryllia."

"No," Kat said. "Caephus sent us to retrieve the mirror from you."

I lowered my eyes so I wouldn't give away the lie.

"There are already five of us," Kat said. "The more of us we involve, the greater the chance we will be discovered by Melchasaar. The best thing you can do for Loryllia is to turn over the Kaptro Teleportation and then stay off the radar."

Jules considered Kat's words for a moment. "If Caephus has ordered it, then I will comply."

He got up again. This time he stopped in front of his grandfather and murmured something in French. Whatever Jules said, it made Grand-père snatch the remote from the snack tray and stuff it under his naked armpit.

"Grand-père," Jules said like he was talking to a toddler. He held out his hand, and then engaged in a full-out stare down with his grandfather. I swear we must have sat there for ten minutes before Grand-père finally gave in. He slammed the remote in Jules' hand, took his dentures from the glass, slurped off the excess water, and popped them in his mouth. He stomped off to a darkened room at the back of the apartment, scratching his French *derriere* all the way. The last we heard of him was a good-bye belch, which lasted almost as long as the stare down.

Jules removed the battery compartment from the remote. We couldn't miss the blue glow spilling out of the plastic control. He shook the remote until the Kaptrofractus fell from the back and into his hand. He clutched it to his heart and cradled it there for a minute before handing it over.

"So this is the end." His face was strained as he dropped the blue mirror in Kat's hand. "*S'il vous plaît.* You will let me know when it's over?" He turned on his heel and followed his grandfather from the room.

"Wow!" Cletus said. "That was almost too easy."

"Speak for yourself!" Andie said, gently prodding her swollen eye with the tip of her finger.

"You know what I mean." Cletus laughed.

"Okay, what's next?" I asked Kat, who had still never shared her entire plan. I suspected she liked keeping the rest of us in the dark. It gave her all the power, and I was starting to resent that.

"Next, we go after the Kaptro Scryor. Of course, it

is the only other fragment on Earth, so it makes sense to get it next. Once we have the Scryor, we can use it to show us where to find the other mirrors." Kat handed Cletus the Teleportation mirror. "You keep this for now. It is best we not reunite the mirrors until we have them all—just in case anything happens. We need to make sure nobody is able to get their hands on the Kaptropoten. This way if we need to separate for any reason, we can still do it."

"That makes sense," I said. "So where is it?"

"It is the last of the three mirrors guarded here on Earth," Kat said. "I believe Stirling keeps it with him at his place in Nevada—in the desert just outside of Las Vegas."

"All right then," Cletus said. "That's enough natterin'. What are we waiting for?" He held the Teleportation mirror in front of his face. "We wish to go to Stirling's house. Everyone grab on!"

I bent close to Andie's ear. "Um, I think I'm supposed to remind you never to do this again."

"Oh no! I can't handle this!" But as the blue ribbons began to spin and dance around everyone else, she panicked and grabbed Cletus' arm.

There was spinning and tingling and stretching and squeezing and then POP, POP, POP…POP, POP!

CHAPTER 18
The King of Vegas and the Queen of Pennsylvania

"In one...two...three!" Cletus put his arms out and, as if on cue, Andie popped in and fainted. He caught her as if it had been scripted all along, and then he tossed her over his shoulder.

The five of us were at the bottom of a very long and very impressive stone and brick driveway. The huge iron gate at the entrance of the drive had a large scrolling letter *V* at its peak.

It was obvious we were somewhere in the Nevada desert. According to Kat, we were right outside of Las Vegas. The view was stunning. We stood about halfway up a ridge overlooking a crystal blue lake that sat nestled between mountains.

"Whew, it's hot!" William wiped his forehead with the back of his arm.

Even though it was closing in on dusk, it had to be at least ninety degrees. Considering the time difference from France, I guessed it was somewhere around eight o'clock in the evening. The steady beat of a bass drum made its way from the top of the hill.

Kat marched up to the gate and pressed the button on the intercom. After waiting only a few seconds, she impatiently buzzed it three more times.

"Names, please," said an arrogant-sounding male voice with an English accent.

"We are here to see Stirling." Kat had every bit as much arrogance as the voice on the speaker.

"Entrance is not permitted unless you are on the guest list. I need your names, please." The voice was even more snooty than before.

"You see here! I do not know about any guest list, but I demand to see Stirling immediately! Tell him Princess Katriana of Flaeritay requires his presence at once!"

I had to smother a chuckle. William was standing behind her, imitating her impatient posture. He mocked her by mouthing everything she said.

Kat didn't turn around or even look. She flicked her fist up over her elbow and nailed William in the chest. It knocked the wind right out of him, and he fell on his knees. Cletus and I busted out laughing.

"Princess Katriana?" the voice asked.

"Yes," Kat said.

"Princess Katriana of Flaeritay?"

"Yes!" She threw us a smug look over her shoulder and marched over to the spot where the gate would be opening.

"Princess Katriana of Flaeritay is NOT on the list." The voice in the intercom seemed to take great joy in that declaration, and then the speaker went dead.

"Well, I never!" Kat stomped back to the intercom and jammed her thumb on the button. She held it in for a good five seconds.

"Names, please." The man sounded like he actually didn't know it was Kat again.

"Now you listen here!" Kat shouted at the speaker. "You are either going to tell Stirling I demand to see him, or you are going to open this gate!" She was just revving up. I felt sorry for the guy on the other end of the intercom.

In the meantime, Cletus decided it was too hot to stand there with Andie flopped over his shoulder. He put a finger to his lips and winked at William and me. While Kat gave the speaker a piece of her mind, he backed up, took three running steps, and hopped over the gate.

Kat continued her tantrum, so I followed Cletus. William climbed on my back, and I jumped to the other side. We were halfway up the drive when we heard Kat's crazed shriek, the brief crackle of electronic wires being snapped, and the last, desperate squeal of the dying intercom.

We were almost at the top when Kat caught up with us.

"I will most certainly be having words with Stirling about this!"

We all had to smother another laugh.

When we reached the end of the circular driveway, my jaw dropped. There were Ferraris, Bentleys, Lamborghinis, Mercedes, Jaguars, and every other fancy car I had ever dreamed of owning. They were parked in neat rows across the front yard. A sprawling desert mansion perched on the side of the mountain. It looked like it had swallowed every house on my entire street.

It was a blend of stucco and stone with sleek walls of glass that almost spanned the entire front of the house.

We approached the front door. The sounds of the bass drum we heard earlier mingled with the melody of the blaring party tunes. The music was coming from the backyard, so we headed that way, rather than take our chances with the snobby butler who hadn't let us in.

Fortunately, Andie was awake now. She complained about a headache, but was well enough to walk without help.

We neared the backyard. Throngs of party guests spilled from the back and around the side of the mansion. It was amazing. I had never seen so many beautiful people altogether in one place.

"No way!" Andie clutched my arm. "Isn't that Kylifer? You know...Kyle Landon and Jennifer Rossi? The actors? The most famous power couple in the world?" Andie hadn't been this excited since Mr. Hencil announced there would be an extra credit project in History class.

"Yeah!" I answered. "And I think that's Chase Brody!" I was awed by all the major celebrities there. "Go Hawks!" I called to the baseball superstar as we passed.

"Please," Kat said. "Demonstrate a little decorum."

Cletus snatched a handful of mini pigs in a blanket from the tray of a nearby tuxedoed waiter. "I could get used to this," he said through a mouthful of mini wieners.

When we rounded the corner of the house, even Kat was impressed by the backyard oasis. A lazy river meandered around the perimeter of the yard and past a cobblestone-lined water slide. In spite of the weather, partygoers relaxed in the steaming hot tub. A huge waterfall covered a secluded cave cut into the stone. Party guests walked across an arched bridge over the pool to a balcony, which gave a view of the tennis courts and private putting greens. The back of the house was almost entirely open to the outside. Its giant glass walls had been slid open to allow the guests to party inside and out. The whole scene was made even more glamorous by the hundreds of spotlights that illuminated parts of the rocks and pool, and cast other parts mysteriously into the shadows.

We began to notice the condescending looks being shot our way as the A-list guests decided our choice of clothing was way too casual.

"What does Stirling look like?" I tugged at my shirt. I was hoping to find him and get away from the critical eye of the crowd.

"Trust me," William answered. "You'll know him when you see him."

We passed another waiter, and Cletus managed to score himself several puff pastries stuffed with some white gunk that oozed onto his face when he bit into them.

We weaved our way through the crowd. Eventually, we spotted a cluster of beautiful women in fancy dresses, wearing lots of makeup and sky-high heels. They each fought for the attention of one incredibly outlandishly dressed man with a dark brown goatee. He was charming his audience with a tale about his latest feat at the poker tables.

Even though this guy was really short, his clothes made a big statement. He wore a silky purple suit jacket with silver stripes down the sleeves. A white ruffled shirt peeked out of the jacket. Even in all those layers, he didn't seem to mind the heat at all.

His pants were the tightest leopard print fabric I could imagine a man would ever want to squeeze into. Pointed black crocodile boots had at least a two-inch heel. On his head was a purple brimmed hat with a speckled black-and-white feather tucked in the band. A large pair of sunglasses with pink-tinted lenses covered his eyes. And the best part of the entire outfit was the thick, gaudy gold chain that hung around his neck. It secured a large pendant that was actually none other than a purple-glowing mirror fragment with a brass plate and etchings.

"Stirling!" Andie had whispered what I was already thinking.

Kat, William, and Cletus all nodded.

"That's a pretty bold move," I said, "hanging his Kaptrofractus around his neck like that."

"That's Stirling for you." Cletus helped himself to a fistful of cheese cubes from a nearby food display.

We stood at the edge of the crowd and listened as Stirling described the last hand of a high-stakes poker game. Apparently, he had called the bluff of world-famous poker player, Duke Lutke, and ultimately won Duke's private jet. The women applauded when he finished his story. One of them called, "Tell us another one, Stirling!" but Stirling had caught sight of our little group.

He passed off his glass to the woman on his left, parted the crowd, and strolled over to us. "Well, well, well…" He came to stand in front of Kat. "My Komitari friends have come to pay me a visit. To what do I owe the pleasure?" The way he punctuated every other word with dramatic emphasis made him sound like a preacher. He reeked of confidence.

"Let's move inside. We can catch up and have a private chat." He led the way into the mansion. We crossed a shiny marble floor through an amazing kitchen, across an enormous three-story foyer, to a private office sporting dark paneled wood on the walls and ceiling. The back wall was plastered from end to end with photographs of Stirling posing with celebrities, athletes, and politicians. In the center of the room, the huge desk held a framed newspaper article from the *Nevada Times*. The article featured a picture of Stirling standing on a poker table in the middle of some casino. His legs were spread and his arms were folded across his chest. The headline read, "Stirling Vates: King of Vegas."

Once the door was closed, Kat said, "I see you have continued your family's tradition of…uh…prosperity."

"So we bend the rules a little." Stirling poured himself a drink from a cabinet along the wall. "Don't even try and tell me you never shape-shift just for fun. Come on now, Katriana. We all use our mirrors every once in a while for a little personal pleasure. My pleasure just so happens to be…lucrative." He spread his arms and waved them to show off the expensive surroundings. You didn't need to be a genius to figure out Stirling was talking about using the Kaptro Scryor to win at gambling.

"Cletus, I know you manipulate the weather from time to time to suit your own purposes." Stirling took a swig from his glass. "It's only natural I might use the Scryor to supplement my income. I just use it for a little…assistance at the casinos. So what?" He tossed his head back and swallowed the rest of his drink.

Stirling set his glass on the desk and walked around to my side. He stuck out his hand for me to shake. "Welcome, Mr. Jackson Sheppard!"

I was surprised. How did he know who I was?

"I've seen your face in the Scryor many times, my friend." It was like he read my mind. "So what brings you all to my humble home?"

"It's Melchasaar," Kat said. It was enough to turn Stirling serious.

"Melchasaar?"

"Melchasaar killed Loryllia, and now he has her mirror. He also sent one of his soldiers to steal the Elementum. Cletus had to use the Tegeris incantation." She obviously didn't care about hurting Cletus' feelings. "He is not even a Komitari anymore."

Stirling's eyebrows shot up. "You lost your mirror?" He filled his glass again and took another swig.

Cletus looked down. "I'm not proud of it."

"Don't worry," I said. "Cletus is going to earn it back. He's a great attendant. He even saved my life once already."

"They made you an *attendant*? Brother, that's low."

That irked me. "I bet my attendant can whoop your attendant's butt!"

Cletus shushed me. "Being an attendant is an honor. I may be ashamed about losin' the Elementum, but there's no shame in servin' another Komitari."

William held out a fist, and Cletus pounded his knuckles in a show of brotherhood.

"Let's cut to the chase," Stirling said. "I have guests who are missing me. Why are you here?"

"We came to get the Scryor," Kat answered. "Melchasaar is getting increasingly more aggressive. Rephael plans to use the Kaptropoten to kill him, so we have been sent to collect the Kaptrofracti."

Stirling backed away. He shielded his mirror with his hand. "I have a big Texas Hold'em tournament tonight. Some of the most high-profile players in the world are here—some real high-rollers." He shook his head. "Sorry, girl, but it's not going to happen—I'm not giving it up."

"Are you joking?" Cletus asked. "You know what Melchasaar is capable of! Are you really that selfish? You would risk the lives of countless innocents to win a stupid poker game? This is what we've prepared for our whole lives!"

Stirling didn't respond. He actually didn't look like he cared at all.

Kat planted her hands on her hips. "We are prepared to take it from you if it comes to that."

Stirling tossed back another gulp. "And what about you, Ark?" He surprised me with the Ark reference. "Are you prepared to fight me for it?"

All eyeballs turned to me. I had never been in a real fight in my life—I was always too afraid of seriously hurting someone. I didn't even like conflict—it made me sick—and just this argument alone had my stomach pitching faster than Chase Brody, the all-star pitcher. It didn't seem right to just show up at some guy's house and then jump him for his necklace. It felt kind of shady. But at the same time, I needed that mirror to save Sebastian.

"You know…I…well…I mean…I guess if I have to." I tried not to commit either way.

"Maybe you haven't heard about my prowess as a fighter." His gaze went to one of the photographs on the wall.

"You were an Ultimate Fighting World Champion?" I gulped. I took in the picture of Stirling holding his championship belt above his head. His left foot used the body of some knocked-out Neanderthal like a footstool.

"Not *were*. Am."

"Like, currently?" I gulped again. "But you're so… short."

"Welterweight," Stirling said.

"Size doesn't matter when you're fightin' Normals," Cletus said with a good measure of disapproval.

"Like I said, I bend a few rules." Stirling was unapologetic. "If you want the Scryor, you'll have to win it in the cage." He pointed a finger at me. "I'll take you."

I gulped a third time.

It was one thing to take on an Ultimate Fighting World Champion—I mean, that would be easier than…

than…taking candy from a Normal. But an Ultimate
Fighting World Champion who also happens to be a
Komitari? My palms started sweating.

"We do not have time for your games, Stirling," Kat
said. "You would be wise to reconsider."

"You think I would be wise to reconsider?" He pretended to laugh. "That's a good one!" Stirling pressed a
button on the phone.

"Yes, sir?" asked a male voice from the speaker.

"Show my guests to the training room. They may need
some, uh…encouragement to go with you."

The doors to the office swung open. Two very large,
very serious-looking men in dark suits entered. My heart
dropped to my ankles when I saw the very small, very
serious-looking guns they had trained on us.

We all threw our hands in the air. Everyone was too
afraid to speak, so I forced a fake cheerfulness. "That
sounds nice. We'll look forward to a friendly bout of
sparring in the training room." My voice was suspiciously
high. "See you in the training room for a friendly bout
of sparring." I sounded every bit like a witless idiot.

It was time to seriously second-guess my involvement
in this whole mess. Yes, I wanted Sebastian back more
than anything in the world. But I never actually considered the idea of fighting or battling. And I surely never
pictured myself at the open end of a gun. I truly just
thought I would go along with Kat and steal the mirror
after she collected all the pieces. And "steal" was probably
too strong a word—"borrow" was probably much more
like it. To be honest, I doubted I had the backbone to

pull any of it off. I was frightened. It made me all the more certain I was absolutely, positively not the Ark. What could anyone possibly want with a scrawny, little chicken-boy?

The two bodyguards ushered us to the basement where Stirling maintained a fully equipped training room. The room was cavernous, with ceilings at least twenty feet tall. In the center of the room was Stirling's very own full-size fight ring, which I discovered was not shaped at all like a ring, but an octagon.

We shuffled through the door like a gang of eighth graders being led into detention. Without a word, the two men left us. They barred the heavy metal doors behind them.

As soon as the doors crashed shut, Andie let loose. "What the heck kind of a Komitari is he? I thought you were supposed to be good guys"—she pointed at each of us—"saving the world from evil and…and…other bad things!" She was so angry she sputtered. "How does a guy like that get to be in charge of a magic mirror?"

William said, "Stirling's family has been guarding the Scryor since the KIA got it back in the fifties. I'm guessing Rephael knows they abuse their power. He probably knows they don't always follow the code— everyone knows about that. But I'm also guessing he's willing to overlook it. Because, let's face it, they have always kept the Kaptro Scryor safe."

"Haven't you ever heard power corrupts?" Andie crossed her arms and frowned.

"Hey, no worries!" Cletus held out the Kaptro

Teleportation and wiggled his eyebrows. "Everyone hold on."

We all grabbed his arm, anxious to get out of this room. But before Cletus could make a wish, one of the bodyguards busted through the door and snatched the mirror right from his hand. The guard left, and the door slammed back in place.

"Aargh!" Andie kicked the door.

"Okay, everyone focus. There's got to be a way out of here." I was determined not to let myself be a punching bag for some pint-sized, purple-wearing egomaniac. I scanned the room. There were no windows. Cletus was one step ahead of me and was finishing his investigation of the only other door in the room.

"Just a bathroom," he shouted from inside the door. "No way out through here either. Unless…Hey, Kat! How would you feel about morphing into a fish?"

And then we heard the toilet flush.

Kat shrieked and strode toward the bathroom, which Cletus had just exited. She broke into a run like she was going to stuff *him* in the toilet.

Cletus threw his hands up. "Kidding! Just kidding! Relax, already."

She stopped short of pummeling him, but shot him the worst stink eye I ever saw.

"So, are you saying we're trapped?" Andie asked.

That thought made me panic. There was no way I was going to stick around here and get the Komitari kicked out of me. I ran to the door we had been brought through. I tried the same kung fu kick that had worked for me twice before. The man in the hall wasted no time in swinging the door open and waving his little gun at me.

I backed off with my hands in the air, "Sorry, I…uh… tripped into it. Won't happen again."

He swung the door shut.

"Now what are we supposed to do?" Andie asked.

"We are going to hope Jax is better at fighting than he is at riding coasters," Kat said.

"Don't get your hopes up! I've never fought anyone before! Everyone just needs to think. We have magic mirrors *and* super strength! We are going to find a way out." But I wasn't sure I believed that. I took a mental inventory of my belongings. For the second time this week, I considered giving my telescope to Andie and my video games to Drake. "Hey, Cletus. How do you feel about chewed gum?"

"Huh?" He looked baffled, but I didn't have a chance to explain.

Suddenly, I detected the muted, but distinctive voice of Stirling on the other side of the metal doors. He was talking to someone whose voice I recognized as the British guy from the intercom. I pressed my fingers to my temple and waited for the voices to tune in.

"Cut them loose in the morning," Stirling told the speaker voice. "After the tournament."

"But, sir," the speaker voice said, "I thought you were planning to fight the young one."

"I was, but I checked the Scryor, and the outcome was not in my favor."

"What do you mean?"

Stirling lowered his voice. I had to concentrate to hear him.

"I saw the Sheppard boy—kneeling in the octagon—holding the Scryor. And me...dead."

"Master Stirling! A fight to the death? You know you cannot change the future. The mirror is never wrong in its predictions."

"Forget about it, Nigel," Stirling said. I could make out a slight quiver in his voice. "I don't plan on having anything to do with Master Sheppard before he leaves the estate. You give them the mirror in the morning and send them out of here. I plan on winning big tonight at the tournament. And I can't think of a better time to announce my retirement from the gambling scene than tonight—right after I win everything from those fat cats." He stopped, but then added, "Don't worry. It'll all be good."

The next thing I heard was a set of high-heeled crocodile boots clicking away from the door. I slumped over the side of the ring. I felt like I got kicked in the stomach.

Me? Kill someone? It couldn't be possible. It was like someone had parked one of those expensive Ferraris on my chest. The mere thought made me nauseous. I heaved a few times. Andie found a garbage can and ran it over to me.

"Are you all right?" she asked. "I swear, Jax. You have the weakest stomach."

"Must be pre-fight jitters," William said, but I could sense his concern.

I couldn't bring myself to tell them what I had heard. There was no way I was going near Stirling—for any reason. I was no killer.

The door rattled. A tall, stuffy-looking man with thinning hair entered the room. He wore a tuxedo with long tails in the back and a crisp pair of white cotton gloves. He rolled a silver cart loaded with plates, glasses full of soda, and a large platter with a shiny silver dome cover. Someone outside tugged the door shut, and the bar clanged as it was dropped back into place.

"Good evening." It was speaker voice, or as I now knew him, Nigel. Kat recognized his voice too. She popped up off the floor like a Kat-in-the-box and started smashing her right fist into her open left palm.

The man had no trouble ignoring Kat. He parked the cart alongside a long folding table set up near the fight cage. Before he could even turn around, Kat grabbed two fistfuls of his tuxedo tails. With one swift jerk, she ripped them from the bottom of his jacket. She balled them up, lifted the silver cover off the platter, and stuffed the torn tails underneath.

"Put *that* on your guest list!"

The man was unruffled. "I am Nigel, Master Vate's personal concierge and attendant." His lip was curled like he smelled something bad. "Master Stirling has graciously ordered your supper. If there is nothing else you require, I will leave you to dine."

Andie snapped. "I'll tell you what we require! We require you let us the heck out of here, or I'll call the police—no! I'll call the FBI! And then I'll call every casino in Vegas and tell them your boss is a weaselly, little cheat." She left out the part that her phone hadn't been charged for days.

Nigel ignored Andie as easily as he had ignored Kat.

"If you can be persuaded to remain as Master Stirling's guests until morning, there will be no fight. He will turn over the Kaptro Scryor prior to your departure."

I immediately seized the opportunity to get out of the fight. "We *could* use a place to bunk for the night." I tried not to sound too desperate. "And dinner *does* sound tempting."

"I suppose we could wait until morning," Kat said. "I think everyone will be glad to hear our fate does not depend on Jax beating Stirling in a fight."

I felt such relief—it was like the Ferrari on my chest had finally driven away.

"There is one stipulation," Nigel said. "You will remain here in the gym until morning."

"Sounds good to me." I'd agree to anything that kept me away from Stirling.

"Not me!" Andie said. "Where do you expect us to sleep?"

"That is for you to determine." Nigel bowed one last time. His back was straight, and his nose was in the air as he walked out the door.

"We got our packs and blankets," Cletus told Andie. "It's a good deal." He lifted the cover from the platter. "Now, let's eat. Anyone like marinara on their tuxedo tails?"

♀ ♀ ∙∞

We were all sufficiently stuffed. To our surprise, Stirling

had given us quite a feast. There was salad and bread, pasta and meatballs with marinara, stuffed chicken breast, potatoes, and green beans. And for dessert, we had a selection of pies and cakes that made my mouth water just looking at them.

After eating, everyone was drowsy. We laid our bedrolls and blankets across the octagon. Within minutes, we all had fallen asleep. Sure enough, it wasn't long before my dreams turned ugly.

Melchasaar had me by the throat. His cold, bony grip allowed me just enough oxygen to keep from passing out.

"Bring me what is mine. I want the Kaptropoten." His evil white eyes began to glow red. He lowered his face until it was so close to mine I could feel the icy chill of his breath on my cheek. "I want…" He smiled and showed his small, sharp teeth. His grip tightened on my neck, and he bellowed, "THE ARK!"

I woke to the sound of my own screams. It must have been loud enough to wake Cletus too.

"You're okay, little buddy. You wanna talk?" He rubbed the sleep from his eyes.

We both sat with our backs against the octagon's cage. I waited for my body to stop shaking before I tried to speak. For the first time, I was terrified I might really be the Ark. And I didn't need anything else to be terrified of.

"I don't think I can do this." I swiped at a tear before it could fall from my eye. "I'm not a hero. I'm about as brave as…as…your pinky toe." I couldn't come up with a better comparison. "And let's face it…we all know the pinky is the least brave toe on the foot."

Cletus looked at me like I had eaten too many tuxedo tails. "Uh…okay, I guess. But I think you might be underestimatin' my pinky toe." He pointed to his left foot, and I'm not kidding, his pinky toe was actually flexing—all by itself. And I swear it—it had its own little pinky toe biceps.

Cletus continued, "All the same, none of us are heroes. We're just a bunch of ordinary individuals who happen to have extraordinary gifts. We're all just tryin' to do the right thing. That's all you can do."

"But look at you. You gave up the Elementum to save Yancy. And you didn't have to come here, but you did—just to look after me—even if it means you might never get to be a Komitari again."

"Do you think I'm foolin' myself?" Cletus asked. "I'm never gonna be a Komitari again—none of us are. Don't you realize this is the end? When Melchasaar is defeated once and for all, the Kaptropoten will be destroyed forever. And Komitari will become obsolete—won't be any need for us anymore."

"And you're okay with that?" I asked.

"No. I'm not okay with it. It's who I am. I'm the guy who talks to animals—the guy who makes the sun shine. I'm a Komitari." He paused. "But, this is what we've been trainin' for our whole lives. And if it's gonna end, I wanna be a part of it. I wanna go out with honor."

I studied his face. "Whatever happened that day? With Yancy?"

Cletus lowered his eyes. "It was bad. I came home— Yancy was stayin' with me—and when I got there he was knocked out. Facedown over the side of the sofa. I didn't even get a chance to help him 'cause I got cracked in the head from behind. Knocked me out too. But when I came to, Melchasaar had Yancy on his knees. Had his hand over Yancy's head. He was doin' a Double A on him—that's what we call an Adficio Animus. It means he's suckin' your soul right out of your body. Said if I told him where the Elementum was, he would spare Yancy. I told him where it was hidden in the kitchen, in my mum's old pot. When he went after it, I invoked the Tegeris incantation, grabbed Yancy, and flashed out of there." He glanced up and said, "I knew I would lose my mirror, but it was the only way to save Yancy."

We sat in silence for a while, and then Cletus asked, "What about you? What made you decide to come with Kat?"

I wanted to tell him about Sebastian, but I was too afraid. "I just…I just need to make things right."

"Then you will," he said. "You're stronger than you think. Remember, the wings of angels can be found on the backs of the least likely people."

My breath caught in my throat. "What did you say?"

"You're stronger than you think?"

"No, not that. The other thing," I said impatiently.

"The wings of angels are found on the backs of the least likely people?" Cletus seemed puzzled.

"Yeah. Where'd you hear that?" The only person I had ever heard use that expression was Mom.

"Oh, I don't know. I think I heard it at the Golden Speculum ceremony, two years ago." He rolled his eyes up and thought for a minute. "Yeah, that's right. Your mother said it in her speech—when she accepted her award."

"Cletus," I clutched his arm. "My mother was dead two years ago. Are you sure the ceremony was two years ago?"

"I'm sure. I was fifteen and it was my first trip to the Isle of Mirrors. Went with my pop."

"How could that be?" I asked. Something wasn't right. Jules' grandfather, Grand-père, had said he saw my mother three years ago at his retirement ceremony. How could Mom be seen at two different events on the Isle of Mirrors if she was already dead? "It doesn't make sense."

"I don't know," he answered. "But I remember hearing shortly after that she died."

"What?" I couldn't believe what I was hearing. "My mom was killed four years ago in a fire at my house."

Cletus shook his head. "Nope. That's wrong. It was two years ago when she got that award. I'm certain."

Suddenly, I felt sick. "I need to talk to Caephus. Surely he knows something about this. Why would Mom pretend to be dead and go to live on IOM...?" My throat tightened, and I added, "...without us. I just don't believe it. I think you're confused, Cletus."

"I have an idea," Cletus said, looking around. "Where are those single-use Kaptrofracti?"

I pulled the set of little mirrors from my backpack and handed it to Cletus. He popped the mini Kaptro Scryor from the plastic.

"Since we're gettin' the real thing in the morning, might as well use this one now," he said. He peered into my eyes. His own eyes were as serious as I'd ever seen them. "How bad do you wanna know what happened to your mother?"

"Really bad."

"Are you sure?"

"One hundred percent."

"Okay then. Here goes." He raised the mini Scryor and stared into its depths. "I wish to see Meredith's last minutes."

The mirror glowed purple. A smoky fog began to swirl behind the glass. When the fog cleared, it showed a scene that played out like a movie clip. I blew out a long breath and tried to prepare myself for what I might see.

There was a bed—or something resembling a bed. But it was much smaller. In fact, it was precisely fitted to the body of the woman who was lying on it. I felt a surge of both excitement and sadness when I recognized my mother. She was as beautiful as I'd always remembered her.

"The way she's layin' there—she looks like a queen… from a fairy tale," Cletus whispered.

"She's from Pennsylvania," I whispered back without thinking.

My mother was perfectly still—almost lifeless. I couldn't take my eyes off of Mom's face, until a glare on the image inside the mirror caught my attention. It seemed to be floating an inch above Mom. I leaned in closer and squinted my eyes to get a better look at what was causing that glare. I was puzzled to discover there was a glass enclosure on top of the bed. It encompassed my mom's entire body. It dawned on me that this wasn't a bed. It was some kind of a casket.

"Cletus," I whispered. I was afraid my voice would make the image go away. "I think she's already…dead."

"I don't…know." Cletus was just as perplexed as I was.

We continued to stare into the little mirror when we both noticed at once the small vapor cloud that formed on the glass above Mom's nose. We turned in unison, our eyes meeting in disbelief.

"She's breathing!" Cletus said.

We kept watching as the little cloud faded and then reappeared several times. Eventually, the image died away. The mini Scryor went blank. I took the little mirror from Cletus and studied it, turning it over and over again. Somehow, it just had to show me something else.

"What does it mean?" I finally asked. "You told it to show us her last minutes. But if those were her last minutes, and she's still breathing…" What could it mean? My mind formulated all sorts of explanations, but only one made sense.

My mother was alive.

CHAPTER 19
A Metal Head and a Hot Foot

Cletus had fallen asleep again. My body was exhausted, but my mind was too busy to sleep. I needed to talk to Caephus at once—find out exactly what he knew about my mom. I was tempted to use the Teleportation mirror to get back to IOM right now. A smarter part of my brain, probably the hamster, told me to slow down. I couldn't lose sight of my goal. First, I needed to focus on getting Sebastian back. Then, I would figure out what happened to Mom.

A slight rattling at the door snapped me out of my thoughts. It was still dark in the training room, but I wondered if it was morning already. I couldn't choose which I wanted more: to get extra sleep, or to get the heck away from Stirling's estate. Considering Stirling had me pegged as a maniacal killer, I picked option two.

I figured the noise was probably just Nigel bringing us some breakfast. I got up, still groggy, and went to wash up in the restroom. A bright light from the hall poured through the crack that formed as the heavy metal door creaked open. I padded into the bathroom, trying not to wake anyone. After a second, a quiet click told me the door had closed.

I was washing my hands when I sensed the floor shaking. I half wondered if they had earthquakes here in Nevada. Once the rush of the flowing water stopped, I could make out a quiet rumbling each time the ground shook. Curiosity got the best of me, and I dried my hands. Before I could shake the last drops of water from my fingertips, a blood-curdling scream jolted me wide-awake.

I ran to the restroom door and peeked around the corner. Suddenly, the overhead lights in the gym snapped on. I couldn't believe what I saw. Cletus and Kat must have sprung to their feet at the sound of the shrieks. Cletus had his fists up, ready to defend or attack, depending on the situation. Kat looked like she was ready to make sushi out of somebody. She had one hand on the hilt of the sword strapped across her back, and her other hand held her dagger.

On the other side of the octagon, where Andie and William had been sleeping, were two enormous Pygmy Gorgs. They held William and Andie prisoners. Huge meaty hands pressed against William's and Andie's mouths, smothering their screams. Both William and Andie were fighting like maniacs to break free, but it was useless. Their frightened eyes pleaded for Cletus and Kat to do something.

On the ground, surrounding the ring, four more Gorgs were ready to pounce on Cletus and Kat. Small streams of Gorg drool pooled on the floor at their feet. I scanned the room and tried to figure out what we were up against. When I checked out the door to the gym, I froze in my spot. Standing there, with his hand on the light switch, was a man so barbaric he rivaled the worst of the world's villains from my favorite video game, *The World's Worst Villains*.

He was dressed in battle armor. A battered and tarnished steel breastplate covered his chest. His heavily muscled forearms were wrapped in black leather cuffs that were dotted with sharp metal spikes. A dark cape hung from his thick neck. But it was the sight of his head and face that seared itself on my brain. I shuddered every time I thought of it. A steel helmet covered half of his head. It literally seemed to have been poured on his skull while the metal was still hot, and then dripped over onto his face. The helmet looked like it had become one with his flesh. It completely masked the space where his right eye should have been. In fact, there was no eye that I could see at all—just a bottomless, hollow hole drilled deep into the helmet.

The skin along the fringes of the helmet, both on his skull and his face, was horribly scarred, like it had been etched with acid. The half of his skull that was not covered by the helmet was marred with long blackened cracks. I couldn't figure out what was stopping his brains from running out.

His other eye was black, like death. It had dark shadows around it that were nearly the same shade. His lips were thin and pale and were pulled back in an evil, ugly sneer.

"A whole collection of brave Komitari all gathered conveniently under one roof," he said. He drew out the words like he had all day to finish his sentence. "How very opportune for me." His words and voice made him sound really educated, which was weird considering his barbaric appearance.

He strolled toward the octagon. His boots tapped a slow and torturous rhythm on the highly polished floor. Slowly, he closed the distance between the door and my friends.

"I believe you have something that belongs to my lord, Melchasaar," he said, stopping at the folding table. He pulled out a chair and sat facing the octagon.

The man leaned back in his seat. His legs were sprawled out in front of him. The way he acted like he owned the place made him even scarier.

My teeth chattered. I was afraid the noise would give away my hiding spot. I clamped a hand under my jaw and held it as still as I could manage.

The man produced a long straight-backed knife. He used it to pick his yellow, rotted teeth.

Cletus and Kat were trying to keep both the Gorgs and this horrifying warrior guy in their sights.

"Draemoch, you have no business here! You are supposed to be rotting in my father's dungeons!" Kat lunged, ready to jump right out of the octagon and attack Draemoch.

Cletus held her back. "We're outnumbered, Kat. Don't do anything foolish."

"Oh, yes," Draemoch said as if he had just remembered something. "How very boorish of me, Princess. You must forgive my insolence. I have neglected to deliver a...

message, if you will. Your father sends his regards." He stopped and studied the tip of his blade. "Sad, really, to see a king reduced to such common behavior. Practically begging for his life. Such a pity."

"What do you want, Draemoch?" Kat asked through clenched teeth.

"Lord Melchasaar no longer wishes to ransom your father for my freedom. As you so shrewdly noted, I am already free." He smiled like he was waiting for someone to laugh at his comment. After a second, the Gorgs did. They laughed deep, doltish laughs. Their big dumb heads nodded their approval.

Draemoch rose from the chair. "I owe that gratitude to the good will of your dear old friends from the north, the Pygmy Gorgs." Now he was using his knife to scrape the dirt from under his nails.

"But you see, my dear, that does provide you with, shall we say…a conundrum." He took three slow steps toward the octagon and then paused. His free hand held something that dangled from a thin cord around his neck. He toyed with the object in his hand. His one frightening eye was trained on it.

"Your mother is already dead. It would be such a shame to lose your father too. But, you see, without me, there is nothing Lord Melchasaar desires from you in exchange for your father's life…unless, of course, you wish to produce all of the Kaptrofracti in your possession. Naturally, I would offer my services as a courier, free of charge. Or better yet, why don't you tell me where Rephael is hiding the Ark."

Kat shrieked and pitched forward. Cletus maintained a lock on her arms, refusing to let her near Draemoch.

"Never! I will see my father returned on my own terms!"

"I was afraid you might see it that way." Draemoch flicked his wrist and snapped the unidentified object from the cord. "A gift, my lady. To help you change your mind."

He flipped the item over the cage, and it skittered across the floor. It came to a halt at Kat's feet. In one swift and unexpected motion, Kat jerked away from Cletus. She snatched the object from the floor. I strained my eyes, trying to focus on Draemoch's so-called gift. A second was all I needed to identify it. It was a severed, bloodied finger, wearing a thick gold ring set with a large red ruby—it was Kat's father's!

"Nooooo!" Kat dropped the finger in revulsion and then catapulted over the cage.

At that, all mayhem broke out. The room designed for practicing Ultimate Fighting became the scene for a whole bucketload of ultimate fights. The four remaining Gorgs ripped the cage from their side of the octagon. With the coordination of hippos in ballet class, they climbed inside making Cletus their target. At the same time, William began thrashing against the prison of the Gorg's arms with a rage I couldn't believe he had in him. His heel must have hit its target because the Gorg dropped William on the floor and doubled over in pain. His two giant hands were shielding the spot where no Gorg wants to be kicked.

Andie had pulled out her little dagger from the gift shop. She stabbed her Gorg captor in the arm. He bellowed in pain and let go with his injured arm, but his other hand still gripped Andie's upper arm. She spun around and started kicking his shins like a World Cup soccer player. Cletus, in the meantime, had his hands full trying to fend off the other four Gorgs. He would land a punishing roundhouse kick on one Gorg, and then another would attack from the other side.

On the far side of the octagon, I could hear the sickening clang of clashing metal as Kat and Draemoch locked swords.

All the while, I watched in horror from the safety of the bathroom. I had no idea who to watch or what to do in the chaos.

Just do something—anything! But instead, I cowered. I was ashamed, but my brain and legs were so numb they were both useless.

It was then that Cletus hurled a Gorg from the octagon and into the heavy punching bag hanging in the corner. The momentum of the Gorg made the heavy bag swing like a large pendulum. On its return swing, it cracked the Gorg so hard it knocked him over. He smashed his giant Gorg head on a nearby dumbbell and was knocked senseless.

When I saw that Gorg get nailed with the punching bag, I had an idea. I wasn't sure how good the idea was, but I was just happy to have any idea at all. I removed the single-use Kaptrofracti from my backpack and pulled out the Kaptro Kinesis.

I stared into the mirror and whispered, "Whack those Gorgs with that heavy bag!"

The mirror glowed orange. In the glass, I saw the heavy bag snap from its chain. The bag, all on its own, sailed into the head of one of the Gorgs. He spun sideways and slammed clean into the Gorg on his right. The two Gorgs' foreheads collided with a nauseating thud. They looked at each other for a moment. Their eyes went blank and then they both toppled off the octagon.

I peered out the door. It was clear that what I had just witnessed in the mirror had actually played out in real life. Cletus' head practically spiraled off his neck. He searched the room, obviously trying to figure out what had just happened.

Yes! I gave a mental cheer. *Score one for the chicken-boy by the toilet!*

That evened the odds for Cletus who was left with just one Gorg to battle. William was still inside the octagon. He ran endless circles around its perimeter trying to escape the Gorg who had dropped him. It would have been comical, the way William seemed content to keep running from the Gorg who was just too stinking dumb to do anything but chase him—except for the fact that his life depended on it.

All the while, from across the room, I could hear the fiercely intense battle between Kat and Draemoch. I wasn't sure how long Kat would last against such a terrifying opponent, especially with the injury to her leg from the Hall of Mirrors.

As for Andie, I could tell she was getting tired. She

kicked and punched at the Gorg. It seemed to find her efforts humorous. Every now and again, he would flick her forehead with his oversized finger, stunning her. He laughed that big oafish laugh, which only made Andie all the madder. She lunged forward and sunk her teeth into his thigh. The Gorg roared in pain. It backhanded Andie with his giant meaty fist. Her head snapped backwards. Her body hurtled across the ring into a segment of the cage that wasn't yet destroyed. She bounced off the cage and landed by the Gorg's feet.

Andie moaned and tried to push herself up. When the Gorg bent to pick her up, I felt a spark of courage fueled by fear for my best friend.

Think, Jax! What could you possibly use to defeat a Pygmy Gorg? Another idea popped into my head. This one was borderline genius. I cracked the single-use Kaptro Metamorphus from the package and didn't waste a second.

"I wish to transform into a *regular* Gorg!"

A burst of red exploded from the mirror. Suddenly, I felt like a huge piece of modeling clay being squeezed and twisted, tugged and molded by some giant unseen hand, until POOF! I watched the floor draw farther and farther away as my legs grew longer and larger and uglier. My hands were huge, and my arms were enormous, not to mention green and hairy. Unfortunately, now I couldn't fit through the bathroom door. I decided a grand entrance was my only choice. Hopefully, it would be frightening enough to shock the Pygmy Gorgs to death. I let out a full-sized Gorg roar and smashed through the cinder block wall.

Everyone froze, except Kat and Draemoch. They continued fighting with razor-sharp focus. William took one look at me and collapsed in a puddle of terror, not far from where Andie lay. The three conscious Gorgs quaked as they stared up at me. I had to be at least eighteen feet tall.

I leaned way, way down. My face hovered right above theirs. "Boo."

The three Gorgs squealed like the Three Little Pigs. They leaped out of the octagon and ran single file across the room. They didn't even bother to open the barred door. Instead, they ran right through it, leaving Pygmy Gorg-shaped holes where the door should have been.

"Doh, Doh, Doh!" I laughed, and it rumbled through the room. It made Andie's body vibrate on the octagon like popcorn kernels in a pan of hot oil.

With my thumb and forefinger, I plucked Andie from the octagon. For some reason, she didn't realize I was the Gorg. She screamed and kicked and wouldn't stay still long enough for me to reason with her. I totally got how King Kong must have felt—oversized and misunderstood.

"Andie, it's me—" But I didn't get to finish. "Owww!" I bellowed in my loud, deep full-sized Gorg voice.

Cletus must have decided Andie needed rescuing. He had pulled a dagger out of his boot and charged at my leg like one very angry queen bee. He plunged his dagger into my knee. And let me tell you—it hurt at least twice as much as the stinger of a very angry queen bee.

I brushed Cletus away, but I must have swiped a bit too hard. He sailed through the air and into the cage, bouncing off the wall just like Andie had. Darn super Gorg strength!

Cletus sat stunned and rubbed his head. I put Andie on the floor beside him. Cletus managed to scramble to Andie's side. He blocked her from me with his body.

I needed to show my friends I was the good guy. I turned my attention to Kat and Draemoch, just in time. Draemoch had backed Kat into a corner. It seemed like she was running out of energy. It didn't help any that she was favoring her injured leg. It troubled me the way she winced every time she put her weight on it.

It only took two giant steps before I towered over the two of them. "Move out of the way, Kat," I said, but I guess I distracted her. She looked at me for a second. Draemoch seized the opportunity. His blade sliced open a gruesome gash along Kat's ribcage. She dropped her sword and fell to her knees. Draemoch kicked the sword away from Kat. He stood over her, poised to thrust one last fatal time.

"Thank you." He tipped his head to me and bared his yellow teeth in an ugly, evil smile. "Now, I'll allow you a moment to reconsider your position," he told Kat. "Your father's life for the mirrors, or I'll splay you where you are from gut to gullet. Such pleasure it will bring me to watch your father's reaction when I return your lovely, delicate finger instead of his own. Right before I slaughter him, that is."

As Draemoch delivered his speech, Kat tried to reach

her sword. She dragged her body closer to its hilt with one arm while covering her wound with the other. When Draemoch took a step toward Kat, I acted. I picked him up by his cape. His legs dangled. He twisted his body, and his sword slashed at my giant green wrist and hand.

William must have regained his wits because he rushed to help Kat. He kept an eye on me and cradled Kat's head in the crook of his arm. He pressed a handkerchief over the gash and tried to slow the flow of blood.

It was right about then I started to feel the same odd sensation of being sculpted and molded that I felt when I transformed into the Gorg. I wondered if it was too late to rethink my brilliant idea.

"Oh no!" I said. The "oh" came out in the Gorg's voice, but the "no" was all mine. My body wiggled and waved. It shrank and within a millisecond I snapped back into my regular, puny-sized frame. I found myself standing there with a chin full of Gorg drool and a fistful of black, leather cape, which, by the way, was still attached to one very creepy and vicious being.

Draemoch's shock flashed across his ugly face. "What's this?"

"Uh…here you go." I stuck the wrinkled, balled-up scrap of cape in his free hand. I started to back up.

Draemoch's expression changed from shock to outrage, and he came at me. "What is going on here?"

Like the chicken I was, I flashed backward and away from him. I should have stopped to look where I was going, because I slammed into the side of the octagon. My lower body stopped cold. Unfortunately, I had been going so fast my upper body fell backward onto the octagon floor. My feet flipped all the way up and over my head. It ended with my toes and face planted on its floor.

"Such speed." Draemoch clapped his hands. "But of course, that must make you... another Komitari! Bonus for me!" He hopped onto the floor beside me. His boot stomped on the back of my neck. My face was pinned down. My windpipe felt like it would collapse.

"Which one are you? Have I hit the jackpot? Dare I say I have found the Ark?"

I couldn't have answered even if I wanted to. My throat made a wheezing sound as I tried to suck air into my lungs. I thrashed about on the floor like a half-dead fish, but he was too strong. I strained to squeeze my hand under my chest and reach my mirror. Darkness pressed in, ready to deliver me from the pain in my throat and my chest. At last, my fingers made contact with the gold velvet bag.

"I wish...Draemoch's...boot...was on fire."

There was a brief green glow as the Elementum lit up and did its job. The pressure on my neck was gone. I rolled to the side and greedily gulped down air. Draemoch hopped on one leg, trying to stamp out the flame that devoured his foot and leg. He ripped his cape from his neck and flapped it at the blaze. I struggled to my knees. I was still weak and disoriented from the lack of oxygen, and the putrid smell of burning flesh was making me sick.

With a final flick of his cape, Draemoch managed to

smother the flames. That psychopath didn't even bother to check his burns. His repulsive face twisted in rage. He bared his teeth and let out a blood-thirsty roar. Cletus and Andie cried out warnings before I had a chance to figure out what was happening. Draemoch had drawn the straight-backed blade from the strap on his arm and hurled it at me. I had no time to react. It whizzed across the octagon, end over end, perfectly aimed to pierce my heart.

Then, from the corner of my eye, I detected a blur of purple rocketing toward me. Just before the blade hit its mark, Stirling dove, shoving me out of the way. There was a gurgling sound as the knife sunk deep in the side of Stirling's neck.

"No!" Nigel cried from the doorway. He rushed to his master's side. He didn't even try to stop Draemoch, who pulled out a round mirror of his own and teleported right out of the room in a puff of black smoke!

I recovered and ran to Stirling who was fading fast. His bright red blood spilled on the bright white octagon floor.

"Why did you do that?" My eyes ached from the weight of the tears I wouldn't let fall. "Why did you save me?"

"Ark," he whispered. I knelt beside him, and he took my hand. "Get Kat back to IOM." His breaths were small and labored. "Rephael can heal her."

"What about you? We'll get you to Rephael too. He'll heal both of you." My voice cracked.

"It's too late. The prophecy…from the Scryor…it's been fulfilled."

I just barely made out his words. He raised the Scryor at the end of the gold chain and pressed it in my hand. One final hiss escaped from the gash in his neck. His eyes rolled back in their sockets, and his head fell to the side.

Nigel's face twisted with grief. He brushed his hand down Stirling's forehead and over his eyes. He lowered Stirling's lids with all the tenderness of a dad. "Go. Go now, and save the princess. One death is enough."

I couldn't stop shaking, but I knew Nigel was right. Even though I was worried about what would happen to us when we got back to the Isle of Mirrors, I knew saving Kat was way more important. I reached around Stirling's neck and unfastened the clasp holding the heavy gold chain. I tucked it in my backpack, being careful to keep it separated from my own mirror.

"William! Cletus!" I tried to sound brave. "Get the girls. We have to go. Now."

Both Cletus and William, who to this point seemed to have been shocked senseless, pulled it together. Cletus helped Andie to her feet. He guided her to where we were kneeling over Stirling's body. William lifted Kat. She was slipping in and out of consciousness. I wasn't so sure she was going to make it.

Nigel reached inside his tuxedo jacket, pulled out the Kaptro Teleportation, and handed it to Cletus. "You'll be needing this."

Cletus nodded to Nigel and then turned to us. "We need to use the Ostiums! Gotta get outside to the moonlight. Remember, the Teleportation mirror won't take us back to the island. The Propius Portal and the Ostium are the only ways in."

I looked at Kat. We had no time to waste. "Then let's do it."

I followed the others out the door and past the unconscious bodies of Stirling's two guards. Nigel's gut-wrenching sob was the last sound I heard before we transported back to IOM.

CHAPTER 20
A Big Mess, Really Big Wings, and a Great Big Battle

For the second time in less than a week, I found myself standing on my Ostium on the bright, sunny beach of IOM. The sun was high in the sky. I guessed it was somewhere around noon. To my left, William had already arrived. He was cradling Kat, who looked like she was barely clinging to life. He didn't waste any time. He rushed up the beach to the path that led to headquarters. We all hurried along behind him. I was glad to see Elweard, who had shown up with the other Peds to take our extra gear.

The elevator at headquarters was full of tension. Of course, we were all worried about Kat. The elevator didn't seem like it was in any hurry to take us to the seventy-seventh floor, and Kat didn't have any time to spare. But still, I could tell everyone—even William, who was terrified for his sister—was afraid to face Rephael.

I asked the question we were all thinking. "So, once Rephael heals Kat, what do you think he'll do to us… you know…for going after the Kaptrofracti?"

Nobody offered up an answer, and my imagination went crazy. How, exactly, did they deal with criminals here on the island? A hanging at high noon? Three years in the joint? One year of mandatory service giving foot massages to Peds? Each possibility was worse than the last.

Before the doors had opened all the way on the seventy-seventh floor, I tried to squeeze through. I was in a rush to get to Zara. "We need Rephael! Right—"

But before I could finish, I slammed into a woman dressed from head to toe in black. Her eyes were hidden behind her dark glasses. She had black bangs cut in a harsh straight line across her forehead. Her lips were lined in a bright ruby red. The force of our collision had bounced me back into the elevator.

"Freeze," those lips ordered. The woman flipped open a badge. "KIA!"

I recognized the Russian accent as the one from the Hall of Mirrors.

Four other KIA agents stood behind her. They all held these small gun-like objects that sported little three-fingered metal claws on their tips. Worse yet, they were all aimed at us. We stopped in our tracks, unsure about what was going on. The KIA lady stomped a black-booted foot in front of the elevator door to keep it from closing.

I stretched my neck around her and tried to get Zara's attention. "Zara! Kat needs to see Rephael, now!"

"Hush!" the lady yelled at me.

Zara didn't answer, but she whispered on her phone, her forehead creased. She hung up and rushed around her desk. The female KIA agent gripped Zara's branch-like arm.

"You are interfering with official—"

Zara smacked her hand away. "Rephael will see Princess Katriana."

William stepped forward but Zara stopped him. "Rephael has ordered Master Jackson to bring her."

The KIA woman's nostrils flared, and she clenched her teeth. "You!" She pointed to William. "Pass the girl to Mr. Sheppard."

William didn't look too happy about it, but he placed his sister in my arms. "Take care of her."

Zara took off down a long hallway. "This way."

I wasted no time stepping past Red Lips just as three loud zips sounded behind me.

"What are you doing?" Andie cried.

I whipped my head around. The other agents had pulled the triggers on their weapons, releasing the claws, which were fastened to thick metal cables. The cables seemed to have minds of their own as they snaked around the bodies of my three friends, pinning their arms to their sides. I swear, they wrapped around Cletus, William, and Andie at least ten times before the little claws bit down on the wrapped cable.

Cletus struggled, but every time he moved or wiggled, the thick metal wire became electrified and he got shocked. It was like a cow bumping into an electric fence! To make matters worse, each time he moved, the metal claw would release its grip on the cable and reposition itself to make its coils even tighter. I could tell he was in pain, especially when the claw nipped at his injured shoulder. He fought on anyway and tried to snap the cable. There was an especially large spark, and Cletus jerked. He lost his balance and fell to the elevator floor. The cable tightened again.

I wanted to help my friends, but I knew I had to get Kat to Rephael. "Cletus! Stop! Don't move! I'll talk to Rephael. It'll be fine. Just do what they say."

Cletus nodded to me. He stopped his thrashing and surrendered himself to the cable claw. The KIA agents got on the elevator and yanked my friends to their feet. Red Lips stepped aboard and the doors closed.

I ran to catch up with Zara. She was already at the end of the darkened hall and standing in front of an enormous door. She rapped hard on the door. Immediately, it swung wide, opened by a stylishly dressed Pedample. Instead of knee pants and the white shirt, this Ped wore a snappy little tuxedo. Across his chest, he had the same brown sash as all the other Peds, but his was covered with badges from top to bottom. He must not have liked the shoes I conjured up, though, because his four-toed feet were wild and free.

Zara turned to me. "Rephael is waiting. You must hurry."

I paused a second and tried to muster up a confidence I didn't have—in reality, my stomach hurt. My heart was so high in my throat I could practically gargle with it. I mean, this was huge—nobody ever saw Rephael, and yet here he was, demanding to see me. I felt like a voluntary prisoner, handing myself over to my own executioner.

I followed the Ped into the room, which was nothing more than a large lobby with another elevator.

He bowed. "Good afternoon. I am Gobric. This way, please. Quickly."

Gobric led us into the elevator. This elevator had a small round mirror just like the one in the main lobby. I watched as Gobric scribbled a "seventy-seven B" in his fresh huff mark. The doors closed, and I waited for the sensation I always got in my stomach when the elevator started moving. I never did get that feeling, because as soon as they closed, the doors bounced back open. Except now we were no longer in the lobby.

"Whoa." I followed Gobric off the elevator and into an amazing indoor garden. An impressive collection of plants, trees, and flowers grew in every direction for as far as I could see. There were tropical flowers and wildflowers, tulips, sunflowers, cactus flowers, roses, and lilies—every color and climate were represented. The sweet scent reminded me of Gram's garden back home.

The pleasant sound of trickling water drew my eye to a magnificent fountain with a large round stone basin. A glorious angel, chiseled from stone, stood proudly in the center of the fountain. His large arched wings were spread wide. His noble eyes were fixed on the heavens. I was so spellbound by the angel statue I almost forgot about poor Kat.

"Hurry along now." Gobric was already several yards in front of me.

He had run ahead to another gigantic door. This door stood as a lonesome structure that someone had just randomly plopped in the garden. The arched door was made of clear glass and was framed in heavy iron scroll work. When I peered through the glass, all I could see was more garden.

The door itself wasn't connected to a wall or anything at all, but when Gobric opened it, it revealed the inside of a very large, very bright foyer. I had to lean around the door jamb to make sure my eyes weren't playing tricks on me. Sure enough, there was nothing behind the door other than more endless garden!

We crossed through the door, and I had to squint my eyes. The room was ridiculously bright and cavernous and white. There were no windows, furniture, or decorations, but at the far end of the room was a very tall escalator. We rode the escalator all the way up, climbing its steps at the same time. At the top, we crossed another extremely large and extremely white room to yet one more door. At this rate, I wasn't sure if Kat would be able to hold on until we made it to Rephael.

Gobric showed me through the door and into a very plain room. A twin-sized bed with white sheets was centered under a window with a view of the garden. A small steel sink hung on the wall, and a mirrored medicine chest was mounted above it. Other than the simple nightstand beside the bed, there was nothing else in the room.

I lowered Kat onto the bed. For some reason, it bothered me that her blood might stain the perfectly white sheets.

"Step outside," Gobric said.

"Will she be okay?" I wasn't sure if I should leave Kat.

"Rephael will see to it."

As soon as I backed out the door, Gobric pushed it shut. I didn't know what to do, so I just waited in the empty white room. It seemed like hours. I was impatient for news about Kat, but I knew that meant it would be my turn to meet with Rephael. After a while, I plunked myself on the floor and slumped against the door. All of my aches and pains began to make themselves known. Especially the cut in my knee where Cletus had stuck me with his dagger.

I was rubbing my neck, trying to relieve some of the tension, when the door opened, and I fell flat on my back. I looked up at Gobric.

"Rephael will see you now."

I scrambled to my feet, brushing the wrinkles out of my shirt and pulling back my shoulders. Anxious to hear about Kat, I crossed through the door to the room. Believe it or not, I didn't end up in the sterile white room where I had left Kat. Instead, I found myself in a fancy living room decorated in shades of white, cream, and gold with humongous furniture. A really cool working replica of a carousel sat on the huge coffee table. On one of the end tables was a detailed replica of a Ferris wheel. I wouldn't call them mini—the Ferris wheel was probably as tall as I was—but they were perfectly sized for this giant room. It made me feel like I had been shrunken down to garden gnome status.

I leaned back into the hall to check for other doors— maybe I hadn't realized that Gobric had brought me into another room—but there was only this one door across from the escalator.

"You wait here." Gobric pointed to a supersized arm-chair with fancy cream-colored material. Then he left through the same door we had entered. I climbed up onto the chair. My legs dangled over the edge, and I stared at the Ferris wheel. It was almost hypnotic, the way the little angel figurine in one of the seats rode it round and round.

The door opened again, snapping me out of my angel-induced trance. I jumped. My nerves were a wreck. But it was just Gobric carrying a tray with a glass of root beer, a pile of cookies, and a napkin.

"No spills." He disappeared again out the same door.

He might as well have said, "Don't think about pea-nuts." As soon as someone tells me not to think about peanuts, then BAM! Peanuts! It's all I can think about! I took my first sip. *Don't spill, don't spill*, I cautioned myself. Well, of course, peanuts! The root beer ran right down my chin and between my legs, leaving a big stain on the cream fabric.

I shot a look at the door to make sure Gobric had not seen. Then, I slid to the side and rubbed the stain with the napkin. But it wasn't going away. I rubbed harder and faster, but the stain was still there. Before I knew it, I was rubbing so fast my arm had become a blur. The friction was generating some heat, and the spot began to smoke. I checked the door again to make sure no one was coming. Whoosh! The spot erupted in flames.

Darn super speed!

I reacted quickly. I tried dousing the flames with the rest of the root beer. Unfortunately, there wasn't enough to put out the fire. Instead, it streamed off the chair and onto the white carpet. My eyes darted around the room to a vase full of colorful flowers on the tall mantel above the large fireplace. I jumped off the chair and had to do a super leap to reach the vase. I yanked out the flowers, tossing them over my shoulder. The water splashed over the flames, this time snuffing them out.

By now, the room was thick with smoke. I was freaked out the smoke detectors might go off. I jerked a large pillow from the mammoth sofa and began to wave it in the air. I didn't notice the large lamp on the table next to the wingback chair. Naturally, my pillow zeroed in on that lamp like my Gram had zeroed in on the Portable Pocket Juicer when it was for sale on Personal Shopping Network. The lamp toppled to the floor, shattering in a million pieces. I panicked, ran to the fireplace, and grabbed the little shovel and brush used for sweeping up ashes. In my rush, I tripped over my untied shoelace and ended up sprawled on the floor in the middle of the broken flower bits and busted lamp pieces. I landed with my head right under the trickle of dripping root beer and vase water. Frustrated, I stuck out my tongue and licked the sticky mixture from my cheek.

Of course, it was at this exact moment the door opened.

"I see you have made yourself at home," a deep, rich voice said.

I hopped to my feet. My cheeks burned.

Gobric glowered at me. "You spilled."

But I was too distracted by the creature standing

behind him. I had to do a double-take, but I was pretty sure the angel statue from the garden fountain was standing right here in this room! The man—or *angel?*— was even bigger than Caephus, which explained the monster-sized furniture. His face was masculine and chiseled, but somehow it was beautiful too. A perfect dimple had been poked right into the middle of his chin. Wavy blond curls covered his head, and his eyes looked like pots of melted chocolate sauce. Even from halfway across the room, I could see my reflection in them.

His angel clothes were different than what I would picture on an angel—they were more like half armor, half toga. The portion above his waist was the armor half—it was golden and sculpted to his body, tracing every powerful muscle in his chest and stomach. A golden sash was tied around his waist and below it hung a draped, knee-length gown of pure white. Laced-up leather warrior boots would have completed the look perfectly, but instead he wore beat up old sandals. And then there were the wings. Their thick layers of soft, fluffy feathers arched high above his head. There were no straps or ties holding them on, so I could tell they weren't fake. And the weirdest part of all was that he glowed! A soft aura of golden light outlined his entire body.

"May I present…the amazing, the magnanimous, the unparalleled Rephael," Gobric said. He stepped to the side and swept his arms in a grand gesture.

I didn't know the correct way to greet an angel, but I didn't want to mess it up. I started to bow, but then thought maybe it would be an insult to show him the top of my head, so I rose and dipped in a curtsy, which instantly seemed way too girly, so I genuflected on one knee, but still wasn't sure, so I ran forward, clutched his hand, and kissed his knuckle, and then thought that might be too familiar, so at last I settled on the double-guns click.

"How ya doin'?"

Gobric shook his head, tsk-ing his disapproval.

"You may relax," the angel said before turning to the Ped. "Gobric, if you will, please see to this mess. Jackson, come with me."

"Yes, um…Your Amazingness…er…Your Unparallel…ed…ness." I took a step in his direction but then stopped. "But first, could you please tell me how Kat is doing?"

"She is going to be fine." Rephael's deep, rich, melodic voice made my chest rumble. I liked how he sounded like he had swallowed a cello. "Right now she is resting comfortably. When she awakens, she will be weak but will recover fully. Come now."

"Can someone tell William how she's doing?" I hoped I wasn't pushing my luck.

"Of course. Gobric, will you please have Ulrich deliver the news to Prince William?"

"As you wish, sir." Gobric bowed and hurried away.

"Thank you." I tipped my head way back to look up at him. His glowing brilliance almost hurt my eyes.

Rephael led me out the door, and we strolled casually around the white room, as though there was no place we actually needed to go.

"Do you know why you are here?" Rephael asked.

"Forgive me, Your Magnanimous...ness." I gulped. "Maybe *you* should tell *me* if I know why I'm here? I mean, can't you and Caephus read minds?"

"Surface thoughts only," Rephael said. "Shallow thoughts are easy to read, but we cannot read your deepest thoughts or desires."

"Okay. Then I'm guessing I'm here because we decided to go after the Kaptrofracti."

He shook his head. "You are guessing incorrectly."

"So I'm not in trouble?"

He shook his head again, but this time, his brown eyes twinkled. "Time will tell."

"What do you mean?"

"Jackson. There are many things you need to learn in order to understand your purpose."

"Wait a minute. This whole Ark thing—it's wrong. I'm not the Ark. You and Caephus—you were right. I'm not special. I'm not threatening. There's no reason Melchasaar would want me dead."

Rephael didn't react to that. "You must listen carefully to your heart to learn what's in your soul. When your motives are pure, unselfish—only then will you fulfill all that is intended for you."

My face flushed hot. Did he know my only reason for being there was to bring back Sebastian? I tried to bury any thoughts of Sebastian deep in my brain so Rephael couldn't read them.

Fortunately, we had made it all the way around the outside of the white room and were back at the living room entrance. Just as we reached the door, Gobric threw it wide open. He bowed to Rephael. I didn't expect the room to be clean yet—I mean, we had only been gone for five minutes, and there was no way that little guy could have fixed such a big mess in such a short time.

I entered and when we crossed the threshold, we weren't in the living room. We weren't even in the bland room with the bed where I had left Kat. Our feet and ankles were immediately swallowed by a blackish, purplish, churning mist. Above, hundreds of glimmering stars winked at us from their home on the ceiling. In the center of the room, with fog swirling around its base, was a lone, mystical mirror. It was as tall and wide as Rephael. Its thick frame was decorated with scrolls, fruits, and cherubs carved into antique silver. Rephael directed me toward the mirror, but several feet short of reaching it, he stopped.

"Go on. Touch it."

I glanced at him and then the mirror, and then held up my hand. I eased forward until my palm should have pressed against its own reflection on the surface of the glass. Instead, it passed right through, creating ripples on the surface like a raindrop in a pond.

I glanced at Rephael again. I'd be lying if I said I wasn't as scared as I was curious.

"Step through it."

"Through it? Are you coming with me?"

"No. This is a journey I choose not to relive."

I was confused by that, but I summoned my courage and poked a tentative toe through the glass. I didn't feel anything peculiar on the other side, so I leaned a shoulder through, and then my other foot. My head followed, and finally my whole body crossed the plane. I turned to look at the glass, but all I could see was my reflection.

Puzzled, I raised a hand to scratch my head, but instead of my right arm going up, my left one went up in its place! I stuck out my right foot, but my left foot went forward! I reached in my pocket and pulled out a yellow and black striped bubble gum wrapper. Instead of reading, "BUMBLE BUBBLE," it read, "ELBBUB ELBMUB!" Everything was reversed like its own reflection!

I wasn't sure what I was supposed to do inside this bizarre mirror world, but in the distance, the insistent ticking of a clock called to me. I headed toward the noise, noticing that my feet traveled along a path. Its cobblestones were worn round and smooth. Eventually, I came upon a lonely grandfather clock just standing there alongside the path. It took me awhile to guess the time because its face was reversed, just like everything else inside this strange place. I finally figured out it was 1:05 in the afternoon.

Under the face of the clock was a digital dial displaying the year. Of course, these numbers were reversed, too. As I watched, the numbers began to roll backwards. Soon, the numbers clicked past 0591 to 2191, past 0381, and past 2471. The dial began spinning so rapidly I could no longer read what the numbers said as they ticked past. Then, suddenly, they clicked to a halt on the year CB 812, which I interpreted to be 218 BC after reversing the numbers.

I had no idea what was going on, so I stayed there, waiting for another clue. Eventually, I continued along the path, hoping to stumble across the next sign. My sneakers made no sound as they ate up the cobblestones. I was flashing around a bend in the trail when finally, up ahead, I spotted a bright ray of light shining on a small wooden podium in the center of the path. A very chunky ancient-looking book rested on it. Just as I was about to touch the cover, the book flipped open. The pages fluttered past, fanning my face with their musty dampness. They stopped flipping at page seventy-seven.

As I stared, neatly calligraphed words began to float off the page. Like everything else, they were reversed. It was almost impossible to translate them. I struggled until I noticed the small mirror resembling a magnifying glass lying on the podium beside the book. I held up the mirror opposite the floating words so I could read their reflection. They floated across the mirror and I read:

AND A MIGHTY AND JUST ANGEL WAS SENT TO EARTH TO WARN THE PEOPLE AGAINST THE DANGERS OF USING MAGIC. THE MAGUS, A POWERFUL SORCERER, HAVING HEARD OF THE ANGEL'S MESSAGE, BECAME ENRAGED, AS HE HAD BEEN USING MAGIC TO BEWITCH THE PEOPLE AND WIN THEIR DEVOTION. HE TASKED HIS LOVER, A BEAUTIFUL AND ACCOMPLISHED ENCHANTRESS IN HER OWN RIGHT, WITH BEGUILING THE ANGEL AND DRAWING HIS ATTENTIONS AWAY FROM THE SORCERER. SOON, THE ANGEL, FORGETTING HIS MISSION, HAD FALLEN DEEPLY IN LOVE WITH THE ENCHANTRESS.

THE ENCHANTRESS CHALLENGED THE ANGEL TO
PROVE THE DEPTH OF HIS LOVE WITH A GIFT POSSESSING
THE GREATEST MAGIC EVER KNOWN TO MAN. THE ANGEL,
WHO LABORED AT WINTER SOLSTICE UNDER THE LIGHT
OF THE FULL MOON, AND WHO USED SANDS OF THE
JUDEAN DESERT WITH THE PUREST OF DEWS, PRESENTED
A GIFT THAT WOULD ENABLE HER TO GAZE UPON HER
OWN UNPARALLELED BEAUTY: THE WORLD'S FIRST
GLASS MIRROR. THE KAPTROPOTEN, WHICH HARNESSED
THE FORCES OF NATURE AND SCIENCE, PROVIDED ITS
OWNER WITH THE POWERS OF TELEPORTATION, KINESIS,
SCRYING, CONTROL OF THE ELEMENTS, CONJURATION,
ENCHANTMENT, METAMORPHOSIS, HEALING, EVOCATION,
AND REANIMATION.

This had to be Rephael and Melchasaar! It was the
first time I had ever heard any mention of an Enchantress.
I read on.

THE ENCHANTRESS ACCEPTED THE GIFT AND OFFERED IT
TO THE SORCERER, WHO USED IT TO ENSLAVE THE PEOPLE AND
EXERT HIS WILL. THE ANGEL, BETRAYED AND HEARTBROKEN,
REALIZED THE GRAVITY OF HIS MISTAKE. HE GATHERED
THE MOST GENETICALLY SUPERIOR BEINGS FROM ACROSS
THE UNIVERSE AND ASSEMBLED AN ARMY TO RECAPTURE
THE KAPTROPOTEN AND DEFEAT THE EVIL SORCERER AND
ENCHANTRESS.

"Enchantress" was the last word to float from the
page. When I looked at the book again, the pages were

blank. I flipped to the next page, but it was blank too. The bright spotlight snapped off, leaving the book in darkness.

Wait! I wanted to know more—like whatever happened to the enchantress?

Either way, at least this finally offered an explanation for my super powers.

Hmmm. Genetically superior. I liked the way that sounded.

Once again, I followed along the path, keeping alert for the next sign or clue. Ahead of me, a large obstacle was parked in the center of the trail. A round, cup-like chair—the kind you would see on the tea cup ride at the BVFD Carnival—blocked the path. What was it with Rephael and his amusement park theme?

Of course, I did what anyone would do—I climbed inside and put my hands on the wheel. When I turned it, the cup started spinning, slowly at first but then faster and faster. Eventually, it spun so wildly my surroundings blurred completely. I squeezed my eyes shut.

"Whoooooooaaaaaaa!" I cried out just in time for the spinning to stop.

I opened my eyes. The tea cup—with me in it—was no longer situated on the dark, misty trail. The path was still there, and the cup was still plunked down right in the middle of it, but the three of us—the path, the cup, and I—had been dumped in some other foreign location. It appeared we had been dropped into an ancient, public square.

The square itself was surrounded by long runs of

columns connected on the tops by big arched cement structures. On one side was a temple, which sat upon a tall base, its steps leading to a deep porch. There were several ancient buildings made of wood, and the roads were roughly paved with stone. A small amphitheater of concrete and stone was located several yards away from my tea cup.

Nearby stood Rephael, and his eyes were glued to the stage. A small crowd of people dressed in tunics and robes scuttled about. Most of them had weapons and were wearing some armor.

Clearly, I had traveled way back in time. I made the connection from the grandfather clock that I must be somewhere in 218 BC.

Rephael looked the same—huge and glorious and proud. It was then I realized his eyes were locked on a much younger version of Melchasaar, who stood on the stage. Just the sight of Melchasaar was petrifying. I flattened myself on the bottom of the tea cup. My breaths came in shallow gulps. I slithered up the side until only the top of my head and eyes showed. I was surprised no one had noticed a scrawny kid in a powder blue mug had just popped in. Maybe they couldn't see me at all—like I was just an invisible observer. This thought made me relax a bit, but I kept my eyes on Melchasaar.

I don't know how, but until now I had missed the beautiful, glowing mirror he was clutching. It shone like it held inside it the sun, the moon, and the stars, and they all blended together in an amazing display of colors.

Standing just past Melchasaar was the most

ridiculously beautiful woman I had ever seen. She wasn't your typical beauty, like Kat. She was small and had wild thick, long red curls, and milky skin. Her eyes sparkled like two huge purple jewels. She was positively... enchanting.

Enchanting? That had to be Melchasaar's girlfriend, the evil enchantress! It was easy to understand how Rephael had fallen under her spell. I continued to spy from inside my tea cup.

I realized I must have come upon the aftermath of a battle. Bodies lay everywhere I looked. Those lucky enough to still be standing were taking care of the injured and helping to drag others out of the way. Behind Melchasaar and the enchantress was a collection of people who I could only guess were Melchasaar's followers. They stood behind him like a group of soulless, costumed thugs. Some held large, spiked maces, while others had sharp tridents and swords.

The hideous hiss of Melchasaar's voice was enough to make me dive to the bottom of the tea cup again. "Your army has been defeated, *Angel*. You were betrayed by the woman you love—my sweet, dear Salome." He held out his hand to Salome who flitted to his side. She tossed a smile at Rephael from under her long lashes.

Melchasaar continued, "You have failed to recapture the Kaptropoten. You have *nothing*. You *are* nothing." He spat on the ground. "Get on your knees, *Angel*." His voice grew louder. "Bow before me! The Kaptropoten is mine, and I am unstoppable!" His thugs joined him in taunting Rephael. Melchasaar raised the Kaptropoten above his head, aiming it at the sky. Smoky, black clouds swallowed the sun, and the winds roared. "Bow to me!"

Salome danced behind him. "That's it, my lord. Go ahead! Kill him!"

Rephael didn't move, but even from way over here, I could see sadness in his eyes. He still stood proudly in the middle of the square.

The mirror exploded in a rainbow of colors as a blinding, thunderous bolt of lightning erupted from the clouds. It connected with the ground just feet from where Rephael was standing.

It filled me with pure terror. Vicious rats gnawed at the insides of my stomach. I felt just as I had when I was dropped into the lagoon in the middle of that lightning storm. My heart raced. I couldn't breathe. I struggled to keep myself from falling out of the opening of the tea cup. Sebastian's small face flashed before my eyes. His look of terror caused my pain, my guilt, and my grief to eat at my entire body.

I clung to the side of the cup, forcing myself to breathe. Beads of sweat dripped on the paved stone. I made myself watch the nightmare that played out like a movie. Strangely, Rephael was no longer looking at Melchasaar, but instead was looking at me.

He can see me? The chocolate eyes locked with my own brown eyes, coaxing me into a relaxed state of chocolate hypnosis. A comforting warmth washed down from the tips of my hair to the bottoms of my feet. Suddenly, my chest was clear and so was my head. The corners of Rephael's mouth twitched but he didn't allow a full-out smile. It was just enough to give me strength, and I waved my thanks for being rescued from my own fear. I blinked just once, but when my eyes reopened, Rephael was standing exactly as he had been, focused on Melchasaar and Salome—just as the lightning struck the ground.

The smell of ozone seared itself in my nostrils. The feathers on Rephael's wings were momentarily electrified. They crackled with static as they stood on end. Still, he didn't move. His act of defiance only enraged Melchasaar, who threw back his head and again trained the mirror on the clouds.

Melchasaar's supporters howled their approval. Salome cackled in excitement as she danced and twirled around Melchasaar. Just as the mirror burst forth in magnificent color, Salome's bare foot caught the edge of the stage. She teetered there, her arms flailing as she tried to prevent herself from falling the five feet to the ground. She toppled over the side landing at Rephael's feet in the precise spot where the deadly rod of lightning summoned by Melchasaar was about to strike the earth.

A pure white blinding flash lit the air as Salome's body absorbed the charge. Sparks fired from her right hand as the electrical current sought an escape from her body. Melchasaar let loose a primitive growl. He leaped from the stage. At the same time, Rephael ran to her side. Her purple eyes were wide, empty craters on her face. She stared at the space in front of her. Her lips moved to speak, but then her eyelids fluttered closed. Her chest rose and fell with quick, shallow breaths.

Melchasaar held up the mirror, releasing a roar so loud it nearly split the clouds.

The power of Healing! I remembered the Big Three powers of the Kaptropoten. *He'll use the mirror to heal her!*

The Kaptropoten shook against its own power, and colors erupted from its center. It whistled like a thousand screaming teapots. My breath caught in my throat, and I waited for Salome's body to surge forward with renewed life. But instead, Melchasaar was greedy. He waited, allowing the Kaptropoten to glow brighter and brighter and whistle even louder, hungrily charging its power.

And then, I witnessed the spookiest thing imaginable. Shivers made their way down my back when out of Salome's still breathing form rose the translucent, ghost-like figure of the enchantress herself. It floated over her body for a moment. And then, in a sparkling, swirling whoosh, it was whisked inside the Kaptropoten!

Melchasaar roared. He released one final bolt of lightning, so powerful that hundreds of mini bolts branched out from its thick electrical core. Before the bolt could reach its target, Rephael raised his hands. Like a lightning rod, he somehow drew every single branch of lightning into his palms, forging them into a mighty and dangerous ball of electrical energy. He paused only an instant before hurling the ball at the Kaptropoten.

For a brief millisecond, Melchasaar's expression was one of pure bewilderment. Then, with the force of a nuclear explosion, the Kaptropoten shattered, sending its fragments flying. The Kaptrofracti glimmered as they soared in multiple directions out to the horizon until finally, they could no longer be seen.

CHAPTER 21
A Broken Mirror and a Mirror That Wouldn't Break

The cup was spinning again, and when it stopped I was back on the path inside the mirror. It was silent, and I sat in the cup for what felt like hours. The intensity of what I had just witnessed weighed on me like a ton of ancient paving bricks.

Why had Rephael sent me here? If I was just going to be sent home, or worse, locked away somewhere here on IOM, then what was the point?

I pulled out the Scryor and stared at my reflection. "Show me the Ark." I waited for the purple mini explosion and the smoky fog to swirl inside the mirror, but nothing happened. My own stupid reflection just kept staring back at me.

Dumb mirror is broken.

I stuck the mirror back in my pack and retraced my steps. My feet operated on autopilot. Eventually, I came across the same small podium. The spotlight was on again, casting the podium in warm, yellow light. I was sure that wasn't an accident, so I picked up the little mirror. Soon, the reversed words floated from the page.

HER BODY, ON THE PRECIPICE OF DEATH, HAD BECOME
TOO WEAKENED TO MAINTAIN THE CONNECTION WITH ITS
SOUL, THUS ALLOWING HER SOUL TO BECOME TRAPPED IN THE
MIRROR. THE BODY OF THE SOULLESS ENCHANTRESS CLUNG
WEAKLY TO LIFE AND WAS TAKEN INTO THE POSSESSION OF
THE SORCERER, WHO FLED WITH HIS FOLLOWERS.

THE DISGRACED ANGEL WAS SENTENCED TO REMAIN ON
EARTH, LIVING IN SHAME FOR SEVEN THOUSAND YEARS OR
UNTIL SUCH TIME WHEN THE KAPTROPOTEN BE DESTROYED
AND DIVESTED OF ITS POWERS. HE TASKED THE SURVIVING
MEMBERS OF HIS ELITE ARMY WITH GUARDING AND
PROTECTING THE FRAGMENTS OF THE MIRROR, ENSURING
THEY NEVER AGAIN BE USED IN PURSUIT OF EVIL AND NEVER
BE REUNITED.

The words stopped floating, the pages went blank, and
the spotlight faded again. Wow! Seven thousand years of
bad luck! I felt such overwhelming grief for Rephael. I
remembered Cletus saying a Komitari's greatest shame
was to lose his mirror. Rephael had not only created
the mirror, but had then lost control of it. That made it
available for some serious evil-doing. I could see why
he didn't want to travel with me into the mirror world.
He obviously didn't want to relive that awful experience.

I also understood why Melchasaar was so determined
to get the mirror back, even after all these years. It wasn't
just about the power—he wanted to free Salome.

I headed toward the grandfather clock and watched as
it dialed the year all the way forward to today. It was still
1:05 in the afternoon. I returned to the giant mirror and

stepped out, eager to see Rephael. I didn't know exactly what I would say to him, but I just wanted to tell him it wasn't his fault. How was he supposed to know the woman he loved was a low-down, dirty thug disguised as a supermodel?

Unfortunately, he was gone. I left the room and clicked the door shut behind me. I was standing there, wondering what to do next, when the door I had just closed popped open behind me. I turned, surprised to see Caephus standing on the other side of the door.

"Where's Rephael?" I asked, leaning around him to peek inside the door.

"Come in." This time, when he opened the door, it was the living room again.

Inside, Kat was sitting in the cream-and-gold chair where I had spilled the root beer. Her legs dangled over the edge of the enormous chair. She was pale—her lips were pasty, and her eyes were duller than usual—but she was alive and sipping a cup of tea. I was so relieved to see her. Before I could even think about upholding my cool-guy image, I ran and hopped up beside her, giving her a quick squeeze. My overenthusiastic hug caused her tea cup to topple from the saucer. It spilled on her leg and ran onto the freshly scrubbed upholstery.

As if on cue, the door snapped open, and Gobric popped through.

"Grrrrrr." He growled at me like a bulldog. I avoided eye contact and instead turned to Kat.

"Thank goodness you're okay."

"I am fine!" She slammed her cup on the end table

and dabbed furiously at the spilled tea with her napkin. Her other arm hugged her bag and her satchel, shielding it against her chest. I think she was afraid Caephus would confiscate her mirror and weapons. She put up a good act, but I could tell Kat was just as nervous as I was. She sure smelled good, though.

I was about to scoot off the chair, but was stopped by Caephus. "Stay."

He studied us for several minutes, his expression blank. I prepared myself for the tongue lashing we were about to receive. I just hoped the courts here were kind to kids. I frowned, but then without thinking, I leaned closer to Kat and sniffed.

"Are you *smelling* me?"

"No." I swiped at a pretend tear. "I'm just all broken up about seeing you doing so well." I faked a sniff.

"Enough," Caephus said. "It appears you fail to recognize the seriousness of your situation." He frowned, and Kat shot me a dirty look. She elbowed me in the ribs.

Caephus continued, "Your actions were irresponsible, selfish, and reckless."

Ashamed, I lowered my eyes.

"Your decision to pursue the Kaptrofracti on your own resulted in Stirling's death. "And," he said to Kat, "it almost cost *you* your life."

His words hit me hard. I had been carrying the responsibility for Sebastian's death in my heart all this time. Now, I had to add the responsibility for Stirling's death too. And on top of that, I was worried about Cletus, William, and Andie.

"I understand you have recovered the Kaptro Teleportation and the Kaptro Scryor." Caephus paused and reached into a satchel of his own. He pulled out a small, orange velvet bag and tossed it to me. I caught it and examined it, not sure what was going on. I loosened the drawstring. Instantly, an orange glow radiated from the bag. Kat and I looked at each other, both too astonished to speak.

"It's the Kaptro Kinesis. After the last session of Council, Phlynnis turned over her fragment before returning to Terreptelan. She recognized what needed to be done. It will save you a trip."

I remembered from the *Dummies* book that Terreptelan was the home of the Kaptro Kinesis and the sculpture heads. Phlynnis must have been one of the sculpture heads sitting near Kat when we were at Council.

"Why are you giving us this?" I asked.

"Go back to your rooms." Caephus ignored me for a second time. "Eat well and get plenty of rest. Council will convene first thing in the morning." He strode from the room, leaving Kat and me to stare open-mouthed at each other. I took one last sniff of Kat before Gobric came back and summoned the two of us from the chair.

After that, everything else was a blur. Gobric led us out the door, down the escalator, out the other door, through the garden, and onto the elevator. I held the Kaptro Kinesis in my hands, afraid of putting it too close to my other fragments. It was then it dawned on me that I had *four* of the Kaptrofracti in my possession. Cletus held the Kaptro Teleportation and, of course, Kat had the

Kaptro Metamorphus. I was so close to saving Sebastian, I could taste it. I just needed time to come up with a plan.

"Go to your rooms," Gobric said.

And then it struck me—I had forgotten to ask Rephael to help Cletus, William, and Andie!

"Wait! Gobric!" I spun just in time to catch Gobric making the "I'm watching you" motion one last time before slamming the door.

Kat and I left the building. I tucked the Kinesis in my pocket, and we headed across the courtyard toward the hotel. Kat's face was still somewhat pale and she lagged behind.

"Why don't you take a break?" I pointed to the bench where Cletus and I sat the day he told me he was a Komitari. She must have felt weak because she actually agreed. We sat, and I explained what had happened with the KIA.

"You let them capture my brother?" Kat exploded off the bench. A vein in her forehead was about to pop even in spite of her recent blood loss. "How could you let that happen? I should have known you would mess things up. If you had not distracted me at Stirling's, I would have never taken that blow from Draemoch! I cannot trust ANYONE but myself! I cannot—"

"Wait a minute!" I interrupted. "First of all, we don't even know what the KIA is doing with them. So calm down." I was irked. "Second of all, I chose to save your life rather than stop the KIA. Without me, you'd be dead. And if you're dead, then you can't save your father. You would *both* be gone. Geez! Cut me some slack. You were the one who dragged me into this mess. Without you, I wouldn't have been involved in the first place!"

Kat seemed surprised when I defended myself. She sized me up and chewed on her lower lip. Finally, she met my eyes. "That is not true."

"Yes. It is true. Don't give me any of this Ark crap. It's not me. And my Gram never even planned to give me the Kaptro Conjuration. The only reason she did was because of the trouble you caused the night the Gorg was chasing you."

"No. It is *not* true. And by the way, the Gorg was not chasing me. He was after you. He was trying to collect the bounty. And do you know why your brother is dead?"

Something in my stomach reached up and tried to strangle my heart. All of my guilt rushed back to the surface. "It was a horrible accident. It wasn't my fault." But I didn't believe a word of it.

"You are right, it was not your fault," she said. "Do you know why the lightning struck the pool that night? Have you ever wondered about that storm? It was unusual, was it not? The swirling clouds? The green lightning?" She seemed almost pleased to be talking about it.

"Did you know? That was how you were sent the Elementum. It came through the vortex. That is how the Tegeris incantation works." She paused for a beat while I digested this new information. "It was Cletus. When he sent you his mirror that night—that is what killed your brother. *That* is how you became involved in this." She looked almost triumphant as she delivered that kick to the gut.

"No…no…Cletus wouldn't—he would never—" I couldn't finish. *Cletus did this to me?* I couldn't believe it. I trusted him. Aside from Andie, he had become my best friend.

I stumbled to the bench and slumped down on it. I ripped the two-toned Elementum and Conjuration mirror from the velvet bag and glared at it. This stupid mirror! I drew back my arm and hurled the mirror at the earth beside the bench. It collided with the ground, spitting up a mushroom cloud of dirt and grass. A three feet deep and three feet wide crater was left in its wake.

I stuck my arm in the hole, stretching to reach the mirror. The cursed thing was still intact—there was not even a chip. I stood and lifted the side of the bench. Kat slid ungracefully into the arm on the other end. I bent and snapped off its metal leg and then let the bench drop, allowing Kat to plunk on the ground with it.

I tossed the mirror on the edge of the pavement. Like a crazed warrior, I stabbed it with the sharp, broken end of the metal leg. I stabbed it again and again, trying to destroy the object that had destroyed my life. It refused to break. Eventually, my arm cramped. My breathing was labored. I sat frozen and numb. After a while, I felt Kat's warm hand on my shoulder. She crouched there beside me, her other hand resting on my arm.

"I'm sorry," she whispered. She drew my head to her, cradling it against her chest. We sat that way for a while until Kat finally broke the silence.

Her eyes scanned the area. She wouldn't make eye contact as she toyed with a blade of grass. "Have you ever wondered if you could bring your brother back?"

My spine stiffened. "Noooo..." I lied. Did she know? I turned the question around on her. "Have you ever thought about bringing back your mother?"

A brief flash of guilt washed across her face, but she quickly disguised it. "Of course not!" I could tell her wall was back up. "A Komitari never uses the mirror for personal gain."

"I know, I know. Any use, no matter how small, has the potential to alter the course of human fate," I said, mimicking Caephus.

We finally started making our way to the hotel.

"So what do you want to do about William and Andie?" I didn't mention Cletus because I was so angry I couldn't even say his name. I realized Cletus hadn't intended to kill Sebastian, but his actions had led to Sebastian's death. I wasn't sure if I could ever forgive him.

"I may have overreacted earlier," she said unapologetically. "The KIA is not a cruel and abusive organization. Yes, they are single-minded and will protect the Kaptropoten at all costs, but William and the others will be given a fair trial. I just do not know how long they will be held before they are tried, and I will not let my little brother rot in a cold cell. Not for any period of time. I am going to need to ask some questions before I can decide how to proceed. You go and eat, and I will be over as soon as I figure out what to do."

I left Kat at her room and went on to my own. I paused before the small identification mirror above the room number and waited for it to scan my features. A buzz and a click meant the door had unlocked. Inside, Elweard was setting the little table for one.

"Welcome back, Master Jax," Elweard said.

"No, no." I waggled a finger. "You're gonna eat *with* me."

This time, Elweard didn't waste a second making a plate for himself. He climbed onto the seat, and before I finished spreading my napkin on my lap, he had polished off his entire plate of Mrs. Putt's meatloaf. I was pretty sure he could have whipped my butt in the Eat the Whole Duck and Your Meal Is Free contest.

He was working on a mouthful of potatoes and was loosening his belt when someone knocked on the door.

"I'll get it." I said.

I let Kat in and she shot a disapproving glance at Elweard. Apparently she didn't approve of me letting a Ped join me for dinner. She crossed the suite and took a seat on the striped chair.

"So what did you find out?" I asked.

"It is rather good news. My source told me the three of them are to be released early tomorrow. He does not know what happened to them, but he is fairly certain they are unharmed and will be free to go in the morning."

"Well, thank goodness for that." I was glad to not have to worry about Andie and the others anymore. I plunked myself on the sofa and grabbed the remote, switching on the magical flat screen.

Kat didn't seem to have anything else to say. She appeared content to just sit there in that chair. I clicked through the channels, careful this time to avoid the

History Channel. When Stirling's face flashed on the screen, I had to stop and watch.

A regular-looking reporter in a navy suit interviewed Nigel, who was trying his best to be brave. He was as dignified as he had been when we first met him.

"Stirling Vates was a good man and a great Komitari who died defending the Kaptro Scryor," he told the reporter. A photo montage of Stirling visiting with sick children at their hospital bedsides, helping to build a house in a devastated flood zone, and presenting an oversized check to a bunch of school kids played out on the screen. The curious thing was that in each picture, Stirling was in the exact same pose, wearing the exact same clothes, with the exact same smile. Come to think of it, that pose looked familiar. In fact, it was the same shot of Stirling that was in the framed newspaper article on his desk. I suspected this was Nigel's poorly photoshopped attempt to rewrite Stirling's history. It seemed like Stirling was still bending the rules—even after he was gone!

The reporter related the details of what had happened earlier in the day. I was glad when he referred to us as "unknown actors" instead of by name.

He mentioned the Gorgs.

"So that Gorg was after me, huh? How can you be so sure?" I asked. "Because to me it looked a whole lot like he was chasing you."

"Well…" she said, "he might have followed me to get to you. But all those other episodes…those accidents that have been plaguing you. They were no accidents. Every one was an attempt by one of Melchasaar's soldiers to capture or kill you."

It still seemed farfetched to me. "Anyway, how did the Gorgs even get from your land to Earth?"

Kat yawned. "The Kaptro Scryor has been stolen many times throughout history. There was a time when the Gorgs came to be in possession of it. They looked into the past and then attempted to copy the magic formula used to create the Kaptropoten." Elweard handed Kat her drink, and she sipped. "They were not successful, thank goodness, but they were able to copy enough of its properties to develop their own teleportation mirror. You might have noticed Draemoch used one too."

I was surprised the Gorgs had been able to copy the Teleportation mirror. That was just one more reason to make sure the Kaptrofracti didn't fall into the wrong hands.

I clicked the channel again and settled on an old comedy, which I hoped would give my mind a break from all this thinking. When Elweard joined me on the sofa, Kat raised an eyebrow, but she didn't say anything. In fact, she even stayed and watched the movie with us. Elweard and I laughed so hard, we cried, and every now and again, Kat broke into a smile. When the movie finally ended, we were each covered in vanilla milkshakes and ketchup from the big food-fight scene, but I knew it would fade in a few minutes. In any case, my mind felt lighter, and I was ready for bed.

Elweard turned down my sheets, fluffed the pillows, and then left.

Kat, on the other hand, seemed like she didn't want to leave. Even when I got up to go to bed, she stayed in the chair, twirling her ring around her finger

"Do you want something?" I asked.

She looked away. "I was hoping I could stay here tonight. On the sofa."

I was not expecting that. Kat wanted to stay here? I gulped. "Why? What's room with your wrong?" I tried again. "I mean, what's with your wrong room?"

"Forget about it." She scrambled to her feet and headed toward the door. "I will go."

I flashed in front of her and blocked her way. "Wait a minute. What's wrong?"

She turned her back to me. "It's the nightmares." Her voice was so low I almost couldn't hear her.

"Did you say 'nightmares'?" My ears burned.

She faced me again, her brows forming a deep ridge between her eyes. She rubbed her temples. "It's Melchasaar. He astral-planes into my dreams—tortures me every night. I just do not want to be alone."

"He astral *whats*?" I couldn't believe Kat was having nightmares about Melchasaar too.

"Astral-planes. It means his astral body—some would call it the soul—leaves his physical body and enters our dreams. He does it to terrorize, influence, and manipulate. It is horrible."

"I have nightmares about Melchasaar every night." I shuddered at the idea that Melchasaar himself was entering my dreams. "You can stay. Definitely."

I grabbed a pillow and blanket from the bed. "You

go ahead and take the bed. I'll sleep on the couch." I had learned a thing or two from my Grandpap about being a gentleman. As soon as my body hit that sofa, I fell into a deep, restful sleep.

CHAPTER 22

*Secret Agents Who Shock and a Friend with a
Shocking Secret*

I awoke to the sound of the door clicking shut. It was morning—7:02 a.m. to be exact. I had dreamt about Melchasaar again, so my deep and restful sleep hadn't lasted too long. I stretched my arms, cracked my neck, and trudged to the bedroom.

Kat was gone. She probably had headed over to her own room to get washed up and ready to go. I dressed and made myself a bowl of Sticky-O's. A few minutes later, the door opened, and Elweard came in.

"Good morning, Master Jax." He had no sooner walked in than Cletus and Andie pounded on the door.

"Hey, Jax," Andie said. "William stopped at Kat's room. What's for breakfast?"

She spied the Sticky-O's on the counter and helped herself to a bowl. "Mmm...so good...I'm starving." She shoveled in a few more spoonfuls. "Jax!" She put her spoon down and grabbed my shoulders. "No one at home would ever believe this, but *I* spent the night in jail. *Me*—the rule follower!"

"Tell me about it later." I shrugged away from her hands. "I have to get ready for Council."

"Us too. But we got a little time." Cletus took the cereal Elweard had poured him and sat beside Andie. "Don't you wanna know what happened last night?" He spooned some milk from the cereal into the cup of coffee Elweard just served him. He took a sip. "Ahhh. That hits the spot. Besides, you have to tell us how Kat is doin' and we're dying to hear about Rephael."

"Kat's fine. Rephael's fine." I pulled on my socks. I was so angry with him I refused to look at him. But even from the corner of my eye, it would have been hard to miss his confused expression.

Andie was still too wrapped up in her Sticky-O's to notice my bad attitude. "You should have been there. It was like a movie. They locked me in this white room with a table and a spotlight and they questioned me for like, hours."

"What did they ask you?" I crammed my foot in my shoe.

"Believe it or not, they only asked a few questions about us getting the Kaptro Teleportation and the Kaptro Scryor. They kept asking about Loryllia. They were demanding that we tell them what we knew about the Kaptro Enchantment. It was crazy! And they asked what we knew about the attempt on Cletus' mirror. They even did this good cop, bad cop thing. But I was so good. I didn't crack. Not even once! There was no way I was going to let them force me to tell them what they wanted to know."

"Could that possibly be because you don't *know* what they wanted to know?" I asked.

"Well, yeah…but even if I did know what they wanted to know, I wouldn't have squealed." She picked up her bowl and slurped every last drop of the remaining milk.

"Why would they think we knew anything about Loryllia's death? I don't even know what the Kaptro Enchantment does."

"Gives you the ability to plant thoughts," Cletus said. "You can tempt, seduce, and, if the person is weak-minded, you can even mind-control."

I ignored Cletus. "Like I said, what makes them think we know anything about the Kaptro Enchantment?"

"Ahem." Elweard cleared his throat from his stool by the sink where he was cleaning the dishes. "If I may…" I nodded and he continued. "We Pedamples…we hear things—we're not snooping, mind you—we just can't help overhearing things when we work." He tugged at the neck of his shirt. "The latest word is the KIA found evidence. They think someone from the island gone and killed Loryllia. They found denarii at the scene." He nodded his big round head, like we were all in on the secret. "And Wicky swears him and Loryllia didn't have any denarii with them."

"Well, that's ridiculous!" Andie said. "I don't have any denarii. Why would they question me?"

"Because everyone else on the island *does* have it," Cletus said. "Doesn't really narrow it down that much." He stood and reached behind him, grasping his ankle behind his bent knee and stretching his quads. "That explains it though. Couldn't figure out what those agents were after last night." He dropped to the floor and fired off a bunch of sit-ups as he talked. "I already answered all those questions from the KIA the same day I sent you my mirror."

That comment made me sick. "You mean the day you killed my brother."

Everyone stopped dead in their tracks. Elweard stopped clanking the dishes. Andie stopped slurping her milk. Cletus stopped doing crunches. They all stared at me with big horrified eyes.

"That's right." I flung the accusation at Cletus. "You heard me. I know how you created that storm when you used the Tegeris incantation. I know how it made a vortex and shot the lightning bolt into the pool. I know how you—" My voice cracked. I went back to tying my shoe. "I thought you were my friend."

Cletus got on his feet. "Jax, I didn't know that was how your brother died. I promise." His voice was strained and his eyes were sad. "I would never hurt anyone. Especially not you. You *are* my friend. We're brothers." He put his hands on my shoulders. "I didn't know—I'm so sorry—"

I smacked his hands away. "Save it for someone who cares." I grabbed my stuff and stormed out the door. Somewhere deep down, I think I knew Cletus didn't do it on purpose. But it was a relief to take the blame off myself and dump it on him for a while.

I flashed all the way to HQ. I was sitting at the conference table for a good fifteen minutes before anyone else got there. Cletus came in and sat next to me.

"We need to talk," he said, but I ignored him.

Andie sat on the other side of me. Nobody else showed up but Kat and William, and, of course, Galen. He was wearing that ugly tweed suit, and it still had that stupid "Hi, My name is Galen" tag stuck to it. As usual, he was shuffling through his papers.

Caephus entered through the huge door and took his spot at the head of the table. "Together, you have in your possession six of the Kaptrofracti. Since the Kaptropoten was destroyed in 218 BC, there has only been one other time that the fragments have been reunited. You are very close to fulfilling Rephael's plan. It is an incomparable privilege and an awesome responsibility—the task is yours to achieve, or yours to fail."

His blue eyes scanned my face. "It must be said Rephael never lost faith in you, Jackson. Nor have I. It was his hope you would discover your own strength. That you would develop your confidence and embrace who you are—on your own. That on this journey you would find the courage you need to serve the Komitari with honor. We needed to be certain you were ready." He paused. "That is why Katriana was allowed to steal the Conjuration and Elementum mirror." Kat appeared offended at the suggestion she hadn't actually stolen the mirror on her own.

Caephus went on. "I say this before the others because it is up to you, Jackson, to lead them on the final stage of this mission. Melchasaar wants you. You *are* the Ark. And as long as Melchasaar is consumed with destroying you, then he is not focused on the Enchantment and the other mirrors. We can use that to beat him—to get the

Enchantment and reunite the Kaptrofracti. But you must be confident in your powers. You have strength beyond what any of the others could even imagine."

All eyes were pinned on me. I couldn't believe all along Rephael and Caephus still thought I was the Ark. And worse yet, if they *did* think I was the Ark, they were totally willing to use me as bait. I had tried so many times to tell everyone I was not the Ark. I definitely didn't *want* to be the Ark; it was too scary to even consider. And anyway, it just didn't make any sense. I wasn't special. I wasn't brave. I wasn't any sort of a threat, and I certainly never did anything to make Melchasaar mad enough to want revenge. Why would Melchasaar waste his time on me? Nope. They were wrong.

Short of taking out a billboard and plastering it with a close-up of my handsome face along with the words, "HEY! IDIOTS! I AM NOT THE ARK," I didn't know what else to do.

I had come full circle and once again decided it was best to let them think I *was* the Ark. That way I got to be in charge. At my first opportunity, I would stick all those cheery glowing mirror fragments back together, get my brother, grab Andie, and head back to Pennsylvania. Maybe I would try to get us all accepted into the witness protection program. All I would have to do is explain to the government about how I was a superhuman Ark who saved the world from an evil sorcerer by breaking the magical mirror that he stole from the angel who tried to make off with his girlfriend. I'm sure they would happily agree to ship Sebastian, Gram, Andie, and me off to Wisconsin to live undercover as a family of cheese tasters named Smith.

It seemed like everyone was waiting for me to say something.

"Well, Rephael was right about the journey," I announced dramatically. "It worked! What has two thumbs and is definitely the Ark?"

Everyone stared at me dumbly. I made two fists, stuck my thumbs out and jammed them in my chest.

"This guy!" I said. "Who's with me?"

Galen shot a worried glance at Caephus, who just sat there scratching his head. Kat rolled her eyes at me—again—and, if I wanted to, I could have reached out and tugged on the tonsils of Cletus, Andie, and William, who were all slack-jawed.

"Well then." Caephus cleared his throat, trying to regain control of the meeting. "I will start by reminding you of one of the cardinal rules of the Komitari Code. Remember, you must *never* use the Kaptrofracti to advance your own interests. Any such use could have catastrophic effects on the fated course of history. And, of course, the increased activity on the mirrors makes it easier for Melchasaar to track you."

I tried to keep my mind carefully blank. I may have been paranoid, but I was pretty sure this was a warning to me.

"Cletus, you will continue to serve Jackson as his attendant," Caephus said.

"No way," I said. "I'll be just fine on my own. I don't need his help. He's already helped enough."

Cletus couldn't have looked any more sad and dejected. I felt a nagging guilt, which just piled up on top of all my other guilt. I managed to squash down that new guilt the same way I squashed the garbage down in the can when I didn't feel like taking out the trash.

"It is not your decision to make," Caephus said. "You need an experienced attendant. Cletus will accompany you."

I put forth a weak challenge. "What if I refuse?" I almost mumbled it.

Before I even finished the question, every one of my mirrors—from my backpack, my pocket, and the velvet bag—jerked away from my body and flew to Caephus. He flipped a giant hand in the air. With the speed of a blackjack dealer, he caught them and laid them on the table, one by one, each several inches from the other.

"You will *not* refuse."

I knew I had crossed the line. I shrank back in my seat and gulped. *Please tell me I didn't just ruin everything.*

"Yes, sir. I'm sorry. You know what's best. I'll let Cletus come with me." And then I asked, "By the way, where... exactly...are we going?"

Caephus rested his hands on the table. "To Melchasaar, of course. We have summoned Jules and Phlynnis to the island. As soon as they arrive, Galen will review the mission with you. But this is it. It should all be over soon enough."

My heart sunk. I knew all along it would eventually come to this, but I had tried not to think about it. I kept thinking somehow I might just be able to get the mirrors without confronting Melchasaar. I had no idea how I was supposed to take on an evil sorcerer who had been pining away for his girlfriend for the past two thousand years.

"Okay." I was a little desperate. "So, I'm just thinking out loud here." I licked my lips. "Maybe, we could just send him a letter. You know, one that says he just won the Magazine Distributor's Clearinghouse Sweepstakes. And it could say, like, 'All you need to do to claim your prize is mail any Kaptrofracti you might have in this pre-addressed and postage-paid envelope.' And then—let me know if I'm losing you here—we won't really send him any prize money." I stopped when I heard the slapping sound Andie's hand made when she smacked her own forehead. I could tell from the way William shook his head at me that no one else was on board with my plan. "Feel free to brainstorm with me here," I said a lot less enthusiastically.

Fortunately, I was saved when the buzzer by Caephus went off.

"The KIA is here to interview Master Jax and Princess Katriana now." It was Zara's voice and that meant the KIA was right outside the door.

I was super nervous. I knew I hadn't done anything wrong, but I had always had this bad habit of feeling totally guilty anytime someone accused me of something—even when I didn't do it. Like the time in second grade when Hank, the school janitor, blamed me for clogging the first floor girl's toilet by stuffing it with Good-Bye Kitty underpants. I hadn't even worn my Good-Bye Kitty underpants that day, but I almost confessed out of pure guilt anyway.

Caephus seemed annoyed. "Send them in."

The door opened and Red Lips and her crew of uptight agents marched single file through the door.

"Caephus." Red Lips bowed to him, and the other agents followed suit. "Thank you for allowing us a few moments with Master Jackson and the princess. We'll try to make our questions brief as we understand you require their services."

"I presume this line of questioning has merit, Natasha?"

"Of course, sir," she answered in her clipped Russian accent.

Beside me, Andie was glaring at Natasha as if to say, "You want a piece of this?" Instead, she tore her eyes away and said to Caephus, "Excuse me, sir."

"What is it, Andrea?"

"I have an idea. We could end this right now." She looked at me and then back at Caephus. "Can't the Scryor show the past too?"

He nodded, already on board with Andie's plan. He slid the Scryor across the table to me. I had figured out exactly what Andie was thinking, and it was a great idea. If it worked, it would save Kat and me a lot of time and aggravation. And it could lead us to the traitor. I raised the mirror in front of my face.

"What is the meaning of this?" Red Lips demanded.

"Show me Loryllia's death," I said. The mirror glowed purple. In unison, five chairs scraped the ground as

Cletus, Andie, Kat, William, and Galen pushed away from the table and ran to look over my shoulder. The smoky, purple fog began swirling in the mirror. Everyone behind me jostled for a better view as the Scryor came into focus.

When the fog cleared, the mirror showed an ultra-modern kitchen with sleek steel countertops and shiny red cabinets. Seated at the counter was a woman, probably about twenty-one. She was pretty, with shoulder-length brown hair, black eyes, and a cute turned-up nose. Aside from her funky sci-fi-inspired wardrobe, she looked very much like she could have been from Earth. She read a holographic version of a newspaper and drank from a metal coffee cup. The space behind Loryllia fell into the shadows, and I could feel the tension building behind me as we all prepared to witness the inevitable tragedy.

Suddenly, there was a glint of silver above Loryllia's head. We could sense rather than hear the thump that occurred as that unknown object was smashed on Loryllia's head. Her body slumped over the counter. The Scryor panned out like a movie camera. The suspense built while we waited to get a look at the attacker. As the view broadened, we could see at first two muscular arms tossing a silver vase to the side. The arms then reached around Loryllia and lifted a pink velvet bag—similar to mine—over her head. It was strange how gentle the attacker was with Loryllia. The light brown leather vest covering the culprit's chest came into view.

I became really uneasy, really fast. Then, we could

make out a familiar chin, followed by a long, thin face. The only thing missing was the characteristic grin. I went numb. It was Cletus!

CHAPTER 23
A Failed Alibi, a Storm in the Sky, a Girl or a Guy?

I couldn't believe it. I felt sick as I watched Cletus open the velvet bag and dump the pink glowing mirror into his hand. He examined it, stuck it back in the bag, and then picked up the vase to rub off his fingerprints. He never noticed the handful of denarii that fell from his pocket and landed on the floor. After returning the vase to its pedestal, he gave the room one last check and sneaked out the window.

The Scryor slipped from my fingers and fell on my lap.

I couldn't even look at Cletus. If I hadn't seen it with my own eyes, I would never have imagined it could be true. An aching knot lodged itself in my throat and it hurt. It hurt so bad I thought I might choke on it. I trusted him—like a brother. How could I have been so stupid? First came the news about Sebastian, and then this. It was the ultimate betrayal—to me, to Stirling, to my mother, to Rephael, and to anyone who sacrificed everything to protect the Kaptropoten. That guilt I had squashed down in the garbage can for making Cletus feel bad…well, now I spat on it! I threw a whole cup full of dirty coffee grinds on it! And then I topped it off with a smelly bowl of tuna fish!—Plus rotten, squishy cucumbers from the bottom of the vegetable drawer! No guilt anymore!

Everyone else was looking at Cletus, their faces a mixture of shock and disgust.

"No!" Cletus said. "I—I—I didn't do it!" At the same time, one of the KIA agents shot him with the claw gun again.

"You're under arrest!" Red Lips barked. "Where is the mirror?"

"I don't have it!"

Caephus shook his head. His eyes were clouded with pain. "Take him away."

"Jax, you have to believe me!" Cletus struggled and fought against the cables, this time seeming oblivious to the shocks. "I didn't do it! Get Yancy!" he called as they dragged him out the door. "I was with him when Loryllia died! He'll tell you!"

Just before the double doors slammed shut, the Kaptro Teleportation whizzed past me. Caephus had summoned it from Cletus the same way he had confiscated mine. The doors closed and it was silent except for Andie's sobs.

"I'm sorry." Her eyes glistened with tears. "I thought it would help."

"You did the right thing," Kat said. "Cletus was lying to us all this time. What a spineless snake! The truth needed to come out."

Galen, who hadn't said a word, stood in front of his briefcase. He stared at his pile of papers, but there was none of the usual shuffling. His face was white. He sank into his chair.

Caephus put the Teleportation mirror on the table with the others. Without another word, he left the room.

I looked down at the Scryor in my lap. Shockingly, it hadn't gone blank yet! It still showed Loryllia's body crumpled over the counter. Suddenly, she started to move! Her hand found the spot on the back of her head where Cletus had struck her.

"Wait! There's more!" I called.

Andie, Kat, William, and Galen rushed back to watch.

Loryllia was dazed. She pushed herself away from the countertop and turned to scan the room. Her face froze. Standing directly in front of her was Draemoch! Draemoch confronted Loryllia, saying something that we could not hear—unfortunately, the Scryor didn't have sound.

"Why is Draemoch there?" William asked.

"Shhh!" Kat said.

Loryllia reached for her velvet bag. She appeared desperate when she realized it was missing. She pleaded with Draemoch, who became more and more aggressive as he closed in on her. Finally, Loryllia's mouth opened in an unheard scream. Draemoch drew his sword. The Scryor went blank, sparing us the gruesome details of Draemoch's final blow.

"I don't get it," Andie said. "If Cletus was working for Melchasaar, why was Draemoch there? Obviously he didn't know the Kaptro Enchantment was already missing."

William said what we all hoped. "Maybe Cletus knew Draemoch was coming. Maybe he was trying to protect Loryllia and keep the mirror safe."

"That doesn't make sense." It was Galen's nasal voice. "If that was the case then why wouldn't he tell Loryllia she was in danger? He may not have killed her, but that blow to her head very well *could* have. And why would he so blatantly lie about it, insisting he didn't do it after we all watched him steal the mirror? He may not be working with Melchasaar, but if he's not, he has some other agenda."

"Galen is right," Kat said. "Cletus stole that mirror, and because of his actions Loryllia is dead."

"But why? Why would he possibly do such a thing?" I asked. I was so shaken by this news. I was desperate for a reason to believe Cletus. "We need to find Yancy. I want to know the truth."

"What truth?" Kat asked. "The Scryor never lies. It is never wrong in what it shows or predicts. Face it. Cletus deceived us all."

I had to find out for myself. I snatched the remaining three mirrors from the table and charged out the door, flashing to the elevator. When the doors parted, I couldn't have been more relieved to see Yancy and Hobart inside.

"Yancy!" I said. "Thank goodness you're here."

"We came as soon as Zara called us." Yancy pushed past me. "Where's Cletus?"

"Zara called you?" I asked.

"Yeah. Told me I was gonna have to step in as your

attendant. She said somethin' bad happened to Cletus. Where is he?" He stretched his neck to search the room behind me.

"The KIA took him. We saw him attack Loryllia in the Scryor. And he stole the Kaptro Enchantment." I watched Yancy to see his reaction. In fact, I watched him get right in my face. He grabbed a chunk of my shirt in his fist, jamming it up under my chin.

"Take it back! Cletus is no killer."

"Okay, okay," I said. "Relax for a minute. That's why we need you." He released my shirt. "Cletus says you two were together when Loryllia died." Everyone else, including Galen, gathered in the lobby to hear Yancy's answer.

"All right, let me think…" Yancy looked up, stroking his lower lip with his thumb. "I remember hearin' about Loryllia's death…" He thought awhile longer. "Ah, that's right. I remember exactly where I was. The day Loryllia died, I would have been visitin' with my Aunt Doris back home. Can't say I recall where Cletus—" he cut himself off, realizing he had just failed to give Cletus the alibi he needed.

Galen's shoulders slumped even more than usual. On his way back to the boardroom, he brushed against me and pressed a note into my hand. He waited there until I looked up at him.

"Jackson. Be careful." His warning was super sincere and not like him at all. He walked off and pulled the double doors closed behind him.

My thoughts were too scattered to give the paper

much thought. I crumpled it up and stuffed it in my pocket.

"Jax." Andie touched my arm. "Cletus did save your life in the lagoon. And mine too—with the Gorgs. And he saved Yancy. He's a good person. There had to be a reason for him to turn like that."

"What reason?" I asked. "What possible reason could there be for betraying your friends and your family? For putting the entire world at risk?"

"People are motivated by all sorts of things," Kat said. "Greed, fame, money. Perhaps he was bitter about losing the Elementum or being forced to serve as an attendant."

"Kat has a point." William sounded like he was trying to convince himself more than us.

"Cletus *was* a wreck when he lost his mirror…" Yancy ran his fingers through his hair. "I don't know—maybe he cracked. I take responsibility. If he didn't have to save me, it wouldn't have ever happened. I should have seen this comin'. I should have been there for him." He sank down on the leather bench and buried his face in his hands.

"All right. Enough of this," Kat said. "We have to find that mirror. We should start with the KIA and find out what they have discovered. With any luck, Cletus has already told them what he has done with the Enchantment."

"You're right." I was just going to have to accept that Cletus was a traitor. Even though I was mad at him, my heart was having a hard time accepting what my eyes had seen in the Scryor. I sighed. "Let's just get it done."

"Look," Andie said. "Maybe I'm making this too easy, but why don't we use the Kaptro Scryor to find where Cletus is keeping—?"

"I do not think that would work," Kat said. She looked at her watch. "We are wasting time here. We need to focus on finding the Enchantment."

"I agree with Kat," Yancy said. "Let's just get goin'. Once you guys get the Enchantment, I can focus on freein' Cletus."

"That's dumb," I said, and Kat sent me a disgusted look. "We could save a ton of time if it does work. The Scryor shows things you can't see, and we can't see the Kaptro Enchantment." I went ahead and pulled out the Scryor. "I wish to see the hiding place of the Kaptro Enchantment."

There was the burst of purple and the swirling fog. As soon as the fog cleared, a fancy bedside table, just like the one in my hotel suite, came into focus. That was it. There was nothing else.

"Pan out," I told the mirror, but it didn't listen.

"Mm-hmm," Kat said arrogantly. "I told you it would not work."

"What do you mean?" I asked. "It did work. Don't all the rooms have the same furniture? It's pretty clear Cletus has it in his nightstand at the hotel. Let's go."

"There's no need for us all to go!" Kat said.

Talk about being edgy! I suspected she was as nervous as I was about finally getting her chance to reunite the entire mirror and fight Melchasaar. I guess I couldn't blame her. After all, we were just a bunch of kids. It was another one of those rare times where Kat seemed just like the rest of us.

She inhaled and blew it out. "William. Andie. You two head to Cletus' room and see what you can turn up. Yancy and Jax. You two come with me to the KIA." She strode to the stairwell and flashed down the steps.

I shrugged. I didn't agree with the plan, but, apparently, that didn't matter. I was just about to follow Kat down the stairs when, as an afterthought, I took the remaining single-use Kaptrofracti from my backpack. I still hadn't used the mini Enchantment, the mini Elementum, or the mini Conjuration.

Yancy interrupted my thoughts. "Don't let me hold you up, 'cause I'll be takin' the elevator. You comin', Hobs?"

I had almost forgotten Hobart was even there. He never said a word, but I could tell he was taking in every detail. It was creepy the way he just listened to everything everyone else said without ever saying anything himself.

"Here, Andie." I handed her the three mirrors.

She took them and tilted her head. "What are these for?"

"Use them if you need them. Just in case anything happens."

"What's going to happen? We're just checking out Cletus' room."

"You're probably right," I said, "but what if Draemoch is on the trail of the Enchantment? Just be careful."

"Draemoch can't get on the island," William said. "But don't worry. We'll be careful."

The elevator doors closed on the three of them, and I zipped down the stairs. I expected to meet Kat at the bottom, but she wasn't there yet. It was overcast and the air was nippy. I jammed my hands in my pockets. *What's this?* I pulled out the crumpled-up note from Galen. After smoothing out the wrinkles, I read:

> Jackson,
> Perhaps now would be a good time to inform you of a very important caveat regarding the Kaptropoten and the power of Reanimation (you would already have learned this had you not bombed your orientation, but let's not dwell on the past).

Man! Everyone just needed to quit busting my chops about that! I read on:

> Above all else, the Kaptropoten seeks to maintain the balance of nature. When one life is restored, another life must be sacrificed. The Kaptropoten chooses the life.
> G-

What? I flipped the note over. Surely there was more to it than that! What the heck was that supposed to mean? My cheeks burned hot. I scanned the area to see if anyone was watching me. Why would he even tell me that? My heart raced. Did he realize I was planning to bring Sebastian back? My conscience couldn't handle worrying about yet another life. I had enough to worry about with Sebastian, and I *had* to resurrect Sebastian. It was the only way to escape the grief and guilt I carried.

I grabbed my gold velvet bag and made a wish. Whoosh! The small slip burst into flames and burnt itself out in an instant. The ashes were swept away by a gust of wind.

Kat approached through the wave of floating ashes. She swatted at them like they were fleas. "Sorry about that. I had to use the restroom."

"No problem," I said. The others had just exited HQ, and I watched as Andie and William headed off toward the hotel. Yancy and Hobart caught up with us, and Kat set off in the direction of the K-Coaster.

"I would have expected the KIA office to be in HQ," I said.

"It is," Yancy answered, "but prisoners are held at the penitentiary—outside of town."

We walked at a pretty fast clip. It started to drizzle, and the sky changed from gray to almost black. I shivered against the chill.

"It looks like it might storm," I said. This weather was making me uneasy. The morning had been emotional enough. I wasn't sure I could handle another lightning storm.

Just then, Kat stopped short. "Oh no!" She looked at her hand. "My ring! It's missing! It must have come off when I washed my hands in the restroom."

"Don't sweat it," Yancy said. "I'll just have Hobs

go back and get it for you. Hobs won't mind, will you, Hobs?"

"I guess not," Hobart grumbled and sauntered off. His lanky limbs made me think of a daddy longlegs spider. He definitely creeped me out.

Yancy grinned. "That's one of the best parts of havin' an attendant."

Kat led us into town and past the sweets shop. The streets were empty today—nobody was out, and it was spooky. The wind howled as it raced down the street and between the buildings. The sign hanging from the IOM Book Repository creaked on its post. Dark clouds devoured every last bit of sunshine, snuffing out any hint of warmth. It was dark enough now to be nighttime.

Eventually, Kat turned between two buildings and followed an overgrown path into the woods.

"Uh...Are you sure this is the way?"

"Yeah. It's pretty isolated," Yancy answered. "They don't want anyone to escape."

It made sense, but it didn't make me any less nervous. I was tempted to use the Elementum to clear up the weather, but Caephus' warning was fresh in my ears.

Soon enough, we were deep into the forest. The eerie stillness of the woods added to the tension. I could barely see three feet in front of my face. Where was super vision when you needed it?

Suddenly, there was the loud snap of a branch. I jumped off the path with a second to spare. A huge, shadowy figure thundered across my path. It trampled the brush in front of me.

"BBBBARRRRUMPH!" It was only an elephant, but no one had told my blood pressure that. I wondered if it would be okay to use my mirror to conjure up a couple of those paddles they use on TV when they want to restart your heart. My sixth sense screamed something bad was about to happen.

"Are we almost there yet?" I asked.

"Yeah. Just a little farther," Yancy said.

As we picked our way through the dark, dense undergrowth, I fell further and further behind Kat and Yancy. It was deathly quiet except for my own ragged breaths and the distant rumble of thunder. The trees seemed to come alive. Their limbs bent threateningly toward me. They clawed at my skin, slowing me down. I ran, trying to escape the evil clutches of the forest, but I couldn't outrun the feeling I was being chased. Fearful of the unseen, I flashed and ran smack into the back of Yancy. The two of us tumbled out of the woods and into a clearing.

I stood and tugged Yancy to his feet. I hadn't realized how much the cover of the trees had shielded us from the cold, blustery winds. But here, without the shelter of their leaves, it was miserable.

Inside the circular clearing, there was just enough light to see Kat. The violent gusts tore at her hair, picking her braid apart. Strangely, it seemed to energize her. She threw out her arms, threw her head back, and spun in a circle.

I, on the other hand, was totally over this. Just then, the sky was illuminated as somewhere far away lightning traveled from cloud to cloud. That was it—I was ready to get the heck out of these woods.

"Come on, Kat," I called over the wailing of the wind. "It's too dark, and it's about to storm. Let's go see what Andie and William found out. We can come back here when the weather clears up." I didn't think there was any chance Kat would agree. I was fully prepared to break Caephus' rule and use the Teleportation mirror to pop on back to the safety of my room.

Kat stopped her whirling. "Sure. We can do that." She was strangely calm. "Just let me show you something. It will make you feel much better. It might even make you want to stay."

I glanced at the dark woods bordering the clearing. "I don't know…"

"Do you trust me?" Even in the dim light, her smile was radiant.

"Yes." I was embarrassed by how easily she could manipulate me.

"Let me see your mirrors." She put her hand out.

"My mirrors?" I blinked.

"You do trust me, right?"

"Yeah…Of course." I knew it wasn't a good idea. But for some reason I really wanted to please Kat—even more than usual. Against my better judgment, I took each of the four mirrors from their different locations. Stupidly, I had forgotten to keep them separated. Instantly, they all rose a few inches from my hand, levitating there momentarily.

"Oh, shoot!" I cried, but it was too late. They each

began to spin and whir like a swarm of very agitated locusts. They spun faster and whirred louder, glowing so brightly they illuminated the entire clearing. At once, they slammed together sparking an explosion that lit the sky with bursts of green, amber, blue, purple, and orange. A rush of air streamed out of the mirror and threw me back, hurtling me into a tree trunk. The blow knocked the wind out of me. I sat stunned and in pain, trying to catch my breath.

The newly formed, multi-colored mirror stopped spinning and dropped softly on the bed of rotting leaves and twigs. Kat ran to the mirror and snatched it from the ground. She dropped it, recoiling when it burned her hands. I peeled myself off the tree and joined her.

"You have to let it cool." I rubbed my lower back and glanced around the clearing. "Where's Yancy?" I hadn't noticed 'til now that he was gone.

Kat didn't give it a thought. "I do not know. Maybe he was afraid."

She stooped to study the mirror. "Amazing," she whispered. "It's seamless. Like the parts were never separated." She stared for a few more moments. "I suppose it needs this too." She pulled the red glowing Kaptro Metamorphus from the leather pack on her back.

For the life of me, I couldn't figure out why Kat would want to reunite six of the seven pieces of the Kaptropoten. Particularly when we knew they couldn't be separated again until the mirror was reunited in its entirety. This didn't feel right at all. The only comfort I had was the knowledge that no one could get on the island without an Ostium. In the meantime, the storm was getting closer.

I backed away, not wanting to be too close when Kat placed the Metamorphus beside the new mirror. But instead of reuniting the Metamorphus with the others, she set it on the ground several inches away from the larger mirror. She laughed a tinkling, giddy laugh. What the heck was she up to?

Kat opened the smaller satchel, which was slung across her chest. I was completely unprepared for what happened next. Kat, wearing a triumphant, self-satisfied smile, pulled out the pink glowing Kaptro Enchantment!

"H-h-how did y-you get that?" I was 100 percent confused. Kat took the Metamorphus in her other hand and stood. She looked at me, the corners of her mouth still pulled in that smirk. Then, before my eyes, the outline of her form began to wave and twist and pull. Suddenly, her body snapped into the exact likeness of Cletus.

CHAPTER 24
A Whole Bunch of Bad Guys

I had no idea what was going on. "Cletus?" I asked.

"Of course not," Cletus said as his outline snapped back into Kat. She laughed again, but there was no humor in her eyes.

"What's going on?" I was too astonished to move. But as soon as my initial shock faded, it became clear what had happened. "It was you!" I accused. "You transformed into Cletus and attacked Loryllia! You stole the mirror!" I clasped my head in my hands, unable to figure out why Kat would have done such a thing. "It was *your* nightstand we saw in the Scryor!" And then it dawned on me. "Cletus was telling the truth!" The thought was devastating. I hadn't believed him. He must have felt so alone.

Kat didn't answer. As if in a trance, she glided toward the newly formed five-mirror Kaptrofracti. She stood poised above it, holding out the Metamorphus and Enchantment as an offering to the larger mirror.

"Kat!" I yelled, and she hesitated. "We aren't supposed to join the fragments until we are ready to kill Melchasaar." Of course, I didn't let on I had planned to join them just a few minutes before we battled

Melchasaar, bring Sebastian back, and then get as far away from here as possible.

Kat turned her attention back to the larger mirror. She bent, setting the Metamorphus and Enchantment beside it. Once again the pieces levitated and spun, joining in a clash so colossal that both Kat and I were blasted outward and into the woods. A brilliant rainbow of light stretched to the sky. My immediate concern was everyone would notice it and find out what we had done. I was the first to recover. I stumbled back into the clearing, approaching the Kaptropoten. My instinct was to cover the mirror and disguise its glow.

Kat saw me move toward the magic mirror. She got up and flashed to it before I could get there. She tried to seize it. Again, she had forgotten about its heat, and she cried out when the burning mirror singed her skin.

I was certain I needed to get the mirror before Kat did. I wasn't sure what she was planning, but if she was capable of attacking Loryllia and framing Cletus for it, who knew what else she might do?

I stuck my toe on the edge of the mirror. The smell of melting rubber from the sole of my shoe filled the clearing.

I need a bucket of icy water, I wished. The Kaptropoten flashed amber. There was a small burst of air, and a cold, metal pail appeared in my hands. I doused the Kaptropoten. When the icy water made contact, it hissed. Steam escaped from the surface. I grabbed the mirror and backed away from Kat. She stalked me, primed to attack.

"Why are you doing this?" I asked.

"I told you before." Her voice was strangely calm against the backdrop of the swirling winds and rolling thunder. "I will do whatever it takes to save my family." She circled, and I backed away slowly, keeping her in my sights at all times.

"Come on," she said. "You know you want to use the Kaptropoten. You know you want to bring your brother back."

The hairs stood up on my arms. It was all true.

"Go ahead." Her soft voice continued to woo me. "All it takes is one…little…wish."

I thought about how easy it would be. This was exactly what I dreamed of from the moment Sebastian died. And yet Caephus' warning played out in my mind, and so did Rephael's caution about having pure motives, and, finally, there was Galen's note about a life being taken.

Just do it! a voice inside my head interrupted. *This is your chance to make everything right.*

I thought of Gram, Grandpap, and Mom. I wasn't sure what they would do, but I wanted to make them proud. Suddenly, it seemed wrong. Was I being selfish? Who was I to decide Sebastian deserved to live and someone else didn't? But then, if I didn't resurrect him I wasn't sure I could live with this suffocating guilt.

"Come on," Kat said. "Do it."

My brain hurt. I wished I had a moment to think about it, but I was alerted to a new sensation. The hairs on the back of my neck joined the ones on my arms, all standing at attention, and I realized we weren't alone anymore. Shadowy figures stepped into the clearing on all sides. I clutched the Kaptropoten against my chest, recognizing it was probably my only protection.

"Greetings," Kat welcomed the newcomers. "I am pleased to see Yancy was able to open the Propius Portal."

"Yancy?" I said it out loud. Cletus' own cousin was a part of this?

Slowly, the ugly and evil faces of Melchasaar's supporters came into view as they moved nearer to Kat. I almost dropped the Kaptropoten when Melchasaar floated into the clearing. He was more terrifying in person than he was in my dreams. I remembered the icy paralysis that had overtaken me in the Four Circles. My knees went weak.

"Princess Katriana," Melchasaar hissed, acknowledging Kat.

"Hello, Melchasaar," Kat said, unable to disguise the distaste in her voice. "Where is he?" Her eyes scanned the group that had come with the sorcerer.

"Patience, my dear Katriana," he drawled.

"No! I have followed through on my end of the bargain. I have delivered the Kaptropoten," she said. "AND the Ark. Just like I promised."

It wasn't possible! *No! No! No!* I wanted to scream. She wouldn't have done this!

Bile rose from my stomach, and I gagged on it. I doubled over and wretched, throwing up right there in front of Melchasaar and all of his goons. They broke into cheers, cackling and screeching their laughter.

"Look at the mighty Ark," one of the women called from the edge of the forest. She bent over, mocking me by gagging and dry-heaving over her shoe. She led the others in a chorus of maniacal laughter.

Humiliated, I stood and wiped my mouth on my sleeve. None of this made any sense. If I was the Ark, then why didn't Melchasaar kill me as soon as he saw me in the Four Circles? I was so grateful for the security of the Kaptropoten.

Suddenly, I became aware of a dull pain somewhere behind my heart. Melchasaar's white eyes were pinned on my chest, and it felt like they were ripping through it, past my heart, and right into my soul. I could feel my soul being penetrated by his evil lust. He sized it up like a prized trophy. Instinctively, I crossed my arms, creating a mock shield against his greedy, laser-like scrutiny.

I assessed my situation in seconds. I was outnumbered by at least twenty. Somewhere in the back of my head, a voice whispered to me, "Stay and fight. For once, be brave. You have to defeat Melchasaar." But who was I to take on all of these bad guys, one of whom was thought to be the most powerful sorcerer of all time? I had no choice but to teleport out of there.

I held the Kaptropoten in front of my face. Just as I was about to wish myself out of the clearing, a desperate voice from the woods screamed, "Jax! Where are you?"

It was Andie. I spun to warn her and that brief second of distraction cost me greatly. The Kaptropoten was snatched from my grasp. Kat had used the opportunity to flash and steal the magic mirror right out of my hands. I was left alone and defenseless in the center of the clearing.

Three of Melchasaar's soldiers disappeared into the woods at the sound of Andie's voice. Two of them burst back into the clearing, pushing in front of them a feisty and kicking Andie. On their heels was the third soldier who had captured William.

"Andie!" I shouted. "How did you find us? You shouldn't have come!"

"We saw the beam of light! We had to come! It's Kat, Jax!" Her eyes shot arrows at Kat. "She used the Kaptro Enchantment on me at the carnival! She had it all along! That witch made me play Skeeball!" At that, she aimed a vicious heel at the shin of her captor. He snarled, and shoved her away from him. Andie stumbled to the center of the clearing. She captured me in a brief hug.

In the meantime, Kat seemed furious. "William! Why did you follow us? I told you to stay away—to keep her busy at the hotel! How do you expect—"

"You never told me you attacked Loryllia!" William said. The wind almost swallowed his pained words. His face twisted. "You only told me you planned to ransom the Kaptropoten for father. And you know I didn't approve of that! You know I didn't approve of you dragging everyone else into this!" He threw his arms wide. "Look what you've done, Kat! When will it end? How far will you go?" His voice finally broke, and he was shoved into the center of the circle with Andie and me.

Kat had the decency to cast her eyes down. "I—I—I will not stop until I have saved my family!" She spun and faced Melchasaar, holding up the Kaptropoten as a threat. "Where is my father?" she demanded.

Melchasaar ripped his eyes from my chest and the pain disappeared instantly. He raised his arm, snapping twice. At his signal, the brush rustled and a tall, very proud-looking man was led out of the woods. He was thin, like he hadn't eaten in weeks. His face was battered and bruised, but still very handsome. His left hand was wrapped in a dirty, blood-stained bandage. Despite the poor condition of his health, he carried himself regally. This had to be Kat's father, the king. He was handed over to Melchasaar, who forced him to his knees. Behind him, limping out of the forest, was the general who had brought him. It was none other than Draemoch, and he clearly had not yet recovered from his burns.

"Father!" Kat said. "Are you all right?"

"I am fine, Kitty Kat." His words were brave, but his voice was weak.

Draemoch sneered at me, his eyes assessing my height, weight, and features. "*This* kid? This *coward* is the Ark? This *boy* who ran from me like the coward he is? Surely, my lord, you can destroy this child with ease."

"Well, YOU couldn't!" Andie said before I could shush her.

Draemoch ignored Andie. He turned to Kat. "You're looking quite well, Princess."

Kat rubbed the spot where Draemoch's sword had cut her. "Why did you send Draemoch to find the Kaptrofracti, Melchasaar? Didn't you trust me?"

"Draemoch was merely my insurance policy," Melchasaar said. "In case you decided to deceive me.

First, turn over the Kaptropoten, and I will release your father."

"Do you think I am a fool?" Kat asked. "You will get the Kaptropoten once I am sure my father is safe."

Melchasaar's thugs began cackling again, finding humor in Kat's demands.

Melchasaar sneered. "How precious—you think you have a choice. I do not negotiate." He held his hand above the king's head. "However, I am certain I can… convince you…to change your mind."

His fingers curled, his hand hovering there. The king's body began to shake and convulse. Kat was stunned for a moment, but I remembered the documentary from the History Channel. He was getting ready to do an Adficio Animus, the soul-sucking Double A. I was terrified, but I reacted before I had a chance to think. I charged at Melchasaar with full speed. Luckily, he hadn't been paying attention to me. I took him off guard, and the impact of my collision knocked him backwards. He flew about ten feet, colliding with the ugly female who had mocked me. The sorcerer was dazed and for now, at least, out of commission. The king collapsed on the ground. William rushed to his father, sheltering his body with his own.

Realizing she had lost control of the situation, Kat sprung to action. At the same time, Melchasaar's supporters attacked. Kat held the mirror. A rainbow of light burst from the mirror as Kat created a mini explosion. It took out three of the soldiers. I turned just in time to avoid being attacked by six of the others who ran up behind me. I leaped into the air, flipping over their heads and landing in front of an extremely large and barbaric-looking man wearing a spiked mask. He swayed his mace like a pendulum as he eyed me.

I didn't have time to dance around with this guy. I mean, there were six more right behind me! And then there was Draemoch, who for now stayed out of the battle. He seemed content to let us wear ourselves out fighting off all the other soldiers.

I jumped high and leaned to the side, swinging my left leg in a wide arc. I landed a hard kick right in his chest before he even swung his mace. He toppled like a tower of blocks. I rather surprised myself with this very polished-looking fight move. I was rewarded with a rush of adrenaline and the slightest bit of optimism that I might possibly make it out of here alive.

"Did you see that?" I asked, hoping Andie had noticed my newly acquired fight skill. And then I realized I must have been halfway delusional because, right now, nobody here—including me—cared how cool I looked while karate kicking a super goon. Five of the six soldiers I jumped over were coming at me again. This time their swords and knives were drawn. The sixth guy grabbed Andie. She shouted and punched and fought like heck to sink her teeth into him. He held her captive with one arm and then grabbed a fistful of her hair, snapping her head back so she couldn't bite him. I flashed, and, like a bowling ball, crashed right through the middle of the line of five and around the back of Andie's attacker. My well-aimed strike between his shoulders took him by surprise and laid him flat. Andie scrambled out of the way and huddled on the ground beside William and the king.

Big, fat drops of rain began to pelt my head and my shoulders. The thunder and lightning were more persistent, signaling the storm was getting closer. I felt the same anxiety that had crippled me since that night at the pool. It grew stronger and threatened to douse the blessed adrenaline that had just started to energize me.

William, who had waited until his father regained consciousness, drew his sword and jumped into the battle. His ability to swing a sword was almost as impressive as my new karate move. He had already taken out two of the soldiers and was battling a third.

Kat continued to use the Kaptropoten. One blast after another exploded from the mirror as Kat trounced each thug who challenged her.

There were only three goons left, one of whom was engaged in a sword fight with William. Another stalked Kat, trying to avoid the fate of the rest of the soldiers who had crossed her. He only lasted a second before she blasted him. The third circled me, mapping out his best line of attack.

I tried not to lose my focus when I heard Kat confront Draemoch. "You will NEVER hurt my family again!"

I had to look. Draemoch had bared his ugly, yellow teeth in a sneer. He strolled toward Kat. "I am looking forward to finishing our encounter without the interference of your cowardly friend."

"It is *I* who will finish our encounter! I will most certainly use the Kaptropoten to finish you off. But not

until you suffer like you have made my father suffer!"
Kat held the mirror in front of her. There was a brilliant
glow of golden light as the Kaptro Conjuration was
called to action. POOF! A knife, exactly like the one
Draemoch had used to kill Stirling appeared in Kat's
hand. Instantly, there was another burst of color from
the mirror—this time orange—and the knife began to
float toward Draemoch as Kat used the Kinesis to control
its movement.

The battle being waged between the two of them was
completely distracting. I kept sneaking a glance, and it
took every ounce of my concentration not to lose sight
of my attacker. I weaved and bobbed, trying to avoid
his sword, which slashed at the air around me. The soldier, who wore a thick metal helmet with holes where
spiked pieces of his long black Mohawk stuck through,
improved his aim with each strike. The distraction cost
me when his sword found my shoulder. It was just a nick,
but I knew I had to end it with this guy. Fortunately, this
time, it was Mohawk guy who was distracted by the clash
of metal. His eyes shot toward Draemoch and when
they did, my kick struck his wrist, causing him to drop
his sword. I rushed at him, dropped my shoulder, and
hoisted him in the air above my head. I spun and spun,
and finally, hurled him several feet across the clearing.
He landed on the pile of goons who had already been
defeated by Kat.

I turned to watch Draemoch, who had drawn his
sword. He was actually fighting the unmanned knife,
which stabbed and thrust as though it were being held

by the most skillful of warriors. He screamed as the blade, controlled by the Kaptropoten, fulfilled its mission and severed the ring finger from his left hand. Kat cried out in triumph, but Draemoch didn't waste any time nursing his mangled hand. He came at Kat, his teeth bared and his black eyes full of fire.

Suddenly, a rainbow-colored explosion burst from the Kaptropoten. It knocked Draemoch out cold. Kat stomped over to his motionless body, pausing along the way to kick mud on the dismembered finger. When she reached Draemoch, she drew back her leg and kicked him in the ribs. She stood over him, nudging his forehead with the toe of her boot. When his head flopped to the side, she spit on him.

In the meantime, no one had noticed that Melchasaar had regained his senses.

Andie shouted, "Jax! Behind you!"

I spun just as a golden flame erupted from Melchasaar's hand. It hit me in the gut like a cannon ball. I crumpled in on myself, clutching at my stomach and unable to speak. Melchasaar floated toward me, gliding like he was on wheels. His white eyes burned a demonic red. I wanted to run, but my ribs felt like they were cracked in a hundred places. Each time I tried to inhale, intense pain shot through my side.

William, who had finally taken out the general he was fighting, rushed to help me. His sword was drawn in front of him. Melchasaar spared him no concern. He swept his arm through the air, freezing William in place—like a statue!

Somewhere, someone moaned, low and deep. It took a second for me to realize the moans were actually my own. I dragged myself upright, pushing through the agonizing pain. I directed a sloppy, poorly aimed kick at Melchasaar. He avoided the strike and slammed me with another fiery blast from his palm, knocking me flat on my face. I clawed my way to my feet, spitting out the blood that oozed from the gash in my lip. I tried again to fight, this time using all of my energy to throw a weak punch. I missed, and Melchasaar stole the opportunity to grab my extended arm. He squeezed effortlessly, just like he had in the Four Circles. I could feel the skin on my arm blistering from the extreme cold of his grip. He suspended his other hand above my head. Andie's screams were carried away by the wind, and the king now held her back from running to help me.

I was so frightened. My only hope was for Kat to come to my rescue with the Kaptropoten, but I could no longer see where she was. As if I wasn't panicked enough, a blinding flash of light preceded a crackle of electricity as a bolt of lightning struck the floor of the clearing. The noise exploded like a shotgun. My body tingled. I was close enough for the electrical current to make the hairs stand up all over my body. All I could think of was Sebastian. I wanted to surrender—to give up. I felt helpless to save myself, much less defeat Melchasaar. I was no threat to him. I was no hero. The faces of Gram, Mom, and Grandpap floated before my eyes, but there was nothing any of them could do to help me.

Melchasaar forced me to my knees. I couldn't help the

weak, "Please," that escaped from my mouth. It seemed to amuse Melchasaar that I might beg for my life.

He laughed his evil, humorless laugh. "*This* is the best Rephael can do? *This* is his army? A Normal, a pathetic attendant, a traitor, and then *this*?" he asked, referring to Andie, William, Kat, and me. "This boy is the Ark? This boy is the mighty son of the wench Rephael sent to *kill my Salome?*"

What the heck was he saying? "Salome…is in…the…mirror," I choked out.

Melchasaar bared his teeth. His grip tightened around my forearm. I heard the snapping of bone before I felt the searing pain.

"Please!"

He seemed to get energy from my cowardice. His hand still hovered above my head, but he hadn't started the soul sucking yet. He released my broken arm and snapped his fingers again. This time, one of his supporters emerged from the woods carrying the delicate sleeping body of the enchantress herself.

King William had recovered enough to speak. "What are you up to Melchasaar?"

Melchasaar ignored the king. "You are nothing more than a weak, spineless coward. Bow before me!" he said, just as another lightning bolt struck the earth. He withdrew his other hand from above my head. His cold bony fingers seized my hand. He then produced a small knife with a shiny mirrored hilt and a sparkling glass blade. It actually glowed.

The king gasped when he saw the knife. He lurched

forward, but his weak knees didn't support his weight. "He has the Vassica!" he called in desperation to anyone who could hear. "Melchasaar, what use have you for the Vassica? Salome's blood runs not through his veins! You need the blood of a trapped soul's descendant to open the Chamber of Souls in the mirror. This boy is useless to you!"

Melchasaar looked at the king and smiled a slow, wicked smile. Then, with the precision of a surgeon, he cut into my palm with the Vassica. I screamed as he meticulously carved my flesh, making a symbol just like the one inscribed on the Kaptropoten. My blood stained the symbol a bright red.

"Your warm blood, young Ark, is all I require to release Salome from the mirror. And once she is freed, you will die, and I will make your mother watch."

"M-my mother?" I asked weakly. I couldn't believe what I was hearing. "Y-you have…my m-mother?"

"Patience, boy. I will have what I need of her soon enough." He looked around the clearing. "Bring the mirror to me! I will be unstoppable!" His eyes returned to mine. "Bow to me!" I remembered him roaring the same words at Rephael.

And then I remembered Rephael staying proud and strong in spite of everything. I remembered Cletus sacrificing everything to save his cousin. I thought of Andie trying to rescue me in the field behind the carnival when she saw me on the Ostium cloth, and then again today when she came to warn me about Kat. I thought of William charging at Melchasaar just now, and Cletus saving my life in the lagoon. And I thought of Stirling giving up his life for me. I remembered Cletus telling me he was not a hero—he was just trying to do the right thing—and I knew. I knew I had to fight. *I* had to do the right thing for Sebastian and Gram; for Andie, William, Stirling, and Cletus; for Rephael; and most of all for myself.

I looked directly into Melchasaar's eyes, and I mustered every scrap of courage I could find. I stared at him, my eyes proud. I ignored the screaming pain in my arm and refused to bow. Melchasaar was clearly enraged. He started the Double A, and I could feel the strength being sucked from my toes and my feet. But still, I stared at him. My legs tingled and went weak, but I wouldn't look away.

"Bow!" Melchasaar roared, but I called on every emotion I had experienced since my brother died, and I fought back.

"I...will...not!"

What nobody realized was while I was locked in a contest of wills that could very well cost me my life, Kat must have sneaked off to the edge of the clearing. It wasn't until the entire ground rocked and a massive explosion of color escaped from the mirror, that everyone recognized what she had been up to.

"Katriana! No!" the king yelled. "It is for fate to decide! Not us!"

But even as he screamed the words, a sparkling, shimmering, swirling mist began to converge from all over the sky. It looked like someone had dumped giant buckets of glitter from the heavens. As it floated closer to the earth, the mist began to take the shape of a human form, solidifying before our very eyes. And then before we knew it, a beautiful older version of Kat appeared right there in the middle of the battle—Kat had used the power of Reanimation to bring back her mother!

Everyone, except for Melchasaar, stopped what they were doing, at first startled by the blast, and then mesmerized by what had just happened. Melchasaar, on the other hand, was so focused on draining my soul, he never broke his concentration and never flinched. If he had, maybe he would have been warned to the danger I saw coming. A bolt of lightning formed in the sky, so large and so powerful it seemed to hang there. Its branches shot out like a giant web, connecting all the clouds.

I drew on every last ounce of my super strength and all of my resolve. With one final surge of pure will, I broke free of the Double A. Just in the nick of time, I rolled out of the way, managing to drag William with me. A split second after Kat's mother appeared, the mammoth bolt struck the spot where I had just been and where Melchasaar's hand still hovered. His entire body, still standing with his hand outstretched, lit with electricity and shook violently. His white eyes bulged and sparks escaped from the top of his head. And then, he collapsed.

"Mother!" Kat dropped the mirror and raced to the queen. William and the king joined the two of them in a crushing full family hug. Andie ran to me, squeezing me in a hug of her own.

"The Kaptropoten chose Melchasaar!" I said. "It was his life the mirror chose to exchange for the queen's!" I couldn't believe our good fortune as I stood over Melchasaar, marveling at our luck.

"Good!" cried Kat. "Now he can stay the heck out of my dreams!"

William came and crouched beside his body. "The mirror didn't choose his life. It wasn't him," he said, "because he's still breathing!"

Right then, the translucent, misty form of Melchasaar, rose from his almost-dead body. It floated there momentarily before it swooshed right inside the Kaptropoten!

"D-d-did you s-see that?" William asked. "And he's still not dead! His body is still—"

He never finished his sentence, but stopped and clutched his side. "Hmmm…" His voice was deliriously calm. He held up his hand, dripping with red. "I'm… bleeding…"

He fell over, and it was then we saw the knife—the same knife Kat had conjured to sever Draemoch's finger—that was lodged in his side. In all of the chaos, no one had seen that Draemoch had regained consciousness and set his sights on William. As Kat and her father ran to help William, Draemoch snatched Melchasaar's body. The soldier carrying Salome grabbed Draemoch's arm, and then, using his teleportation mirror, they disappeared in a cloud of black smoke.

CHAPTER 25
Smoke and Mirrors

The smoke hadn't even cleared before Kat flashed to the spot where she dropped the Kaptropoten. She grabbed the mirror and then flashed to William's side.

"No! No! No! Nooooooo!"

The king and queen rushed to their son. His mother scooped him onto her lap, cradling his head and rocking him as the rain washed away his blood.

"My baby! This should never have happened!" She pressed her lips to his forehead and sobbed. "Why? Why?"

Kat held the Kaptropoten above her head, and I could tell she was having trouble holding on to it. It shook and rocked against her grip. Despite that, she clutched the mirror.

"Heal my brother!" But nothing happened. "Heal my brother! Bring him back!"

We all waited, but there was nothing.

"BRING HIM BACK!" She had lost all control. The mirror rocked and jerked and Kat stumbled trying not to drop it.

The king came to huddle behind his wife, holding her as she held her son.

"Enough, Katriana! That is enough!" His voice was tortured but strong. "It will not work! The Kaptropoten has chosen, and the Kaptropoten's decision is final." He buried his head on his wife's shoulder, smothering his sob. The mirror lurched again, and Kat finally dropped it. She rushed to her brother's side.

"Then let us take him to Rephael!" She began pulling William from her mother's arms. "He will heal him!"

The queen grabbed Kat and shook her. "He is gone, Kat. It is too late."

Kat stood and began pacing. She flashed back and forth across the clearing, her behavior frighteningly unstable.

Andie drew up beside me, her tears mixing with the raindrops as they fell silently to the ground. An ache formed in my soul. I knew just how William's family felt. Empty.

For the first time ever, I agreed with Andie's saying: Rules are made for a reason. We had been told not to use the mirror for our own personal gain. We had been told not to use the mirror for Reanimation. But Kat had been willing to gamble with fate—and all along, so had I. But now look what happened.

"Is his soul trapped in the Kaptropoten?" I shuddered at the idea of William being stuck in there with Melchasaar and Salome. I could think of nothing worse.

"No." The king's voice wavered. "He died too quickly. His soul would have been freed from his body instantaneously. There would have been no time for the mirror to claim his soul. He was spared."

It was hard not to notice the mirror shaking and vibrating on the ground. The foliage beneath it began to smoke, in spite of the rain, which still soaked us.

"What's happening to the mirror?" Andie asked.

The king took one look at the mirror, his expression changing from grief to concern.

"There is too much energy trapped inside. It is becoming unstable and it needs to be destroyed or the souls of Melchasaar and Salome will escape."

I didn't want to think about what would happen if Melchasaar and Salome were let loose on the world as a team. Turns out, I didn't have to think about it because I was interrupted by a voice coming from the trees.

"Jax," the voice called, and then Cletus shot into the circle. I was so glad to see him.

"Cletus! I'm so sorry! For not trusting you! I should never—"

"Forget about it! Listen to me, Jax! It's Kat! She—" But then he cut himself off when he came upon William and his family. "What…what happened here?" His eyes widened as he took in the scene.

It was Andie who answered, her words bitter. "Draemoch killed him."

"Oh…oh…," Cletus said. He wasn't processing the news. And then he noticed Kat's mother for the first time. "Your Majesties." He bowed. "I am so, so sorry…" He couldn't bring himself to say it. "Might I ask?" He looked at the queen. "How is it you come to be here?"

The queen turned her head, and her beautiful green eyes, shimmering with tears, identified Kat.

"You did this," Cletus said to Kat. "You did all of this."

Kat once again seized the Kaptropoten, which was becoming even more difficult for her to hold. The mirror exploded in a burst of brilliant amber as a pair of thickly insulated gloves appeared on Kat's hands. I guessed she had conjured them there to protect her hands from the mirror's intense heat.

"It's time to end it, Kat." Cletus held out his hand. "Give me the Kaptropoten."

She backed away, like a cornered lion.

"No!" She was becoming more and more agitated by the minute. "If I keep the mirror, nothing like this will ever happen again. No one will ever be able to hurt my family again!" She faced her parents. "Mother. Father. Come! I am not leaving without you. We will use the mirror to go far, far away from here."

The king stepped forward. "Kitty Kat, Melchasaar's soul will not be contained in the mirror. It needs to be destroyed. Please. Give the Kaptropoten to Cletus."

"No!" She reeled forward as she clung to the mirror.

The mirror started whistling and threw Kat off balance as she tried to keep it away from us. There was no way we could risk the time it would take to bring that mirror back to Rephael to be ground to a dust—it was too unstable. I knew something needed to be done. I searched around until I found a large rock, which I held in my uninjured arm, poised to throw at the mirror.

"What are you doing?" Kat was close to hysteria. "If you destroy the mirror, you will never get your brother back. Go ahead. Put down the rock and I will

conjure him up for you." Her voice was suddenly calm
and lilting again. There was a burst of pink from the
Kaptropoten, which meant she had called upon the
Kaptro Enchantment. And once again, I felt such a desire
to please her. Logically, I knew I was being seduced
by the mirror, but I wasn't sure I could resist. In fact, I
realized she had used the mirror on me when we first
arrived at the clearing. I didn't even want to think about
how many other times she might have used it to make
me her puppet. The mirror jolted forward, but Kat fought
hard and brought it under control.

"Go ahead. Drop the rock."

I lowered my arm and one by one my fingers loosened
their grip on the rock. Kat smiled at me and the mirror
shook violently. "Go ahead." Her voice was hypnotic.
"Let's bring Sebastian back. Together."

The Kaptropoten whistled like a train. I strained to
hear Kat's words.

"You know you want to. There is *nothing* we wouldn't
both do for our families. You are just…like…me." She
smiled, right as I was getting ready to drop the rock.

But she had chosen the wrong words. There were a
lot of things Kat had done that I would *never* do.

"I am NOTHING like you!" I yelled, knowing what I
was about to do would destroy my dream of resurrecting
my brother. I missed him still. I would love him always.
But it was not for me to decide.

Just at that, the mirror shook free from Kat's grip.
I hurled the rock at the falling mirror with the speed
and precision of a torpedo. It intercepted the mirror,

smashing it with explosive force. The Kaptropoten shattered with the power of a nuclear blast, just like it did when Rephael had directed the tremendous ball of lightning at it. Seven fragments soared off into the atmosphere and disappeared out of sight.

CHAPTER 26
Sheep and a Courtyard; Mom and a Mirror

I could barely hear Caephus' words over the cheer of the crowd. All of IOM had come out for the big ceremony. Most were probably there on the off chance they would get a rare glimpse of Rephael than for anything else.

"This is a day of firsts here on the island." Caephus' big voice boomed from the large stage erected high above the courtyard. Galen and I sat to the left of the podium. To his right, two easels held the framed portraits of William and Stirling.

"For the first time in the illustrious history of the Kaptropoten, multiple Golden Speculums are being awarded—three today to be exact." He waited for the applause to die down. "For the first time, a non-Komitari recipient has been chosen to receive this unparalleled honor." Once again the crowd cheered. "And for the first time, the Golden Speculum will be awarded posthumously."

The crowd erupted in applause, rejoicing in the idea that William and Stirling would be recognized for their sacrifices even after their deaths.

Below, in the front row, Cletus and Andie cheered

me on while Cletus waved a big foam No. 1 finger with the slogan, "Jax Has Our Backs!" I still felt guilty when I thought about how I hadn't believed Cletus back at HQ.

On Cletus' shoulder sat one very large and very regal magpie. It was Prince Vihtori, and he was here like everyone else to watch the ceremony.

King William and Queen Kathleen sat beside them, with their two younger children, Princess Ryann and Princess Phallon. They were much more serious than the rest of the crowd, but they both wore brave smiles and applauded politely. It had to have been so hard for them to lose two children on the same day.

For me, it was kind of awkward sitting up there in front of everyone. All I did was break the mirror—and my arm. And a few ribs. I didn't actually defeat Melchasaar. As long as Draemoch kept Melchasaar's body alive, and if the fragments were rejoined, there was the chance his soul could escape from the mirror and reunite with his body. But I was being awarded the Golden Speculum anyway. I guess the fact that I had stopped Melchasaar from getting the mirror, stopped Kat from taking off with the mirror, and stopped Melchasaar's and Salome's souls from escaping the mirror *was* a pretty big deal. I was actually proud of myself—enough to finally stop punishing myself for that night at the pool. I did the right thing out there in that clearing, just like Cletus would have.

Shattering the Kaptropoten had made me feel free somehow—like I could finally accept that Sebastian was gone and that I was not to blame for the horrible accident. And, of course, all along I had known deep down that it wasn't Cletus' fault.

Caephus went on and on about the "great tradition" of the Golden Speculum. I was too excited about going home to pay much attention. As soon as the moon came out tonight, Andie and I were heading back to Beyhaven, and I couldn't wait to see Gram.

At one point, Galen hung the medal around my neck. "Mission accomplished," he said before surprising me with an awkward hug.

King William and Nigel accepted the medals for William and Stirling. The ceremony ended to thunderous applause from the crowd. No one seemed at all disappointed they wouldn't get to see Rephael today. There were enough festivities planned to make up for that.

I bounded down the steps to join Cletus and Andie, but was surrounded by swarms of people congratulating me and shaking my hand.

"Hey, mister! Will you sign my poster?" It was Kat's and William's seven-year-old sister Phallon. She wore a wooly white headband with sheep ears attached. It was amazing how fast the gift shop here had manufactured those posters of me. Someone had done a great job of photoshopping me holding a shepherd's crook. Judging by the sheep ears, Phallon must already have joined my new fan club—Sheppard's Sheep. I shook my head just thinking about the sign-up table Cletus had set up in the courtyard this morning.

"Become one of Sheppard's Sheep!" he had called to anyone who passed. "Sign up for a one-year membership, and we'll throw in this 'Just the Facts, Jax' notepad with glow-in-the-dark pen for free!"

I took Phallon's glow-in-the-dark pen and scribbled my name across the corner of her poster. I guess she probably didn't really understand what had happened to her siblings. King William stood behind her and waited for me to finish.

"Your Majesty," I said. "I'm real sorry about…everything. I really liked William…a lot."

"No, son." His handshake was firm. "It is I who am sorry. My daughter placed you in great peril." He lowered his eyes. "I will never understand what motivated her to behave in such a way. We raised her to be just, to be honorable, to be…" He couldn't finish. I'm sure he was hurting, so I almost hated to ask him the next question.

"What will they do to her? The KIA, I mean."

"After her trial, she will likely spend the rest of her life in Cartica, the island penitentiary." His voice cracked just once. "It would be a fair sentence."

The queen and Princess Ryann, who William had said was twelve years old, joined the king and Princess Phallon.

"Hi, Jax," she said, smiling at me from under her lashes. "You know, you'll get a chance to work with me in a few years. After I become a Komitari. I'll show you all my moves, if you want. I've been practicing."

"Ryann," the queen said. "Leave Jackson alone." She smiled at me, her green eyes clouded with sadness. "I do want to thank you—for saving Katriana's life when she was wounded by Draemoch. You are a hero to my family no matter the outcome." She clasped my hand. "We owe you a debt of gratitude."

Ryann continued to smile at me like a lovesick sheep. "Yeah. You are so totally a hero." It was definitely weird.

By then, Cletus and Andie had managed to push their way to my side. Cletus tore off a fluffy chunk of cotton candy he had bought and laid it on his tongue. He clapped me on the back. "So, what did it feel like havin' Caephus hang that medal around your neck?"

"I have to admit, it felt pretty cool to think my mom got this exact same award." I studied the mini replica of the Kaptropoten—this one had a golden plate instead of a brass one—and I wondered if I would have a chance to ask Rephael about Mom before I left tonight.

Andie must have read my mind. "I can't believe Caephus told you the information about your mom was classified. What the heck is that supposed to mean?"

"I don't know," I said, "but I'm going to do whatever it takes to find out."

"And did anyone ever tell you why Melchasaar even wanted you in the first place?" Andie asked.

"Well, apparently, I *was* the Ark. Caephus said Melchasaar *did* have a bounty on me. I guess Melchasaar had some kind of sick vengeance plan. He blamed my mom for trying to kill Salome a few years ago. Plus, he planned to use my blood to release Salome's soul from the mirror. That's why he had that knife—the Vassica. You need that knife and the warm blood of a descendant of the trapped soul to open the Chamber of Souls in the Kaptropoten. But Caephus said Salome never had any children. So Melchasaar was somehow trying to use me as a substitute."

Andie's and Cletus' eyebrows shot up, and I knew what they were thinking. "No." I shook my head. "I'm NOT a descendant of Salome. I asked, and Caephus was 100 percent sure." I changed the subject. "Are you two packed yet?"

Cletus nodded. "Yeah. My Ped, Jurgen, took care of it for me. It'll be strange travelin' alone, though. Without Yancy."

"Do you think they'll find him?" Andie asked. "I mean, I just can't believe he betrayed you like that. I know he's your cousin and all, but what a jerk! To think he and Kat conspired to steal the Elementum from you! And that Kat pretended to be Melchasaar and faked the whole Double A thing with Yancy. She really had this whole thing planned out."

"Yancy would be a fool to ever come out of hidin'," Cletus said. "Guess I never realized how jealous he was. Don't know if I'll ever be able to accept what he did—all just to be a Komitari."

"What happened to Hobart?" I asked. "Can't he go with you?"

"Didn't you hear?" Cletus asked. "Hobs wasn't really an attendant. Can you believe he was actually KIA—undercover? It was Hobs who got Caephus to free me. Then he and Caephus went to close the Propius Portal while I came to help kick some butt. Too bad they didn't get to it before Draemoch escaped."

I didn't even want to think about Draemoch right

now. "Then who will you pick to be your new attendant—now that you're a Komitari again?"

"Don't know yet. Gonna have to figure it out soon, though. Who knows how long it'll take the KIA to track down the Kaptrofracti? And then we'll be called back to duty. What about you? You know who you're gonna pick?"

"No, but at least I have a month to decide. Remember what Caephus said in his speech? The entire island will be on lock-down for the next thirty days—until they complete the investigation."

Andie tapped my arm. "Here." She handed me the single-use Kaptro Elementum and Kaptro Conjuration. "You can have these back."

"Thanks." I tucked them in my back pocket. "Where's the mini Enchantment?"

"Oh. I thought I told you. That's how I figured it out about Kat. When we got to Cletus' room to search for the Enchantment, there was already a KIA agent stationed outside his door. I used the single-use Enchantment to make him let us in. When I saw how he was acting..." She smacked her hands together. "Bam! It hit me. I realized that's how Kat got me to play Skeeball at the carnival."

Cletus smiled and wiggled his eyebrows. "I dig a girl with brains." Andie made the freshly-ground-earthworms face. "Now that's enough natterin'. Let's go."

We had just turned to leave when I got nailed in the cheek with an individually wrapped, flying Ding Dong.

"Hey!" I spun to find the culprit. A huge posse of

frenzied Sheep had gathered and begun chucking Ding Dongs at me. They must have thought it was a good way to get my attention—and they were right. I felt kind of dumb, but it didn't stop me from signing a dozen posters, accepting each of a dozen Ding Dongs, and stuffing them in my hoodie pocket.

"Come on." I tossed a couple of cakes to Cletus and Andie. "Let's get out of here."

The moonlight bounced off the gently lapping waters of the lagoon. Andie and I stood crammed together on my Ostium. Elweard handed us our packs.

"I'll be seeing you soon, Master Jax."

I had decided not to have him come home with us to Pennsylvania. I didn't think I could explain to Drake and the other kids at school about the four-toed, hairy-chested baby staying in my room.

Several feet to my left, Cletus stood with Jurgen on his Ostium. To his left were the two sculpture heads, Phlynnis, and her attendant, Thorna. Beyond them were Jules and Rémi. They, too, were heading home after having stayed on the island for the ceremony. Galen and Caephus stood farther up the beach by the path to town and were there to see us off.

"Mission accomplished!" Galen said in his whiny voice before we left them and stepped aboard our Ostiums.

We all pulled out the little dummy mirrors Caephus had given us to use until the time when we would be called to find our Kaptrofracti. Apparently, the Ostiums would work with any mirror. I looked into mine, relieved to be heading home. I had finally forgiven myself for Sebastian's death. It wasn't my fault, and I couldn't hold myself responsible for fate's decisions. I felt like a new kid, and I couldn't wait for Gram to see that.

The winds began to swirl. As the golden flames lifted from the cloth, I took one last look at my new friends. I had no idea how long it would be before I saw them again.

Right before the transport happened, my ears were assaulted by the high-pitched noise and static that meant my super hearing was about to kick in. The world had already begun to spin and the flames licked at our bodies. The static faded, and Galen's voice came in loud and clear.

"When do you think we should tell him about his mother?"

"How do you tell someone," Caephus asked, "that for the past year his mother's soul has been trapped inside the Kaptropoten with the soul of Salome and now with Melchasaar's?"

"WHAT?" I shouted.

But then Andie and I were being stretched and tugged and sucked through the tube.

The next thing I knew, we were standing in the field behind the dark and empty BVFD parking lot. There were no signs of the carnival, which must have packed up and left town several days ago.

Andie blinked at me. "Thank goodness we never have to do *that* again," she managed to say before collapsing in my arms.

The night air was crisp and clear. It was like nothing

had happened—like everything was back to normal.

Mission accomplished.

Except now there was a new mission. I wasn't sure how I would break the news to Andie, but this would not be her last trip on the Ostium.

We were going back. We were going to save my mom.

Sharon Warchol grew up in the suburbs of Pittsburgh, where Steelers football is its own religion. Traces of her hometown are sprinkled throughout *The Seven Mirrors* in the IOM headquarters building, the Volunteer Fireman's fair, Cletus' slurred "ings," and beyond.

Having spent most of her career as a middle school teacher, she firmly believes that you are what you teach—which would make her a hormonal, acne-covered, talkative pest with a head full of insecurities and a heart full of possibilities. Fortunately, she's since gotten the acne licked.

Sharon is now a full-time professional wife, and the mom of three fantasy-loving book zealots, who devour her stories as fast as she can write them.

To learn more about Sharon, visit her website at www.jaxsheppardbooks.com